THE CURSE

OF THE

FLORES

WOMEN

THE CURSE

OF THE

FLORES

WOMEN

A NOVEL

ANGÉLICA LOPES

TRANSLATED BY ZOË PERRY

AMAZON**CROSSING**

Text copyright © 2022, 2024 by Angélica Lopes
Translation copyright © 2024 by Zoë Perry
All rights reserved.

Previously published as *A maldição das flores* by Editorial Planeta do Brasil in Brazil in 2022. Translated from the Portuguese by Zoë Perry. First published in English by Amazon Crossing in 2024.

Published by Amazon Crossing, Seattle

www.apub.com

Amazon, the Amazon logo, and Amazon Crossing are trademarks of Amazon.com, Inc., or its affiliates.

ISBN-13: 9781662516139 (paperback)
ISBN-13: 9781662516122 (digital)

Cover design by Ploy Siripant
Cover image: © Mads Perch / Getty; © benntennsann / Shutterstock

Printed in the United States of America

For
Lygia, Hilda, Celina, and Sonia,
who went before.

For
Gabriela,
who was with me all along.

For
Cecília,
who followed after.

1

It was always an act of rebellion, albeit invisible.

We knew there was a risk in what we were doing, and perhaps it was precisely the danger of being found out—small at first, barely evident to anyone's eyes, intertwined with the threads of patterns we flaunted so discreetly on our lace handkerchiefs and veils—that emboldened us to take even greater risks.

We weren't all related, but we were united by the art of transforming thread and woven tape into lace. Here, on this patch of land where minor details matter more than big events, where the red clay ground is as cracked and lined as my Tia Firmina's face—both sculpted by time and sorrow—where the fate of women is cut-and-dried, like the imperfect reverse side of the only story woven exclusively by our own desire and determination: lace. No other path wholly belonged to us.

My friend Vitorina was the one responsible for making us the keepers of this knowledge, when she stood at the top of a ladder and spied the secret that had come all the way from the capital.

"What are you doing up there, girl?" Hildinha asked when she saw her daughter lurking at the eaves above the guest room.

"Leave me be, Mother. I'm trying to learn something that will be of great value."

Thanks to Vitorina's curiosity, the lace technique that had adorned altars in Europe for centuries, a cloistered secret, known only to nuns inside convents in big cities, made its way to our little town, Bom Retiro.

A matter of chance, a loose thread of fate, brought by the cousin of a cousin of another cousin of Vitorina's, who, after her secret was stolen, never forgave my friend for her disloyalty.

The girl worked as a kitchen maid inside a very strict convent. After several years of good service, she'd earned the nuns' trust, and they taught her the art of lacemaking. At first, still unsure they could trust her, the nuns only taught her the basic stitches. It was only later, after observing the strength of the girl's character and considering her worthy, that they showed her the more elaborate ones.

Vitorina's distant cousin had a "knack for lace," as they used to say, and knew how to be discreet, an indispensable quality for the keepers of that secret. When the girl announced that she was going to visit relatives in the countryside for the holidays, the nuns warned her:

"If you're going to make lace when you're back home, stay out of sight."

Always respectful of her superiors, the girl obeyed their orders. To keep her promise, made before the saints, that cousin of a cousin of another cousin of Vitorina's only made lace when she was alone in the guest room, with just a yellow tallow candle to light her work.

But at the top of a ladder, determined to find out what her cousin was doing in that room with the windows shut in the midday sun, Vitorina was watching.

She watched so closely that she was able to memorize her every move.

Hunched over a cylindrical pillow, her guest plaited threads into designs made up of all kinds of stitches: buttonhole, broom, tower, rib. Spider, moon, popcorn.

Sunset, lovers stitch, and—my favorite—the bottom-of-the-basket stitch, which enchanted me not so much for its shape, but for its name, which seemed to offer both a threat and a promise. An unknown, unexplored place that could hold fortune or hardship, where you might equally find a silver coin or a scorpion, something only revealed to those with the courage to take risks and stick their hand inside.

Of course, the stitches weren't actually called that back then. They arrived here in the Pajeú River valley with foreign names, names we never learned. But, as we became familiar with them, we were able to identify their similarities with things in the world, baptizing them one by one, as if we'd always owned them.

In the afternoons I spent hunched over my pillow, I tried to imagine what name I might give a stitch if I happened to come up with one of my own. Not that I had such ambition. But, in a moment of carelessness, the needle might get tangled in the thread, go where it shouldn't, and voilà: a new stitch is born.

It would be the first stitch created in this hot country, and not in the foreign land from where the first ones came, an ocean away from the Sertão, brought over by nuns and spied by Vitorina from the top of a ladder.

Creek stitch, dew stitch, dawn stitch.

Those were the names I had secretly chosen to christen my first stitch, which might never be invented. Son of the high-altitude Caatinga, the region where Lampião was also born, who, back then, in the year of grace of 1918, was just starting his life of crime, and of whom we would only hear about in Bom Retiro years later. A rambunctious story about men, so different from our story, that took place almost imperceptibly, between silences and whispers.

I always believed that when I laid eyes on my newly created stitch, I'd know exactly what to call it. Just like mothers do with their children. Those who don't risk giving their offspring a name that wasn't meant to be. You choose Nonato in honor of his grandfather, but the boy insists on looking like a Casemiro for the rest of his life. Hence the abundance of nicknames in the world. After all, things choose their names, not us.

As soon as the cousin of a cousin of another of Vitorina's cousins returned to the convent, the secret Vitorina spied from the eaves was passed on to anyone willing to learn. In no time, a small group of women, myself included, began to meet daily to make fine tablecloths, doilies, placemats, and napkins.

It didn't take long for one of our pieces to make its way to the capital, a gift offered to a lady from a good family, who showed our work to another lady from a good family, who, in turn, over shortbreads and afternoon tea, showed it to another lady from a good family.

"See how perfect it is? It's from some backwater near Serra Talhada, but it looks like it was made in Europe. Do you think there's any way to place an order?"

Orders were quickly made.

When ladies from good families show an interest in something, someone always seizes the opportunity to take a cut.

Weeks later, a gentleman in a dark suit arrived in our town, sweating more than the local men who worked the land, announcing his intention to buy our work at a good price, for us and for him.

Tia Firmina was responsible for dealing with the man. Because she was the oldest of the group and because she didn't have children to steal her time, she could devote herself to taking orders and bookkeeping and then sharing the earnings equally among us.

"If not for me, this guy would be putting one over on all of you. He tried to get a formal tablecloth for a pittance. What a bunch of hogwash! Lucky I'm here to defend our interests," she boasted.

When the first coins brought by the man in the dark suit were placed on the table, we were so engrossed in admiring them that the moment seemed to go on forever.

It was like they didn't belong to us. Like museum pieces, with a sign that says "Do Not Touch" beneath them.

"All that's ours?" Vitorina asked, as if she couldn't believe it.

Until then, lacemaking was just a pastime for us, something to do on sultry afternoons. Some of us made lace for ourselves, creating gowns for balls that would never take place in our little town. Others made bedspreads for hope chests for marriages yet to be arranged.

The exception was Tia Firmina, who devoted her time to making her own burial shroud.

"I shall enter Heaven with the elegance Our Lord Jesus Christ deserves," she announced, seeming a bit too anxious for a moment everyone tends to want to defer.

As far as we knew, money was the exclusive affair of the men, who worked the land and tended the cattle. Be they bosses, landowners, or cattle owners. Be they laborers, henchmen, or peddlers. Be they our husbands, fathers, or brothers. The money was always theirs.

We women were just the ones who cleared the table for them or ordered other women to clear the table for them. It was these men's names, recorded on our birth and marriage certificates, that determined our place in the world.

It was like that with most, except with my family.

Many believed the Flores family was cursed, victims of a hex cast by a gypsy in times past. But for us, living without men around was just life as we knew it.

"They don't stick around for long, poor things," my mother had explained to me and my sister, mourning my father, who died of malaria before he reached thirty-five.

She had loved him deeply, just as she had loved her father, my grandfather, and later her son, my younger brother, who didn't even make it to his first birthday.

My mother had been taught by her mother, who, in turn, had also been taught by her mother, that the men in our lives would always just be passing through, hurried visitors who arrive with the announcement that they won't be long. A coffee at most, thank you, already taking their hat to leave.

They married us, they were born from our wombs, but after a few years they simply left, preoccupied with whatever important appointment came next. Some died of natural causes, some were killed, others died following disagreements or high fevers. They died young or in middle age, but we never saw their wrinkled faces, or their hair whitened by time.

As good hosts to their lives, we knew it was our duty to make them as comfortable as possible during their passage through this world and to offer them an affectionate farewell when the final hour arrived. Knowing our time together would be brief, a feeling of longing tightened across our chests from the moment we met them.

When my mother first kissed my father, during a celebration on the Feast of Saint Agatha, the enchantment she felt for the boy was tangled in the anguish of knowing that when they shared their first kiss, that would be one less kiss on the not-very-long list of kisses they were meant to share. She needed to enjoy them as much as possible.

With the same ease with which we dealt with their arrivals, the moment we placed a white rose on their tombstones, we would try to put the house in order for the arrival of the next visitor. Soon a new cycle would begin, which would end in a departure as premature as the previous ones. Accustomed to that already-familiar way of life, we didn't suffer or question that fate, which people called "the curse of the Flores women."

Whether out of compassion or malice, it was common for the residents of Bom Retiro to give us looks when they passed us on the street. The good people of that place felt sorry that we had no one to take care of us, assuming that because we were women, we'd need more than ourselves to survive. The most wary were convinced we'd committed some sin to deserve such a punishment. "Don't be fooled. Someone did something" was what they used to say about us, and not always behind our backs.

My mother refused to be tainted by the things we sometimes overheard in church.

"The life you're given is the life you have," she taught us. "Going against fate only adds to the pain. We must follow the path that is laid out before us."

"Those people don't know a damned thing." Tia Firmina couldn't stand it, outraged by the gossip. "May they have as much pity for themselves or for those in need. What in God's name would we need a man around here for? Someone belching and complaining about the consistency of the marmalade? What would be the value of having an albatross like that getting in the way?"

My aunt was proud to have dedicated her life to a single male figure: Our Lord Jesus Christ. And maybe that's why she suffered less than my mother, who carried, buried deep inside, but evident in her eyes, the mourning of widowhood and the loss of her only male child.

"At least I loved them immensely. Longing is better than emptiness," my mother reassured my sister and me whenever Tia Firmina suggested we should follow a religious life to avoid the tears to come.

"It's their choice, Firmina. Leave the girls alone."

But my aunt couldn't stand it: "They won't be happy, Carmelita. That's for sure. And besides, having a nun in the family guarantees entrance to Heaven. I'm saying this for your own sake, because my soul is already more than saved."

Despite the number of wakes we'd witnessed in that house, we lived happily. Our men were with us in pictures on the wall and in our memories. Some tender, others harsh. Others were neither. About my father, I remember the pipe that I believed was an extension of his hand and that gave the house a warm, woody smell. And his whistle.

He was the one who taught me and my sister Cândida to recognize birds by their song. We'd often spend afternoons on his lap, while he whistled the melody of an orange thrush or a great kiskadee, so we'd know how to tell them apart. Today, even so many years after his death, I can hear my father's whistle in the song of every bird.

Although our family name was originally Oliveira, we were called "the Flores girls." The confusion started in part because of the well-tended garden we had in front of our house and because we lived on the way to the parish church. At the time, whenever a traveler who had just arrived in Bom Retiro asked for directions to the church, people generally replied: "Go to the house with the flowers and turn right."

In the beginning, our house was just a house with a garden of touch-me-nots, wood roses, monkey combs, white hollyhocks, and purple spider flowers. But over time, after it had been repeated so many times, and never corrected, our house with blue windows came to be known as Casa das Flores, even though it was Casa das Oliveiras. The flower garden became our surname, and, over time, we incorporated it into our documents as well.

It was precisely because we were the Floreses that the residents of Bom Retiro didn't find it strange that the tragedy that occurred was connected to the house with blue windows where our group of lacemakers would meet.

"That's some Flores business," people used to say.

But we didn't deserve the credit. Everything that happened at the beginning of the year 1919 was born out of the anguish of my friend Eugênia, née Damásio Lima, who was about to become Mrs. Medeiros Galvão.

2

Rio de Janeiro, 2010

Alice had decided to go to a party the night before and then to a bar in Lapa.

At the bar, Alice had drunk as much as she wanted because the beer was cheap and exam week at the university had been stressful. Her decision to drink without limits had somehow prevented her from being able to decide the best time to call it a night.

Such that, nearly afternoon on that Saturday, Alice's most recent decision had been to drag herself out of bed to her bookshelf to get two painkillers and a bottle of water. But she couldn't even do that, as the pills slipped between her fingers and rolled under the bed.

Still lying down, she looked in the mirror hanging on the wall in front of her, which reminded her of another decision she'd made, a few days earlier: dyeing her hair blue.

She smiled to herself, approving her new look, and felt a little dizzy. She knew that soon her mother would knock on the door to make her get up and nag her about coming home drunk the night before. But Alice had already made up her mind not to listen to her and just go, "Uh-huh." Her mother also drank, and she also went out to have fun, so she couldn't criticize her. Equal rights under that roof. That was the deal.

"Alice?" Her mom had arrived faster than she expected. Or maybe her hangover had messed with her sense of time. "Get up."

"I can't," Alice growled, or maybe dreamed that she did.

"We have a visitor. Fix that face and come on."

Alice made the decision to not obey her mother and rolled back toward the wall, aiming to get a little while longer under the duvet, which didn't happen.

"Didn't you hear me, girl? Your aunt wants to meet you."

"Aunt?"

Alice put the pillow over her face to shield it from the light streaming through the curtains her mother had just opened.

"Your aunt from Pernambuco. Come on."

Alice vaguely remembered having relatives in a state she'd never been to, and her brain began to make some mental connections.

Her grandmother had come from Pernambuco when she was young and barely talked about her origins. After her grandmother's death, Vera, Alice's mother, who was born in Rio, concocted a plan to use her frequent flyer miles to finally discover the land of her ancestors, but that never actually happened. The miles were spent the day before they expired on a two-night package to Buenos Aires, a trip Alice and Vera spent arguing.

The aunt, whose name was Helena, information Alice only found out when they were introduced in the living room, was a nice lady with high cheekbones that seemed to want to leap out of her face. At apparently eighty years old, she was more energetic than Alice was at eighteen.

"This is Alice, Tia," her mother began, making a face at Alice. Having her daughter come out into the living room looking so disheveled, wearing only a T-shirt and panties, had failed to meet her expectations, as usual.

"I sent you a link to her graduation pictures last year, didn't I, Tia? She's studying communications now. But she skips all the days that end in -*day*," joked her mother, and neither of the other two laughed.

Vera was already indulging in her favorite pastime with Alice, a little good-natured goading, so that if confronted by her daughter later, she could always say, "Wow, I can't even joke around with you."

Her mother also brought up random topics to fill the silences. She probably hadn't sent her any photos, but her aunt politely pretended to remember.

"Of course, I've seen the pictures, what a nice party. You looked beautiful, Alice."

Alice made another attempt at smiling, and as her mother's eyes grew wider, she ventured saying something nice. Proper etiquette dictates that we be kind to our aunts, even if we were unaware they existed until just minutes ago. Even more so when those aunts flashed a big grin Alice didn't deserve, since she was still being rather rude, checking her phone with one hand and peeling last night's mascara from her eyelashes with the other.

"What's up, Tia? How was your flight?" Alice asked, starting the conversation as she flopped onto the armchair, legs splayed over the armrest, making her mother even more uncomfortable.

Alice knew she'd hear a litany of complaints once their visitor left, but deep down, she couldn't resist taunting Vera. She liked to see her disconcerted like that. Besides, she had too much of a headache for good manners.

Vera and Alice waged a silent and never-ending war of wills: on one side, a mother trying to force her daughter into a suffocating mold. On the other, a daughter struggling to stretch and grow beyond the boundaries imposed by her mother's wishes. It was an extremely tiring dynamic for both but one that repeated on a loop, because neither of them knew any other way to coexist.

Alice consciously pushed the limits of what Vera deemed acceptable behavior, going beyond what was natural. She was deliberately rebellious, so her mother would have no doubt that any attempt to change her would be in vain.

"Tia Helena," her mother began again, making a point of emphasizing their guest's name so that Alice wouldn't make any blunders. "You came to Rio for a party, is that right?"

"For the golden wedding anniversary of a childhood friend who moved here at a young age. And I figured since I was here, I ought to pay you a visit. I even brought some souvenirs! Want to see? Some typical things from the North."

Technically, this aunt lived in the Northeast, and not the North, but back when she was born that's what people used to say, as if the country were divided into just two halves: North and South. With a swiftness that made Alice dizzy and reminded her of the painkillers lying under her bed, Tia Helena took small packages from a bag. A fridge magnet, a straw basket, and even a cake were passed into the hands of a grateful Vera, who behaved in an annoyingly childish way in front of her aunt.

"Oh, you shouldn't have. Oh, how beautiful. Did you carry all this with you on the plane? And this delicious-looking bolo de rolo? I can't believe it!" She celebrated each gift as if it was the most precious item on the planet.

When her mother got up to serve the cake, Alice looked at her phone out of habit to check something she didn't need to see. Just a *hey, stranger* in her inbox from a professor who was trying to get her into bed.

As Vera sliced the bolo de rolo, dozens of millimetric, almost transparent layers revealed themselves, showing off the contrast between the buttery layers of cake and the pink guava filling, cut so precisely that the knife was nearly clean. A delicate art that Alice admired, but she saw no reason to go to all that trouble. It would be much easier to cut one nice, thick slice than to do all that over and over.

After coffee, the aunt took what appeared to be the big gift, carefully wrapped in tissue paper, from her bag.

"I also brought a family heirloom," she announced solemnly. "It's for you, Alice."

Alice put her phone aside, thinking she hadn't heard correctly. "For me?"

"Yes. You're a Flores, after all," she said, unwrapping the package herself. "See, it's a veil. It belonged to your great-grandmother, who was a lacemaker."

With a care Alice found over-the-top—it was lace, not crystal—her aunt laid the veil proudly on her lap, but Alice couldn't manage to smile back as social rules demanded and her mother certainly wanted.

"A veil?" Alice externalized her uneasy surprise when she saw it in front of her. "I hope it's not for a wedding."

Vera squirmed uneasily on the sofa, hearing what she would classify later as "incredibly tactless behavior" around "such a kind lady, who just wanted to please you, but I wouldn't expect anything different from you, Alice. I don't know who you learned to act like that from. It wasn't from me. I'm very polite, I care about other peoples' feelings, unlike you, who always wants to hurt everybody." But Alice would only hear that part later.

"Alice!" her mother said, scolding her with a look that even now, at eighteen, transported her daughter straight to her childhood, when Alice felt abandoned for the first time in her life.

They had been staying at the beach house of a couple of Vera's friends when, busy in the kitchen, Vera asked Alice, then six years old, to get her a tampon from the bathroom.

Proud to have been given such an adult task, Alice was expeditious. As soon as she'd located the tampon in Vera's suitcase, she ran out into the yard, eager to hand it over as if to say: "I did it, see how responsible I am, see what a good daughter I am?" But instead of the expected praise, the look on her mother's face destroyed Alice's feeling of goodwill. In her childish innocence, Alice had handed over the tampon in front of the other adults, never imagining that this would embarrass her mother so much that she would stop talking to Alice for the rest of the day.

She had never felt so wronged. If Alice didn't even know what a tampon was for, how was she supposed to know she shouldn't hand it out in front of other adults? Her mother had made the request without any provisos. She had waited for her mistake to blame her, a habit Vera perfected over the years that followed, without even giving it much thought. That was how Alice, from an early age, came to understand that no one would lead her down already-tested paths. She didn't have her mother's emotional support and would have to take her own risks to find out how to defend herself, fully aware that there would be no safety net if she fell.

Tia Helena sensed the tension between Alice and Vera and started to talk about the ninety-year-old veil, attempting to ease the discomfort in the room.

"It's not a wedding veil, don't worry. It's a mantilla veil, to wear to Mass," she explained.

Alice was about to say, "Yikes, even worse!" but stopped short. Not for her mother, but for her aunt. She didn't want to prove her mother's theory that she behaved aggressively around everyone. She wouldn't give Vera the pleasure.

"I take it you're not religious either," said Tia Helena.

"You got that right," Alice replied sarcastically, and then, half regretting her candor, praised the gift: "But it's pretty, I can use it for something else. Thanks."

"You don't have to wear it if you don't want to," said Tia Helena, reassuring her niece. "I just needed to bring it. Ever since it was made, this veil has been kept by the youngest female in our family. My job was just to pass it on. You can do whatever you want with it. Keep it in a drawer and never open it again, upcycle it—isn't that what you say nowadays? For a while I thought it should belong to your mother, but it took me so long to get to Rio that I think it should belong to you now, Alice. I'm sorry, Vera, my dear," Tia Helena lamented to her eldest niece, who tried unsuccessfully to hide her disappointment. "It's tradition, you know what I mean."

"Of course," Vera said, trying to minimize her disappointment at being passed over, but quickly moved on to disparage Alice. "Anyway,

I'm the one who'll end up taking care of it. Alice doesn't care about anything. No one can get into her room because of all the mess. It's a pigsty." Alice felt those words like blows. Right, left, cross, *blam, pow.* But she wouldn't fight back, she'd just wait for the signal that the round was over. "She'll lose it in a couple of days, you'll see. Such a beautiful antique, held on to for so long. What a shame."

Tia Helena didn't seem to take Vera's predictions or Alice's alleged shortcomings seriously. "Your only duty is to pass it on to your daughter," she said to Alice.

Alice laughed out loud. This woman really didn't know her at all.

"Or some other younger relative," Tia Helena said, correcting herself, noticing the annoyed look on her niece's face. "Like I'm doing now."

Alice thought about how she wouldn't do any of that. There was still a long way to go for one of those scenarios to come to pass, and if it did, she certainly wouldn't remember the strange assignment she'd just been given. Even so, she reassured her aunt with a "Leave it to me," and then, considering her role in the visit complete, she got up to go back to her room and forgot the veil on the arm of the chair.

"See! Didn't I say she doesn't take care of anything, Tia?" Vera bragged as Alice went back to get the gift. Her head was still throbbing. She really needed to find those painkillers.

3

Bom Retiro, 1918

"What is that preposterous webbing, Eugênia?" complained Tia Firmina, referring to the lace Eugênia was making that afternoon. "Just one stitch after another, no patterns, no shamrocks, no birds. Have you ever seen such a thing?"

"That's just the way I felt like doing it, Firmina. What's the matter with that?" Eugênia replied with a hint of sass, never pausing her needle.

That afternoon, when we had corn cake for lunch and the April breeze made its way timidly through the balcony door, Eugênia stitched at random, not following the design she'd drawn from a pattern she chose the day before.

"The gall of this girl!" Tia Firmina went on, unhappy with what she considered sloppy work. "You're just making a row of stitches. Better to rip them out now so you can at least reuse the fabric. We'll lose money that way. Eugênia, are you listening to me? Where's your head? The moon?"

"Perhaps, Firmina," Eugênia replied curtly, again with none of the respect my aunt expected. A girl Eugênia's age should never address an older, wiser woman that way. The affront riled my aunt even more.

"Is that any way to speak to your elders? I should like to see you keep up this willful act once you're married."

Eugênia suspended her needle in midair, as if that might stop the progress of time.

Until just a few weeks ago, Eugênia's life presented her with no great worriment, and she spent her days leafing through the fashion magazines her mother ordered from the capital and selling raffle tickets for the Feast of Saint Agatha, our town's patron saint. At fifteen, the sheriff's only daughter, she wanted for nothing. She had too much time on her hands, too few chores, and despite her yearning for something exciting to happen, she didn't envy the chores of other girls who, like me, had to bake bread, tend the garden, and care for the animals.

Because she thought she was destined for a future that was grander than ours, Eugênia wasn't worried when Colonel Aristeu Medeiros Galvão, a recent widower with two small children, came to visit her home.

Eugênia told me later that, at the time, she was even pleased when she learned they would be receiving guests. Her mother had been so busy that morning preparing delicacies that she barely had time to explain the reason for the scheduled visit.

When the church bell rang eleven, Eugênia heard someone clapping at the gate. The Colonel was known to be a man of his word, someone who honored his commitments. He never arrived early or late for an appointment.

"Please, after you. Make yourself comfortable, Colonel. My, my, isn't it hot out today? And in the middle of April! Have a seat here, it's cooler. How charming your little ones are. Come inside, children. Would you like some cajá juice? We have shortbreads, too. Fresh out of the oven."

Eugênia's mother was not acting herself. She seemed a bit impatient, a bit subservient, a bit flustered, nervously wiping her hands on the skirt of her dress, constantly searching for Eugênia out of the corner of her eye.

"Eugênia, my dear. Go fetch some juice and cookies from the kitchen. Go on now. And show the children around the yard. They must be eager to stretch their legs after the trip. Make haste, girl, did you hear me? That way, children. Go with Eugênia, go on now."

The children obeyed the lady of the house. They walked toward Eugênia, who grinned at them with a slightly morbid curiosity. The two had recently lost their mother, and, in her romanticized fantasy, Eugênia imagined the Colonel's children would look like pale and teary-eyed orphans. Ready to welcome the little ones in their grief, Eugênia grew somewhat frustrated as she watched those rosy-cheeked children running around excitedly and playing in the backyard.

"Come! I'll take you to see the swing."

"Thank you, ma'am," the older boy said politely. Eugênia found his formality amusing.

"Oh, come now, what do you mean by that? *Ma'am* is only for my mother. You can just call me Eugênia."

"My father told us we had to call you *ma'am*, ma'am," the boy explained, and Eugênia tried to clear up what she deemed a childish misunderstanding.

"I'm sure your father was referring to my mother. I'm just Eugênia, okay? Why, we're almost the same age," she said to the boy, who grinned, relieved he didn't have to treat her with so much deference.

After lunch, when her presence was requested in the sitting room, Eugênia still didn't think much of it. She imagined her father would ask her to fetch some coffee or that soursop liqueur, which they'd been keeping for years for important visits such as this, still sealed at the back of the china cabinet. It was the look in her father's eyes, more elusive and fearful than usual, that told Eugênia that something was about to happen.

Standing in the door to the small parlor, Eugênia was given the news that had darkened her eyes ever since. The Colonel had asked for her hand in marriage, and her father had gladly given it.

"You won't find a better husband around these parts," said her mother, trying to convince her daughter. "You hit the jackpot, and you'll soon regret those tears."

Good looking, the Colonel wasn't much older than thirty and could provide Eugênia with all the comforts she deserved at his ranch, Fazenda Caviúna.

"And you'll have the children," her mother insisted, continuing to list the benefits that, according to her, Eugênia wasn't mature enough to see at that moment. "Motherless, the poor things!"

Eugênia should have some compassion for those little angels, who needed someone to care for them, as much as her daughter needed a purpose in life. In less than a year, Eugênia's mother was sure, she would hardly remember those little ones were not her own flesh and blood, and, who knows, perhaps another child would be on the way.

"What a blessing that would be. My grandchildren, heirs to Caviúna," her mother mused.

But that was not the life Eugênia had imagined for herself.

Their mother's death had been a blow to the Colonel's children, but they were rosy cheeked and giggling as the swing went higher and higher. They didn't need her, just as she didn't need the Colonel's ranch. Eugênia liked living in town, where she could show off her new dresses at Mass and see people in the streets.

Still standing at the door to the parlor, listening to her father tell her about the decision that would change her life forever, Eugênia felt short of breath. Before her, Colonel Aristeu sat in respectful silence, not appearing particularly interested in his future bride. He'd gone there in search of his life's missing piece. A life that, until a few months ago, had been running smoothly—food on the table, clothes pressed, family in the front row at Sunday Mass. But things had broken down, and repairs were urgently needed.

That afternoon, the Colonel may have just been assessing whether the sheriff's daughter could fill the hole left by his late wife, who'd departed this life before schedule, causing so much disarray. If he made a good choice, in a few years he might not even realize that this second wife was a substitute, not the original.

No one had asked Eugênia a thing. It wasn't in the interest of the men present, nor her mother—who by then was already saying prayers in the bedroom, asking the Lord Our God for everything to go as planned and for the Colonel not to change his mind about his intentions for her daughter—whether Eugênia agreed to this fate, decided in her absence.

If they'd consulted her, Eugênia would have said no. She didn't want to be the Colonel's wife, or the mother of those children. She'd been raised as a pampered only child. She had never been punished, nor was she taught domestic chores, like hanging the linens out to bleach in the sun or shucking corn, separating out the best kernels for cornmeal and leaving the rest for the chickens. Eugênia was a girl with wishes and desires, and being the new wife of Colonel Aristeu Medeiros Galvão was not one of them.

"Well, don't just stand there. Come and say hello to your fiancé," she heard her father order her, still stunned. Instead of obeying him, on an impulse, Eugênia turned her back and ran further inside the house, an act considered a great insult to the Colonel.

The sheriff almost took his belt to her. Eugênia was saved from the whipping by her mother, who pleaded with her husband, arguing that girls were prone to outbursts like that. "I'm sure the Colonel will understand. It was just all the excitement with the news, what else could it be?"

Ashamed of his daughter's bad manners, the sheriff, who was tough outside the home but soft-hearted when it came to his family, hung his belt on the doorframe to warn Eugênia that there would be no backing down from the engagement that was already agreed upon.

Deep down, he blamed himself. His weak grip on the girl had caused him to be embarrassed in front of the most powerful man in the region.

Even without physical punishment, the sheriff did not forgive his daughter and ordered that Eugênia not be allowed to set foot outside the house for the next few weeks. She wouldn't even be allowed in the yard. Maybe Eugênia would come to her senses. She would only be allowed out on the street again if she began to behave as a young woman who was spoken for should, and expressed her sincere apologies at the Colonel's next visit.

"She'll apologize," her mother had reassured her husband on her daughter's behalf. "Marriage will make her more mature; you'll see. It happens to all of us. I cried too when my father brought you in by the arm and announced our marriage, and I'm still here, aren't I?"

The sheriff was surprised. In nearly twenty years of marriage, he had never been told that detail.

"It's what youngsters do! Now, drink this liqueur, and tomorrow everything will be different."

When she was finally released from her punishment, after a formal apology to the Colonel on her fiancé's second visit, Eugênia showed up to our house to resume her lacework. The piece she had been working on was still half finished, but Eugênia was no longer the same. Our friend seemed to have forgotten the craft of lacemaking. Once so meticulous with her pieces, Eugênia had lost her knack from sadness. Instead of those lovely arabesques and curlicues, she now made shapeless designs that tried my aunt's patience.

"The Colonel isn't that old, Eugênia," Vitorina said, trying to cheer her up. "He's quite handsome, and, what's more, he's rich! He can take you to see the sea in Recife. Or maybe even to Europe? Just imagine, you'll get to see Paris!"

Silent, Eugênia seemed not to hear Vitorina's musings.

"You're lucky," added my aunt. "Would you rather stay single? Die young? Fall for some lowlife and lose your way? You should be raising your hands to the heavens. I'm going to tell you the truth, Eugênia, since your friends don't have the courage to stand up to you. That sulky face of yours is a great ingratitude toward your parents, who have made a nice arrangement for you with the Colonel, thinking only of your own good. But God will send a punishment. There's no other fate for those who spit on things as you have since this engagement was sealed."

But Eugênia already felt punished by God, and that's why she just continued to make her lace in silence, with a melancholy air, and in that unusual way, with no designs, like an apprentice still practicing the basic stitches.

"No one will buy that lace," my aunt complained once more, as she leaned over to examine Eugênia's work more closely. "It won't even do for the display case."

"I won't sell it, Firmina," my friend said at last, mid-sigh. "I'll make it into a collar for the dress I'll wear to Mass."

When she heard that, Tia Firmina sat up straight: "You're going to wear that mess to church? Show off that shoddy work in front of everyone? Whatever for? To tarnish our name? Well, I can't wait for this wedding to take place. Your husband will set a bridle on you. You can count on it!"

This time Eugênia did not respond to her taunts. She let out another sigh, one of the many she made lately, and went back to her lace.

She finished the collar that same afternoon and, to our surprise, when Sunday came around, she entered the parish church with a confident smile, showing off her work, stitched onto her dress in a way that looked a little uncomfortable, not unlike the bridle my aunt had mentioned.

With an engagement ring on her finger, Eugênia started to dress differently. A betrothed woman, she no longer wore braids or ruffles. She was expected to wear her hair tied back in a bun and dresses in a neutral color, straight cut. The Colonel and his children also attended Mass, but this time they sat in the same pew as the sheriff with his wife and daughter, announcing their engagement to the whole town. Anyone looking on from afar could picture the portrait of the family they would soon form.

Eugênia's collar, made with that unusual lace, didn't attract the attention of anyone besides us lacemakers. In the eyes of someone unfamiliar with the craft, Eugênia was wearing a lace collar like any other. Perhaps a bit more discreet, in line with her new status as a fiancée.

But right as I was leaving the church, Eugênia ran up to me, in a state.

"I need to tell you a secret."

Her eyes shone as I hadn't seen in a long time.

"See if you can figure out my intentions with this collar."

Before I had time to ask her what she was talking about, Eugênia turned over my palm and, in one swift movement, placed a folded piece of paper in it. Then, she closed my fingers tight, and gave me a knowing smile before running off toward her father, now calling her at the door of the church.

I only mustered the courage to see what was written on that paper when I got home. Admittedly, I didn't understand it right away. In the note given to me by Eugênia, there was only a series of letters in rounded handwriting alongside symbols drawn in pencil.

It was only when I looked at them more closely that I recognized the shapes of the drawings and understood what was going on. Eugênia had assigned a letter to each stitch of our lace. My friend had created a code. A code in lace.

Eugênia had started by using the first letter of each stitch. The angel stitch represented the A; the butterfly stitch, the B; the chain stitch, the C; until, because there were no stitches starting with all the letters of the alphabet, she began to make her own tweaks. For the Z she chose the bumblebee stitch, for the X the cross stitch, and soon she'd covered the entire alphabet.

The day after we ran into each other at Mass, when we met to make lace at my house, Eugênia wore the same collar as the day before, now attached to a cotton blouse.

"So?" she came over to ask me, discreetly, so the others wouldn't hear. "Did you figure it out?"

Immediately, I looked at her collar more closely, now trying to decode it. When she realized what I was trying to do, Eugênia laughed, taking pleasure in it.

"Today you'll have an extra challenge beyond making your perfect lace. Don't worry, I'll sit right in front of you to make your life easier."

"What are you two whispering about?" Tia Firmina wanted to know, and Eugênia made up something about an order we had to finish that week.

While Eugênia chatted with the others, I took the opportunity to adjust my pillow, placing the paper with the code under the piece I was working on, taking care so that no one would notice.

That day, after every stitch I made, I'd raise my head slightly, allowing me to check the sequence of stitches on Eugênia's collar and compare them with the code.

The first stitch was an *I*, the second a *T*. It took me a while to identify the third letter, because I needed to see through the lines of my work. As I worked my needle up and down, I deciphered Eugênia's message and memorized the combinations, until, after the first half hour, I no longer needed to look at the paper.

Once I'd figured out the first line, I dropped a spool, which hit the floor with a thump and rolled all the way across the room, until it reached the porch.

It pains me to marry. That's what the collar said.

My sister Cândida, who was playing outside, heard the spool hit the stone floor and, following the direction of the sound, groped around until she found it and handed it back to me.

"Here you are, Inês," she said, holding it out to me with her delicate, tiny hand.

"Sometimes I'd swear that girl can see," Vitorina said, and my mother bragged:

"Cândida can see better than most people. Don't be fooled by her eyes."

"What color is this thread, Inês?" my sister asked.

"It's white, like a white monjita bird," I replied.

My sister understood colors as they corresponded to birds. I knew how much she admired the song of that bird, so common in the semi-arid Caatinga region, also known as the little widow, and it occurred to me to use it as an example to explain white.

Now recovered from the shock, I glanced back at Eugênia and realized my friend was expecting a reaction to her message, but my first instinct was to pretend to concentrate on threading my needle.

When you spend a lot of time in silence with the same people, you develop an ability to sense their moods through their breathing. Even when we were often distracted or lost in thought, the other lacemakers and I remained attentive to each other's movements, as if we were part of a single body.

Eugênia knew that in a lacemaking circle not a single sigh went unnoticed, so, in order to distract the others, she brought up something that would divert everyone's attention from my obvious nervousness: the Cine Teatro Guarany, which was being built in the next town over, Triunfo, modeled after the cinemas of the world's great capital cities.

"We'll have moving pictures, concerts, operas, and elegant balls," Vitorina said, listing them off. "Progress is making its way here."

"Well, I think it's a waste of money. Whatever do we need a cinema for, for God's sake?" asked my aunt. "So people will believe in happy endings?"

The ensuing debate between them bought me some time to decode the rest of Eugênia's collar.

When I finished, my heart was racing. I tried to smile but couldn't.

"Inês?" Vitorina had noticed I'd stopped working, and my aunt came over to check the lace I was making.

"You've barely started, Inês. You're always ahead of the others."

When she bent down to peer at my face, she got worried. "Why, you're as white as a sheet. Is it that time of the month, by any chance? You know you can't make lace when you're on your period. The hand gets sluggish. How many times do I have to tell you?"

Seeing me in such low spirits, my mother put her work aside and got up to make me some beef broth, boiled with the bone, to ensure I'd recover quickly.

"Why didn't you tell me you were feeling poorly, dear?" she asked affectionately, leading me to the sofa, while Tia Firmina took away my work and complained about how fragile girls were these days, with none of the robustness of the women of olden times.

"You fall apart over nothing, a bunch of weaklings. Bring some of that broth for everyone, Carmelita. Or we'll have to finish the bedspread ourselves. And, if that's the case, the profits will only be shared among those who worked on it. I will not reward softies."

I accepted the doting that surrounded me, while I repeated to myself the words that had so surprised me on Eugênia's collar.

> *It pains me to marry,*
> *no right to say no.*
> *On the outside, I seem quiet,*
> *but I'm screaming within.*
> *Veil, ring, and collar,*
> *a lifelong slave.*

As I sipped the broth that was so hot it burned my tongue, I looked at Eugênia's neck. I no longer saw a lace collar before me, but the hopeless outpourings of a woman condemned.

4

Eugênia vanished from our lives shortly after the afternoon I deciphered the message on her collar. As her wedding day approached, she simply didn't show up one day, then the next, until her consecutive absences began to interfere with our production, forcing Tia Firmina to ask the man in the dark suit for an extension on the delivery time for some orders.

After a month, when we no longer counted on her presence, and were used to not hearing her breath in our circle, her mother appeared at our door.

She'd come to tell us that her daughter would no longer be attending our lacemaking afternoons. She was far too busy with wedding preparations and no longer had time for lace. In fact, in the midst of so much activity and appointments so her daughter's wedding ceremony would go perfectly, she herself had made a great effort just coming out here to let us know. What's more, Eugênia now occupied a new social position, very different from our own. The groom was a very wealthy man, as everyone knew, and it wouldn't be right for a colonel's wife to continue stitching tablecloths to be sold at bazaars for a few pennies, don't you agree?

We preferred not to answer that question, and, after a few moments, the silence that had taken over the room was broken by my aunt, who, somewhat offended by the comments she'd just heard, quoted a passage of scripture.

"'He that tilleth his land shall be satisfied with bread.' That's not just me saying so, it's in the Bible, in Proverbs. Hard work has never been cause for shame," Tia Firmina said firmly, without disguising her disdain for Eugênia or her family, who had been deceived by the easy life Colonel Aristeu's fortune dangled before them.

On my aunt's list of virtues, hard work was second only to faith. Eugênia, who had never been very fond of either of those things, was now lost forever.

"We'll miss Eugênia very much," my mother lamented. "Ask her to come round to visit after the wedding."

But Eugênia's mother swiftly dismissed the idea.

"I'll give her the message, Carmelita, but I can't promise anything. Once she's married, Eugênia will have to devote herself entirely to her husband and children, those poor little orphans. And Fazenda Caviúna is too far from town for her to keep coming into Bom Retiro with the same regularity. My husband and I will even have to make the trip out there to see her, but I plan on spending entire seasons at Caviúna, especially once my grandchildren are born."

"That certainly won't be any great sacrifice for you," Tia Firmina said, needling our visitor, but she didn't seem to notice.

"Of course I'll miss my home, but Eugênia will need me to guide her in household tasks and mothering. My girl is so inexperienced. But I'm sure she'll miss everyone here," she assured us, bringing an end to the conversation. "Eugênia has always been very fond of you all. So much so that she asked me to bring these scented sachets as a parting gift. Look, she made them herself."

On the table, Eugênia's mother arranged half a dozen heart-shaped lace sachets with each of our initials. They gave off the citrus scent of lemongrass. We were all moved by the kindness of Eugênia's gesture and the quality of her work. There was even a sachet for Cândida, who, feeling the lace with her well-practiced little fingers, identified two different

Cs. The one with the most texture was surely for her, the other for our mother. She was also the one who realized that the sachet with the letter *I*, for Inês, was simpler than the others.

"Yours came undecorated, Inês," Cândida said, and I quickly snatched the little bag out of everyone's sight, to put an end to the matter. I knew why my sachet wasn't like the others, and I didn't want to call attention to it.

With all the gifts handed out, Eugênia's mother considered her task complete and announced that she must be on her way, as the cake tasting would be held that same afternoon.

"There are so many details to sort out. You can't imagine how exhausted I am. I never thought that marrying off a daughter would be so much work! You'll see, Carmelita. Although . . ." She stopped herself short before she said what she was really thinking, something along the lines of "I suppose it's best the Flores girls didn't marry."

"Although what?" my aunt repeated inquisitively, sensing the hidden intent behind our guest's remark.

"Although, the longer the girls stay single, the more company you'll have, Carmelita!" said Eugênia's mother, trying to steer the conversation in a different direction. "Can you believe I cry myself to sleep every night over my daughter who hasn't even left home yet?" she said, lying to cover up the faux pas she'd nearly made.

My mother smiled politely and, accompanying our visitor to the door, offered to help with whatever was needed before the wedding.

"You can count on us. In fact, we would be delighted to make the lace for the bride's veil. If you haven't already ordered one, of course."

"Ordered where, Carmelita?" Tia Firmina asked, almost offended. "Even the brides from Recife come to us. We have more orders for veils than we can handle. Especially now that we're down one of our lacemakers. Luckily, Eugênia wasn't the most devoted of makers. She won't be missed much. If it had been Inês, well, then we'd be in very bad shape."

"The veil could be our gift for the bride," said Vitorina, excited about the idea.

But Eugênia's mother turned down the offer.

"Thank you for your kindness. But Eugênia insists on making the veil herself. You know how stubborn she is. She wants to make it with her own hands. She said it will be a surprise for the groom. And she's oh so devoted to her plan! She's been spending her days locked inside her room, toiling away. I keep telling her she won't have any color in her cheeks on her wedding day, but she doesn't listen."

Tia Firmina agreed that Eugênia did have a difficult temperament but praised her change in attitude toward marriage.

"Glad to know that the girl is being less disobedient. It was high time for Eugênia to mend her ways and stop complaining. No husband will put up with a wife who sneers and scoffs at everything. Madam, forgive me for being so frank, but your daughter moaned to us about things that amounted to nothing more than childish stubbornness."

Eugênia's mother smiled, a little embarrassed by her daughter's behavior, which she knew well, and then, seeming to remember something very urgent, she turned.

"Oh goodness, it's after three! I really must be going."

She wished everyone good luck, stressed that she was counting on our presence at the ceremony, and left, certain she would never again have reason to return to Casa das Flores.

As soon as Eugênia's mother left the house with the blue windows, Tia Firmina and Vitorina went to a corner of the room to talk about the rudeness of that woman who had barely touched the cake we'd served her. I took advantage of the fact that the two of them were engaged in conversation and that my mother had gotten up to take the untouched tray back to the kitchen to look more closely at my sachet.

The paper with Eugênia's code was hidden inside a book in my bedroom, but I remembered most of it and was able to decipher the message on the sachet with the letter *I*.

It was one short sentence. A message.

So I can be sure
I can count on you,
wear yellow to my wedding.

"Why are you studying that sachet so closely, dear?" asked my mother, now back in the sitting room, noticing my faraway look.

"I'm just looking at the stitches, Mother," I replied, half telling the truth. She came closer to get a better look.

"Well, they aren't as pretty as yours. But none of ours are. Better not let your aunt hear us," she joked, and we laughed.

The unwanted title of best lacemaker in the group was like an uncomfortable garment for me, the kind that fits but we didn't choose. Most of the time, I tried to downplay any compliments I got, even though I knew my lace was always the first one sold from the display.

"We have to wait for Inês's stock to run out before ours starts to sell," Vitorina would joke after a bazaar or a visit to a buyer. "As long as there's one of Inês's hankies lying around, my pieces just sit there at the bottom of the trunk."

"Don't be silly, Vitorina," I replied. "You were our teacher, and don't you forget that."

But she just shrugged, because she didn't really want to be the best.

My naturally calm demeanor, combined with a mind not given to wandering, made me a natural. Unlike the others, I could spend hours in silence, with my attention focused on the lace, the never-ending up-and-down of my needle, finishing off one stitch after another with the same regularity as my breath, in endlessly repeating cycles.

At the end of the day, when the piece was finished, it felt like I'd just woken up from a dream, the kind that slips away from us like water between our fingers in the first moments after we wake up. Many times I couldn't even remember the design I'd just made; I was so lulled by the continuous movement that it led me into a trance. Maybe that was why I didn't develop a particular attachment to any of the pieces I made, and sometimes I even wondered whether I'd made a christening gown or a tablecloth the day before.

"How could you have forgotten that nightgown, Inês? You spent days toiling over it," said Eugênia in astonishment.

But I really didn't remember. The final product didn't matter as much to me as it did to Eugênia, always enthusiastic about the possibility of new designs.

"I was thinking about stitching some butterflies in flight for this dress, Carmelita. We've never made butterflies. What do you think?"

My friend also couldn't stand it when she had to redo a single stitch.

"Can't I just leave it the way it is, Firmina? You can barely see the flaw, it will take me hours to redo this hem," she whimpered, always complaining about what a waste of time it was going back down the same path.

Unlike my friends, starting over didn't bother me, since it was precisely the repetition that intoxicated me. Though it was guided by my hand, the constant to-and-fro of the thread seemed to have a mind of its own and took me places I'd never seen before and that perhaps didn't even exist. This almost mystical stupor, to which I surrendered daily, was more valuable to me than the pride of seeing my piece finished. That's why, as soon as I'd finished one job, I would immediately start another, like an addiction, an escape.

Vitorina was even less cut out for the work than Eugênia. She had too much energy pent up inside her to sit still for so long. We usually started work at nine in the morning, and before eleven there she was, pacing back and forth, offering to go to the kitchen to get some juice, or to close or open the windows, saying "It's so hot today" or "It's definitely going to rain today, don't you think?"

"Do whatever you want, Vitorina, but be quick. It makes me dizzy seeing that girl fidget like that," my aunt would complain, and Vitorina would take the opportunity to get up once more to go to the bathroom, get some fresh air on the porch, or people-watch.

"You may not believe it, Firmina," Vitorina said with a clever air, trying to make excuses. "But if I don't stretch my arms a bit, they'll get stuck, and tomorrow I won't be able to work from all the pain in my joints. Orders will be delayed because of me. Is that what you want?"

My mother was more like me. Her hands created pieces almost as highly praised as mine. Tia Firmina's were also impeccable, with a perfection achieved thanks to pure stubbornness. Her determination to produce something that was a cause for exaltation was such that, in the end, she made works of art.

Even Cândida tried her hand at a few stitches. With her tiny fingers, she would feel along the tape until she figured out where the needle should enter. Then, with the other hand, she would make sure of the exact spot to push it back out. She recorded with thread, even with very simple designs, things that she only saw in her mind.

"Even the blind girl is faster than me," Vitorina said, poking fun at herself when she saw what my sister had made. "I'm going to give up this life as a lacemaker and go back to helping my father in the store."

"Don't do that, Vitorina," said my mother. "It's his money there. This money is yours."

"Besides, it was thanks to your snooping that we learned the stitches," Eugênia added, and Vitorina shuddered, squirming in her chair.

"Don't say that! My cousin threatened me with the fires of hell over that. She swore she'd ask the nuns to pray to God to punish me for my wrongdoing."

"Oh, what nonsense!" exclaimed Tia Firmina, offended. "She's the one who sinned. That fool was the one who allowed herself to be watched. It's not your fault your cousin broke the vow of trust she'd taken. And, if God allowed the secrets of making lace to reach us, Our Lord Jesus Christ must have had His reasons. We're just doing His will, Vitorina, and therefore we are all forgiven."

The resoluteness of those words comforted us. Aside from the parish priest, no one understood more about God's ways than my aunt.

Devoutly pious, she was proud to say it was her own youthful hair that cascaded over the shoulders of the statue of Saint Agatha on the church altar.

"It's in a better place there. On Saint Agatha, it's still the honey color of my youth. On me, it'd have already turned all white."

Because she was so active in parish affairs, she was secretly offended she hadn't been consulted by Eugênia's family about the details of the upcoming religious ceremony. Not even to choose the wedding canticles or readings.

"If Eugênia weren't so stubborn and would let us make that veil, no one would be able to take their eyes off her as she entered the church. With eight hands we'd finish it in no time. In the center, we'd stitch hearts and pairs of doves, to represent the bride and groom's love. Above, two rings intertwined, as a symbol of marriage, an unbreakable sacrament. Around the edges, a frame of orange blossoms, known to bring good fortune. But that ungrateful girl doesn't deserve such a veil. And if she doesn't want it, who am I to insist? Let her be. Maybe we can make a veil like that for another bride?"

Vitorina soon piped up: "Only if it's for me, Firmina. Because no boy from around these parts wants to risk death from the curse of the Flores women," she joked, mischievously, speaking just for the sake of speaking, with no intention of offending me or Cândida.

"Stop being silly, girl," said Tia Firmina, stiffening in her chair. "There is no curse."

"That's not what people say," Vitorina replied.

"Those are people with nothing better to do," Tia Firmina said, but Vitorina insisted:

"If it's not true, how do you explain why all the men who've passed through this house never made it to see their grandchildren?"

"So now I have to explain myself to you? God decides when it's our time to go. Please."

"We lost our men on account of life, Vitorina," my mother intervened after a while. "That's just the way it is."

"Even so," Vitorina continued, unable to drop it. "You'd have to be very brave to court Inês or Cândida."

"Well, I don't care about that curse," Cândida confessed, feeding a cardinal that had made a nest on one of the columns in the sitting room. "I never want to leave this house. Who will take care of my birdies if I'm not here?"

"Are you listening to what this girl is saying?" Tia Firmina got even more upset, now putting her lace aside. "Do you see what you've done, Vitorina? Are you satisfied? You've scared the child."

"I wasn't scared, Tia," Cândida assured her. "I've heard that story many times. It was a gypsy who cursed our great-grandmother, wasn't it?"

"Hogwash!" said Tia Firmina, getting up, more indignant than ever and calling an end to that afternoon's session. She didn't like hearing the family name mixed up in superstition. "I won't sit here and listen to this nonsense. Now if you'll excuse me."

That night, Tia Firmina didn't come down for dinner. She sent a message through Cândida that she'd been hit with a bad case of heartburn after the afternoon's conversation, and she spent the days that followed blaming Vitorina for churning up the acid in her stomach.

Deep down, however, my aunt was burdened by the secret she'd heard from her grandmother and that she'd never had the courage to share with her younger sister. Cândida and I were the fourth generation doomed by a plot she believed in wholeheartedly and one that was far from over. For many years to come, the Flores women would live under the edge of that sharp, invisible dagger, and, for this reason, Firmina prayed the Salve Regina every day for the women not yet born, but who already shared with her, and with us, the same unhappy fate in love.

5

Rio de Janeiro, 2010

Alice came home from the march with her eyes stinging from the pepper spray. *Sons of bitches,* she thought, and then she scolded herself. It wasn't their mothers she wanted to offend but the cops who'd attacked the peaceful protesters downtown.

Assholes, she corrected herself mentally. *They're all a bunch of assholes.*

Underneath her T-shirt, you could still read part of the message she'd painted hours ago on her bare chest with gouache, distorted somewhat by the curve of her breasts: "Not One Less." It was a warning to the world. If just one woman was a victim of violence, the rest would come together and demand justice.

Now, the fabric of her T-shirt almost completely covered the words, displayed with pride that afternoon, during the demonstration organized to draw attention to the attack on Kaylane, a twenty-four-year-old pharmacist, that had taken place earlier that week.

Her attacker, a bitter ex-boyfriend unhappy they'd broken up, had been waiting for her to leave work, holding a bottle of gasoline. There had been no argument. Maybe Kaylane hadn't even seen him when he came up from behind. She just felt her body get unexpectedly wet and then the heat consumed her all over. Twenty-five-year-old Cleyton, an administrative assistant, had thrown an open plastic bottle of gasoline at the person to whom he'd sworn eternal love up until the previous day and, without hesitation, lit the match.

According to a homeless person who was nearby, Cleyton had allegedly taunted the young woman before setting her on fire: "Nobody will want you now, you slut!"

Lying in a hospital bed on the brink of death, with 80 percent of her body burned, was Kaylane's punishment for having decided she didn't belong to Cleyton, who had no record and was considered a quiet and hardworking young man by all who knew him.

If Kaylane wasn't his, she wouldn't be anyone else's, either, and, to ensure no other man would ever love Kaylane, Cleyton deemed it necessary for his ex-girlfriend's body—its scent and curves so familiar to him—to be deformed by fire. It was his way of guaranteeing he'd never be replaced. If his ex-girlfriend died in the fire, it didn't matter. The effect would be the same. Cleyton had already lost Kaylane, and the choice had been hers. Arrested in the act at the scene, Cleyton cried on TV, claiming he only did what he did because he couldn't imagine a life without Kaylane.

Son of a bitch, Alice thought again as she recalled the case and scolded herself once more. Cleyton wasn't a son of a bitch, he was a murderer. You had to give things their proper name. "Murderer," she repeated under her breath.

Her friends texted her to come out to the club, but Alice was in no mood for chitchat and talk about diets. She took off her T-shirt and saw the words pulsing on her body reflected in the mirror, backward. She lay down on the bed exhausted, and, as she put her head on the pillow, she bumped the tissue paper package she'd been given days before.

Remembering what it was, Alice scowled. A mantilla veil, something that combined the two great tools of female castration: marriage and the church. She was so annoyed she tossed the package aside, wanting to get rid of it. A corner of the lace slipped out from the tissue paper.

To Alice's surprise, instead of mildew or mothballs, as she'd expected, the scent of flowers filled the room. The fresh scent, which piqued both her curiosity and her senses, made her tug the lace back toward her and spread the veil out on top of her.

The light from the bedside table pierced the lace, casting the shadow of the woven stitches onto Alice's skin. On her chest, over the remnants of those fighting words, "Not one less," you could now also see the same shadow that lace had made a hundred years earlier. Alice gave in to temptation for a moment and let her veil fall over her face to smell the perfume. She took a deep breath but was soon gasping.

Despite its delicate appearance, the veil was also a prison.

Its lace was like an iron fence wrought to stifle thought. There was no freedom in a mantilla veil. For a moment, Alice felt sorry for the veil's former owner, an ancestor whose name she didn't know. She didn't even know what mark that poor woman had left on the world, subjugated by everything that veil represented.

Alice concluded that they were all prisoners: the ancestor who'd kept the veil; the pharmacist Kaylane, just twenty-four years old, in the hospital on the brink of death; her mother, with her face rendered almost inert by Botox, always boasting to maybe feel bigger; and even her, who, despite her blue hair and the motto written across her chest, still called a murderer a "son of a bitch."

In 2010, the world may have changed, but it was also still very much the same. Alice tossed the veil aside once more to rid herself of that feeling of powerlessness, and, in doing so, a small piece of paper flew out from between the folds of the lace, like a moth escaping a net. After gliding for a few seconds in the air, it landed on the rug at the foot of the bed.

At first Alice ignored it, thinking of all the effort it would take to find out what it was. A forgotten note, a shopping list, an old dry-cleaning ticket that had accidentally made its way into the package. But her curiosity was destined to grow until she got answers, and being restless by nature, the type who peeks at the answers before starting a crossword, Alice knew she wouldn't be able to ignore that piece of paper for long.

After a few moments, tormented by all the possibilities her mind came up with for that tiny intruder on her bedroom rug, Alice gave in. She stretched as far as she could without having to get out of bed and, with some juggling, grabbed the paper off the floor.

Unlike the veil, which was a pristine white, stored with care by the relatives who had kept it all those years, the paper was yellowed with age and perhaps as old as the veil itself.

Alice didn't understand it right away. It wasn't a note, or a shopping list, or a dry-cleaning ticket. None of the possibilities she'd imagined were correct. In neat handwriting, there was a column of letters written in pencil alongside geometric designs that looked like exotic hieroglyphs.

Alice concluded it was an exercise by a child learning to read and write, and this answer tamed her curiosity. She even had the urge to crumple it up and throw it in the trash, but she didn't, believing she had no right to throw away a piece of paper that was who knows how old.

When a cool June breeze blew through the window, Alice felt a shiver in her shirtless chest, still bearing traces of paint. It was because of the cold, but also because of the feeling of helplessness that day's events had given her.

She'd woken with hopes of being able to make a difference, she'd experienced the euphoria of shouting slogans, believing everything could change if they all shouted loud enough, until they were heard. But soon after came the hustle and bustle, the police crackdown, the suffocating pepper spray, taking refuge in the bathroom of a restaurant until things settled down. And then, a lonely ride home on the metro, where most of the passengers, with their eyes glued to their phones, remained apathetic, comfortable in their routine, without slogans written across their chests, without knowing the story of Kaylane, without ever imagining that Alice had a dead relative who'd once owned the veil she was now holding.

Alice drew the lace across her to shield herself from the loneliness that washed over her for a moment and immediately regretted it: the paint on her chest would surely stain the fabric. *Well, fuck this shitty lace,* she thought immediately after, without pausing.

Prison walls are meant to be graffitied. If her aunt had wanted the veil to remain intact, she would have kept it in a drawer seven hundred kilometers away from Alice. If there was a reason that veil had been passed down for all those years, a reason Alice still didn't understand, she could use it however she wanted. If the veil was her responsibility now, she felt entitled to do with it as she pleased. Including untying the ends and fraying the whole thing. Just like Penelope, fed up with waiting so long for a man who went out for a spin and took thirty-five years to come back. That asshole. "Asshole." That's more like it.

A veil is, first and foremost, threads woven into a pattern, but Alice strayed from any patterns. That lace, once used to worship the saints, now warmed her nonconformist breasts. What had once been someone's prison now served as her shelter. It was proof that things could change. Even though she felt drowsy, enveloped in the peace the veil brought her, Alice couldn't sleep. Kaylane was lying in a hospital bed, with burns covering 80 percent of her body.

6

Bom Retiro, 1918

That time of year, the quaresminha shrubs were still green. Contrary to what one might think, it's the leaves and twigs, not the flowers, that, when boiled in a wide, shallow pan over a flame, release a yellow pigment often used by the elders to dye thread and fabric. The secret was in the amount of water. You had to use very little, unless you wanted a pale yellow, almost beige.

For over an hour I'd been concentrating on controlling the height of the flames, fanning the wood with a fan made of juçara palm fronds, trying to keep the embers from going out. Beside me, my mother sighed loudly, on purpose, so I would be sure to pick up on her dissatisfaction. She couldn't bear my sudden desire to change the color of my dress.

"It's still new, Inês. It's a sin to dye it. There are no stains to cover up."

"I wore this dress to the parish's fiftieth anniversary celebration, Mother. I don't want folks to think I only have one," I explained, weakly, since it was hard for me to lie. Even more so to her.

My mother understood the reason, but she didn't agree with it. I wasn't the type to worry about frivolities like wearing the same dress twice; but as it was not like my mother to impose her will on others, she kept quiet.

"What color is yellow again, Inês?" asked Cândida.

"The color of a canary."

Cândida had just put out a piece of scarlet eggplant for her birds, which were beginning to swoop around the house in search of the food my sister left for them everywhere. At Casa das Flores they lived uncaged, making nests on top of the shelves, flying from one room to another and perching on the chandeliers. They were both a responsibility and entertainment for Cândida, who treated them like her children. Birdsong and the rustling of wings filled the world of darkness my sister inhabited with infinite sounds.

"If yellow is as beautiful as a canary's song, you're sure to catch everyone's eye at the party, Inês," she said and, after reflecting for a moment, added: "If I were to change the color of my dress, I would dye it red, the color of the cockerel's plume."

My mother laughed as she imagined an eight-year-old girl dressed in red at a wedding.

"Your dress will be white like the dove of the Holy Spirit. It's more appropriate for your age," my mother explained, and Cândida just scowled.

Doves had a clumsy coo that was aggravating to listen to, but perhaps the dove to which our mother was referring, and which represented the third element of the Holy Trinity, was different. Its song might sound like a heavenly chorus.

Though I trusted my mother and sister completely, I couldn't let on that my dyeing the dress was a response to the message Eugênia had sent me on the sachet. My friend wanted to know if she could count on me, and, without even realizing the extent of such a commitment at the time, I considered it my duty to give her some peace of mind.

Eugênia's distress was understandable. A loveless union with an older, unfamiliar man would plant the seed of fear in anyone. Especially in a soul that had dreamed of other paths in life.

On the other hand, nothing prevented Eugênia from eventually growing to like her future husband. That's the way most marriages went, wasn't it? Perhaps all that anguish over their arranged marriage was just one piece of a great love story, something Eugênia would look back on years later, finding humor in her immaturity in those first years of marriage.

Over time, Eugênia might come to find admirable qualities in the Colonel and grow fond of him. And there would still be the orphans to keep her company.

While I didn't think marriage was supposed to be a punishment for women, a part of me was relieved by the knowledge that, as a Flores, I would never be forced by my family to marry. In the house with blue windows there was no talk of marriage. Fatherless from a young age and widowed before she was even twenty-five, after her third birth, my mother had learned it was possible to live without a man around.

The money she earned at her job as a clerk at the infirmary had always been enough for us, and after we started our lace business, we began to enjoy some luxuries: eau de cologne from the capital and bonbons wrapped in gold paper brought by the man in the dark suit.

Like my mother, Tia Firmina also seemed content to live surrounded only by women. Since she was young, she would say she was married to Our Lord Jesus Christ and had strong bonds of friendship with her devotional saints. She didn't want for company, and, so, that affection was enough for her.

"No love is greater than God's. No protection is more powerful than that of the angels. We don't need men to defend us," she taught Cândida and me, still small, and since then we have confirmed that there is no greater truth.

"But angels are men," Cândida said at the time.

"That's where you're wrong. The body is a worldly shell. Divine creatures like angels are neither male nor female. They are not made of flesh, like human beings. They are made of light."

Despite not knowing the meaning of the word *worldly* at the time or sharing the same understanding of the concept of light, I remember the look of enchantment that washed over Cândida's face when she imagined this divine pantheon of winged beings my aunt had described in such rich detail.

Though it wasn't Tia Firmina's intention, that conversation caused us to start imagining angels always in female form. If they didn't have a defined gender, it was fair for people under their protection to choose how they looked. The form we imagined became one of a beautiful and affectionate woman guarding our path.

◆　◆　◆

Strangely, when I stopped being a little girl and took on the shape of a young woman, I didn't have romantic daydreams, or any real or imagined desire to fall in love, like I saw with Eugênia, for example.

I remember one day on the Feast of Saint Anthony, when Eugênia appeared holding an apple, excited to teach me a ritual she'd overheard from some older women who worked in her house. She was eager to try something that promised to reveal a clue from the marriage saint about her future husband.

"Now, pay attention, Inês. You have to peel the apple all in one go, like a ribbon. Then we take the whole peel and throw it in a basin of water. But be careful: the basin must be virgin. Like us. If you do this with faith in your heart, the letter the peel forms in the water will be the same as our future husband's first initial. Got it?"

Upon hearing the explanation, I smiled in disbelief. A gimmick like that would never lead to a reliable result. I even tried to argue that there were several letters that simply couldn't be formed from one continuous piece of apple peel, like an X or a T, for example, and that curved letters like C or U would have an advantage over others, and it was more probable for them to appear floating in the basin, but Eugênia wouldn't listen to me.

Instead of agreeing with me, she sighed, annoyed, scolding me for doubting Saint Anthony's power.

"Your lack of faith is what's kept the Flores women alone all these generations. If you believed, Saint Anthony would be able to free you from the curse. Saint Anthony has great powers and can make an apple peel into any shape. Besides, who would want a husband whose name starts with an *X*? I can't even think of a name starting with an *X*."

"Xerxes, Xavier," I replied, even though I didn't have to.

"God help me, Inês. I would never marry a Xerxes. Come on, I've got a basin with me. Do you want to do it, too? I have two apples. One for me, one for you."

"I really don't care to," I said, declining her offer. Eugênia didn't insist, imagining that, as a Flores, I had no real plans to get married, so as not to carry the blame for the death of an innocent man.

"Then hand me the knife and be quiet. I need to concentrate."

With her eyes closed, my friend began the ritual: she made her request to Saint Anthony "with faith in her heart," as she had explained to me was necessary in order for the ritual to work, and tossed the peel into the water. The letter that formed, curved as I had predicted, was an *S*.

"See, silly? It works." Eugênia clapped her hands, victorious, and spent the following months dreaming of a love story straight from the movies: a young man from the capital, a handsome student, maybe a doctor, maybe of noble stock, from Recife or even Rio de Janeiro, by the name of Silvio or Solano would knock on her door late one afternoon, perhaps asking for information, perhaps injured and in need of her care, and he would fall in love with her as soon as he laid eyes on her.

"Solano has a nice ring to it. Or maybe Santiago or Sebastião would be better?"

"It might also be Sergio," I suggested, not even believing her story, just playing along.

"Yes. Sergio is nice. We'll wait for him, then. He should arrive before the next Feast of Saint Anthony. That's how these rituals work."

Before a year had passed, however, Eugênia was already engaged. Out of solidarity and compassion, I never reminded my friend about that day, but I confess that the *S* floating in the basin of water came to mind when we learned of the arranged marriage to the Colonel.

As I had warned her that afternoon, not all letters could form from one continuous apple peel. *A*, for Aristeu, was one of them.

In addition to dyeing my dress yellow, I decided to add a detail that would reaffirm my solidarity with the bride. A collar, similar to the one Eugênia had made months before to show me the code, which would also carry a message.

On the eve of the wedding, I sat in my room while Cândida slept and pinned it to the dress, just before we left, so it wouldn't attract the attention of Tia Firmina or my mother. Because it was just a short phrase, I could make bigger stitches, which would ensure Eugênia would be able to see them even from afar.

"Trust" was the message on the collar. Not exactly in God, as I might have added, but in the ability of the future to be better than the present.

I truly believed that suffering could be turned into a gentler, more pleasant feeling. That's what happened when my father passed away. After I watched him perish following two feverish nights, his absence created such a void in our lives that I was sure I would never be able to smile again. However, with time, the weight of those difficult memories was diluted until they were overshadowed by sweet memories of the good times.

That was the lesson I wanted to pass on to Eugênia with my collar. That anguish, happiness, suffering, and peace were like seasons. They came and went, out of our control. They changed the world around us and then left for a new cycle to begin. Just like our men.

When my mother saw me ready for the ceremony, she smiled in approval.

"You were right, Inês. It does look like a new dress. Especially with that new collar."

She was wearing an old dress, but still in good condition. It was dark gray, the color of the green-winged saltator.

Cândida ran her fingers across the lace of my collar.

"Is there no design?" she asked, surprised when she didn't recognize any specific shapes.

Tia Firmina, who came rushing from inside the house dressed in a heavy black dress, like a smooth-billed ani, sarcastically interjected: "It's the latest fashion. Young folks these days no longer follow tradition. I can't wait to see what Eugênia's come up with for that veil she insisted on making herself."

"I'm sure it's beautiful, Firmina," my mother opined. "Eugênia is talented and determined."

"Too determined. That one is going to give the Colonel hell, poor man. As if the suffering of being a widower weren't enough," she added, as she took her mother-of-pearl rosary. "Come on, let's go! I don't want to lose my front-row seat. I conquered that seat throughout a lifetime in this parish, and I refuse to give it up. I'm not interested in the importance of the groom and his guests. He can call the shots out there on his cattle ranch, but not here in the land of Saint Agatha."

7

Bom Retiro, 1918

The tears streaming down the bride's face seemed to suggest she was overcome with emotion as she entered through the main door of the parish church in her white dress, wearing a beautifully crafted veil.

Contrary to what Tia Firmina had predicted, and what I myself had expected, Eugênia's elaborate veil depicted a variety of floral designs stitched to perfection, doing justice to our reputation as the best lace-makers in the region.

There was, however, one detail that few noticed but that didn't escape my eyes. In the center of the veil, forming a square no more than thirty centimeters wide in the middle of Eugênia's back, was a set of stitches resembling a chessboard.

Arm in arm with the sheriff, Eugênia stepped elegantly down the red carpet toward the altar. I noticed her searching for me, and, when she finally spotted me in my dyed canary-yellow dress, she smiled discreetly in gratitude for my answering her request.

I was only able to study the veil more carefully once the bride had passed our row, and it took me the entire homily to decipher the words Eugênia had felt unable to say aloud, but which she had decided to make real in her lace.

> *Instead of congratulations,*
> *Give me your condolences.*

Instead of smiling, cry for me.
This is my funeral Mass.
They have taken my life from me.
I am dead.

I put my hand to my chest, upset by what I'd just read. I squeezed Cândida's hand, and she pressed mine in return, even without understanding the reason for my unease.

"What is it, Inês?" she whispered, sounding distressed.

"It's just the emotion of seeing Eugênia, dear. Don't worry about me."

Nothing about the bride's behavior betrayed the desperation on her veil. After the ceremony, when the bride and groom finally came over to greet us, Eugênia appeared to be fine. She thanked us for our presence alongside her now-husband, Colonel Aristeu Medeiros Galvão, who gave us a sidelong glance, without any interest.

"Beautiful shade of yellow," Eugênia said, praising my dress. "The collar looks nice on you, too. But now that I'm getting a closer look, I don't think it's really my style."

Her comment would have sounded rude to anyone who overheard, criticizing a detail on a guest's dress, but we both knew the hidden meaning of our words, as well as those other words, in lace. As in times of war, we protected ourselves by speaking in code. The bride was referring to the message on my lace collar, in which I'd asked her to "trust" and, imperceptibly to the others, she was refusing my advice.

Taken aback by Eugênia's rejection of the idea that her situation might improve, I was about to reply that she could "at least try it on. Perhaps the collar would suit you, who knows?" but there was no time. My mother interrupted our conversation, not imagining we were talking about something else altogether:

"Of course the collar would look nice on you, Eugênia! You have such a slender neck. It would look ever so elegant."

"Hear that, Eugênia?" I agreed, still speaking ambiguously. "Maybe it's a matter of making a few alterations?"

But, before she could answer that it would never fit, the Colonel cleared his throat impatiently beside her.

The newlyweds still had to go around the entire hall to greet their distinguished guests from other cities, and we were talking about dresses.

"Let's go," he ordered Eugênia, touching her elbow.

I saw my friend's body stiffen to his touch, though it was brief. Eugênia looked at me steadily, as if she were going to scream, revealing to everyone there what she really felt, but then she seemed to abandon the impulse, allowing herself to be led, obediently, and smiling at the group next to us. She greeted her guests with the same studied intonation she had used with us.

I saw Vitorina a while later, wearing a dress the shade of a bluebird's feathers. She was accompanied by her brothers—she had so many that I sometimes got their names mixed up. They were all very close in age and took turns doing similar tasks. Vitorina's father owned the only general store in Bom Retiro, and the family could have been rich if there weren't so many of them. The boys worked in the family business, serving customers, traveling to other places in search of goods, and going to markets in the region, peddling vegetables, dried beef, sausages, and tobacco, then returning a few days later in an empty truck.

As the youngest in a large family, Vitorina enjoyed a certain amount of freedom in relation to the other girls in town. Her mother was older by the time she was born and, tired from chasing after the four older boys who were always setting fire to the rugs and breaking the china, Hildinha was more lenient when it came to raising her youngest. After spending all day scolding the older ones, she didn't have it in her to tell the girl to sit up straight at the table or to teach her etiquette or the piano.

The time she did spend with Vitorina, Hildinha set aside as a chance to rest from her role of being a mother. She even allowed herself to be lulled into afternoon naps as she watched the girl playing make-believe, wrapping herself in pieces of cloth and pretending she was in other times and places.

Vitorina was a joy that Hildinha could not deprive herself of, and, for that reason, she treated her daughter as a grandmother would a granddaughter. Until the birth of her youngest, she only had her husband and sons for company, and at the time, she was a little fed up with life, without knowing exactly why. Everything around her irritated her—the noise in the house, the taste of the food, the customers without manners, the hot weather, the cold weather—until her daughter arrived and the world became sweeter. Hildinha was finally able to use the ribbons and ruffles she'd ordered for her previous pregnancies but had never taken out of their boxes. She was nearly fifty when she fell pregnant with her and had thought her body was already done with the role nature had intended. The little girl's rosy lips and long eyelashes made everything turn surprisingly colorful, as it never had been, not even in her youth.

That is why, when the girl began to show the curves of a young woman, Hildinha tried not to think about the possibility of her youngest getting married. Deep down, she refused to accept that time would lead Vitorina to wish for a destiny other than that of being hers.

Secretly, Hildinha dreamed of Vitorina staying close by, keeping her company in her old age. Even if she never spoke this desire or even thought about it clearly, it was evident in her gestures and the way she nagged her.

With increasing frequency, Hildinha was forced to alter her daughter's dresses, as the girl's breasts no longer fit. Even so, she still bought her sweets and treats as if Vitorina were ten years old and teased any boy who approached her pride and joy.

Her eldest son was already married with two children. The second was engaged. So she wouldn't be wanting for grandchildren. Her husband was so quiet that Hildinha couldn't bear to live alone with him in that house. Not after Vitorina. She'd gotten used to the girl's singsong voice, which echoed off the walls, multiplying by a thousand and making it seem as if a party was being held in the next room.

Even though he was busy managing his business, it didn't take long for her husband to realize that his daughter's company alleviated his wife's bad moods and rheumatism, and, in a silent agreement there was no need to sign, he allowed Hildinha to cultivate the illusion that their daughter would never grow up.

At the age of sixteen, Vitorina still walked around barefoot, free of strict rules of behavior. Two young men from town had even gone so far as to inquire about arranging a meeting, but Hildinha had chased them off for their audacity, tallying such a long list of those poor men's faults that they never set foot in the general store again, forced to ask their relatives and neighbors to buy whatever supplies they needed.

Knowing her mother was so disturbed by the idea of her entering a relationship, Vitorina kept to herself the affection she had recently begun to feel for the primary school teacher, a shy, serious-looking young man who had recently arrived in Bom Retiro.

She'd met him as a customer at the store, on one of the rare occasions she helped out her brothers after becoming a lacemaker. From that day forward, every time Vitorina saw the young man arriving at the establishment, she would run over to assist him, even though it wasn't her duty.

The schoolmaster usually bought a cut of dried beef and two potatoes, as he lived alone and didn't need more than that. *Prudent and responsible*, Vitorina thought admiringly, starting to fall in love.

"I'll cut the meat for you. In fact, I'll do more than that. I'll give you an extra piece as a courtesy for being such a good customer," she kindly offered, but the schoolmaster refused, embarrassed, insisting on paying the fair price.

"I'd never want to cause you or your father to lose money."

Fair and honest, Vitorina marveled, and she wouldn't rest until she gave him some sort of gift: a piece of toffee or a box of alfenim sugar paste candies.

"You'll accept this sweet treat, won't you? It's on the house."

Embarrassed, the schoolmaster took her offer.

And so, between one purchase and another, a mutual regard was born, which would soon become more than that. Vitorina now felt a strange flutter in her chest every time they met. Whether it was in the store, at Mass, or on the street, she began to stumble over her words and thoughts, which was unusual for her.

Dropped packages, miscalculations—whenever Vitorina was around the schoolmaster, she felt like she was being graded in some way and would be overcome with nervousness while doing simple arithmetic. "One liter of milk, one hundred grams of black-eyed peas"—she tried so hard not to make a mistake that her sums came out all wrong.

Once, the schoolmaster kindly offered to help, and Vitorina felt her cheeks burning with embarrassment. *He must be thinking I'm a fool for getting such a silly sum wrong,* she lamented as soon as he left. Disappointed in herself, she sulked for the rest of the afternoon, only regaining her confidence at the end of the night, after she correctly recited the times table without looking at the printed card she still kept from her school days.

In the beginning, when Vitorina and the schoolmaster were first getting to know each other, this unbridled feeling frightened her a little. Because she was raised in a family with many siblings, who were not in the habit of judging her, Vitorina had never been embarrassed in front of boys, like other girls her age. Because it was such an unusual and unexpected feeling, Vitorina decided it was love, and, therefore, the next step was to make the schoolmaster's heart her own. Ever since she was born, she had always gotten everything she wanted, and this would be no different.

As he occupied a respected position in town, the young man had been invited to Colonel Aristeu's wedding to Eugênia. Not being a local, however, he spent most of the party alone and somewhat out of place. Many people greeted him politely but didn't stay with him for long.

"How have you been? I hope my children aren't giving you too much trouble. Say hello to the schoolmaster, son. Now let's go, the schoolmaster shouldn't have to put up with you on his day off. Enjoy yourself."

On these occasions, as Vitorina looked on, the schoolmaster would smile and let them go, always polite and measured in his words and gestures.

Even with my heart aching for Eugênia, whom I watched from afar as she walked around in her elegant white gown, now without her veil, it didn't take me long to realize, from the way Vitorina drummed her fingers on her punch glass, that my friend was about to act. As I said, we knew each other's breathing.

One of Vitorina's hallmarks was always doing whatever she wanted, without fear of consequences. That's how she discovered the stitches for making lace, perched on top of a ladder. Hildinha spoiled her, making her believe the world was hers, and, for Vitorina, there was no other truth on earth.

"I'm going to go over and talk to the schoolmaster, but I can't let Mama see me," she said, right after the bride and groom left the party. "If she finds out I'm besotted with him, she'll start selling the poor man flour with woodworms. That is, if she doesn't poison his olive oil or mix ground glass into his sugar. You have to help me, Inês."

I was surprised by her request. At that point, Odoniel, the youngest of Vitorina's brothers, approached us. Knowing what his sister was like, he could also sense she had something brewing.

"You better not be getting up to any of your tomfoolery," Odoniel scolded her as he approached. "Mama is in fragile health."

"Don't go meddling," she said, cutting him off brusquely, lacking the ceremony that befitted siblings.

Odoniel was a little embarrassed to have been told off like that in my presence, but I didn't act surprised; I knew that in this family Vitorina was the one in charge.

Odoniel was my friend's fourth brother, and often, when we were making lace on the porch, he would drive the store's truck by the house with the blue windows and honk three times to greet us. "There he goes, late, as always," Vitorina mumbled affectionately, waving to her brother.

"I just want to dance, Odoniel," she insisted, flustered, as the band started to play Forró music. "What's so wrong with that?" she asked.

"I'll dance with you, then," offered Odoniel, trying to spare his mother's nerves and tame his sister's excitement.

In that moment, I admired Odoniel's efforts to ensure Hildinha's peace of mind.

"Heaven forbid! You have two left feet. If I dance with you, I'll leave the party crippled. I'm going to dance with the schoolmaster, who's so skinny he must be as light as a feather. But I can't be the first one out on the dance floor. Mama will be suspicious. Let's do this: You dance with Inês. Then the dance floor will fill, and hardly anyone will notice the schoolmaster and me among all the other couples. Come on, take Inês's hand and go dance with her!"

Odoniel looked as baffled as I felt.

"You just accused me of having two left feet, and now you want me to dance with Inês? Some friend you are."

"It's just that Inês is closer to your height," Vitorina said, trying to make excuses, now in a more pleading tone. "Go dance, please. Mama will see you, and that will distract her."

Sensing our hesitation, she tried once more, this time appealing to our compassion:

"You know very well that if it were up to Mama, I'd die a spinster. I want to have children. Clever children who know math. The schoolmaster is perfect for my plan."

Odoniel looked at me awkwardly, weighing the proposal, but he didn't have the courage to make the first move.

"That's fine by me," I said, stepping forward. I watched a wave of relief wash over him. Vitorina smiled and gave me a hug.

"You're an angel, Inês!" Turning to her brother, with a pleading look on her face, she said: "And you, go on and prove you care about your sister's happiness. Dance with Inês right in front of Mama so she won't see me in the back."

As she said this, she placed Odoniel's hand over mine so we wouldn't waste any more time. That was the first time I'd touched a boy, but I didn't realize it until years later. That day, I was more worried about my two friends: Eugênia, about to start her new married life, and Vitorina, who would soon break Hildinha's heart.

Odoniel led, and I tried to follow the rhythm of the music, and, as soon as we got used to each other's movements, I met the eyes of my mother, who placed her hand on her chest, in a mixture of surprise and enchantment. A smile crept across her lips, perceptible only to those who knew her as well as I did.

Like my mother, almost everyone there turned to watch us, perhaps lamenting Odoniel's sad fate, risking his own early death by getting so close to a Flores woman.

"You know why they're all looking at us, don't you?" I asked Odoniel, who nodded.

"They're already ordering my coffin," he said jokingly and then assured me: "Don't worry, I don't believe in those things."

"I don't think one dance will put you in any danger," I joked back, with a moxie that made Odoniel miss a beat.

"Thanks for letting me know," he said finally, and I smiled at him.

Roused by our example, other guests got up to dance, and soon the party came to life. Odoniel and I watched Vitorina from afar as she walked up to the schoolmaster, pretending to want to refill her punch glass, and struck up a conversation. Vitorina gesticulated gracefully, leaning in closer to the schoolmaster. She was dogged, but not too forward. The young man remained reticent and even took a step back, perhaps to ensure he kept proper distance from an unmarried young woman.

"Unfortunately, I'm absolutely hopeless at dancing. I could never forgive myself if I were to put you through that, miss," he replied, excusing himself.

"Don't be so modest! I noticed from over there you were bored so I came to save you. It's my mission to cheer you up. Come on, let's go."

He doubled down: "I appreciate your concern, Miss Vitorina. But I don't deserve your offering. Thank you anyway. Please do excuse me." He backed away from Vitorina, who was rattled that he had thwarted her plan.

When I saw my friend walking away from the schoolmaster, I stopped dancing immediately.

"I think we've done our job."

Odoniel was taken aback.

"Wouldn't you rather wait for the song to end?" he suggested gently, then added: "So as not to raise suspicions that we're covering something up."

I smiled at him, flattered, and decided it wouldn't hurt to keep going. Dancing with Odoniel had almost made me forget about Eugênia, who by then was on her way to the Colonel's ranch to become the new Senhora da Caviúna.

8

The Colonel was known to be a quiet man, and few people in Bom Retiro could say they had, in fact, ever heard his voice. Whenever someone spoke to him, always close to his ear, he would nod in a way that expressed neither agreement nor disagreement, just a sign the message had been heard.

His constantly furrowed brow seemed to indicate he was always mulling over very important matters, which the local folk would never be able to understand: the price of cattle, the trip he would have to make to the capital, the political situation in Pernambuco, the gang of cangaceiro bandits led by Simão Pereira, threatening local order. All sorts of topics that, in his mind, didn't merit being shared with those around him.

The Colonel and his fiancée met only twice more before their wedding day, and both times Aristeu had been silent, perhaps thinking about these very important matters. Their meetings took place in the sitting room of the girl's father's house, and, on both occasions, the groom didn't say a word to Eugênia. In turn, Eugênia, indignant at being forced to marry a stranger, had also decided to remain silent, which didn't seem to have affected the groom's disposition in the slightest. Unlike Eugênia—who would snort loudly from time to time to indicate her annoyance with the situation and tap her feet on the ground to try to make the time pass more quickly—Aristeu maintained that same far-off look, reflecting on his very important matters, which had nothing to do with the girl sitting in front of him.

Eugênia's mother, lurking in the hallway, trying to overhear their conversation, was surprised by their silence during these visits and by the fact that nothing she served had been touched by her future son-in-law. Not even the mulberry liqueur, which she'd special-ordered for him.

"Did your fiancé not like the refreshments? Did you insist he at least have some liqueur? Oh, Eugênia! You should have said he had to try the cookies, that you made them just for him. Poor man, by now he must be on an empty stomach and offended by your bad manners."

"There's nothing poor about him, Mama. And the Colonel won't be dying of starvation any time soon, either. There's no shortage of cattle on that ranch."

"Eugênia!"

"It was all I could do to keep from walking out."

"If your father hears you," her mother scolded her, shaking her head, upset by Eugênia's rebelliousness and the food and drink left untouched on the table. "That stubbornness of yours won't get you anywhere. Soon you'll have to take care of the Colonel as your husband. If you weren't so headstrong, maybe you could start preparing now, while you still have your mother by your side to teach you."

"How kind of you to be so concerned about my happiness, Mama. It's truly moving," she replied sarcastically, and then took a bite of one of the cream cookies, which she hadn't baked.

At the bride and groom's next meeting, Eugênia was even more upset because the wedding date was drawing near, and because her father had forbidden her to make lace with us. Determined to test the Colonel's limits, she stomped loudly into the kitchen to get the tray of refreshments. She coughed and cleared her throat to break the silence and, at one point, took off her satin shoes, which, being new, pinched her pinkie toe. But Aristeu didn't react to any of these minor provocations. He just sat there, motionless, staring at something on the wall opposite, perhaps thinking about politics or the price of cattle. After another hour spent in those doldrums, Eugênia dared to let out a loud sigh, so it would be clear she was bored. But even that didn't make the groom-to-be react.

When there were other people around the couple, the silence wasn't so oppressive. Even with the two of them sitting silently as usual, there was always someone paying homage or bowing and scraping to the Colonel. "What a beautiful evening, don't you think, Colonel?" or "I heard the dry season should start earlier this year. Is that true, Colonel?" Those offhand comments, which weren't even worthy of a response, filled the room and lessened Eugênia's unease.

And even after the wedding, it was in that same silence, which had grown into a tangible presence between the couple, that the newlyweds traveled for the first time to Fazenda Caviúna. Eugênia crossed the threshold of the imposing front door to the main house, thinking only of the suffering her new condition would bring. She saw herself as an intruder in that parlor, personally decorated by Aristeu's late mother, the first madam of those lands.

She felt like bursting into tears, but soon the children descended, the staff came to introduce themselves one by one, and the atmosphere filled with warm welcomes. When she glanced over, Aristeu was no longer there, and, relieved, Eugênia calculated she would only see her husband hours later, when dinner was served.

Fortunately, according to Dorina, who'd overseen everything around there since the Colonel was a boy, Eugênia would have a room of her own. The Colonel had his habits and routines and didn't mean to share his place of rest with anyone.

Eugênia had intentionally decided to keep on the same clothes she'd worn to leave the church and kept them on after retiring to her bed-chamber at night. Not changing out of the clothes she'd been wearing when she came from the city gave Eugênia the illusion that her presence in that house wasn't permanent. The dark green dress, given to her by an aunt, belonged to her world. The idea of undressing and putting on her wedding nightgown seemed to Eugênia a betrayal of her own self, as if she were surrendering to the life she'd been forced into.

On the other hand, that sense of security was fragile. She noticed when she entered the room that there was no key in the lock, and she knew that soon her husband would open the bedroom door, intending to consummate their union. To quell the dread inside her chest during that torturous wait, Eugênia decided to stitch a few words on a rag, in the code she'd invented.

First she stitched *fear*, then *hatred*. Words that summed up what was going through her head at that moment. Alone in the room that had once been her mother-in-law's, Eugênia was afraid for the future and hated everyone and everything. Her husband, who had chosen her as if she were a cog in a machine; her father, who had handed her over as if she were a cog to be sold; her mother, who so admired that machine called marriage; the guests at the ceremony, so satisfied and secure to find all the gears to be working. The only thing she didn't hate was us, the lacemakers, who didn't want or fit into any kind of machine.

Several hours later, when she heard the doorknob turn, Eugênia paused her needle. Without even looking up, she sensed her husband's presence like a lantern singeing the air in the room. The sound of Aristeu's boots walking toward her was deafening. His footsteps, the creak of the wooden floorboards, his heavy breathing, and then, the first words he'd spoken to her since their engagement:

"Get undressed."

The crudeness of his order chilled the blood in Eugênia's veins, and she resumed stitching the final letter of *hate* as if she hadn't heard him. In her mind, such a demand was an affront. It was humiliating. She was a girl from a good family, she hadn't chosen to be there, she'd never wanted to be this man's wife, she owed him nothing, and, therefore, she wouldn't fulfill her marital obligations.

Faced with a wife who refused to obey him, Aristeu came closer and grabbed her wrists, with a brutality Eugênia didn't imagine him capable of, he was always so respectful in her parents' sitting room.

"Get undressed," he repeated, tugging hard on his wife's arm.

"What do you think you're doing?" Eugênia began to argue, but her husband covered her mouth with one hand, while the other groped at her flesh.

"Didn't your mother explain what happens between a husband and wife?"

In fact, her mother hadn't explained it to her, but Eugênia knew about things, for she had ears eager for forbidden matters. She'd heard dozens of whispered conversations in the kitchen about the escapades of some girl in the city, who, later on, would be called "lost." She'd also already had the opportunity, on a visit to a farm, to watch some animals copulating, a scene that made her very uneasy, believing that, when it came to human beings, made in the image and likeness of the Creator, things surely didn't happen the same way.

She also remembered once, as a child, when she saw two buckets of water being thrown to separate a couple of stray dogs, joined by their private parts, right in front of the general store. There was no forgetting Vitorina's father's reaction—cursing the dogs, he accused them of driving the customers away with that lack of composure on the sidewalk.

Just thinking about something similar happening in that bed, Eugênia began to flail.

"Get away from me!" she screamed, managing to break free and lean against the corner. "Get away from me or I'll go berserk!"

Contrary to what she expected, Aristeu looked more surprised than furious. He never imagined he would have to fight to get what, in his opinion, was his right.

Eugênia noticed that her husband was hesitant and pleaded with him: "Don't do it, I beg you."

But he had a job to do.

"The maids will need to strip the bloodstained sheet tomorrow," he said and, in one quick motion, turned Eugênia onto her back and hiked up her skirts.

Eugênia tried to free herself again, to cry out for help, but her husband covered her mouth once more and, in her ear, whispered: "If you scream like a calf, you'll never get the respect of the servants."

Plunged into despair by what was about to happen, on instinct Eugênia sank her teeth into her husband's hand, and he released her for a moment. That was enough time for Eugênia to reach out her arm and grab the little sewing scissors lying on top of her lacework.

In his astonishment, Aristeu's eyes followed Eugênia's movements, perhaps finally realizing his new wife was not a spare part that had come to fix the machine of his life. Eugênia had desires and was as wild as the ocelot he'd once shot after hours waiting in ambush on top of the mountains.

"If all you care about is some blood on the sheets, here you go."

And with that, Eugênia stuck the sharp edge of the scissors into the palm of her hand and let the blood pour out. Looking down at the crimson stain on the bed, the Colonel was momentarily stunned. His hair was disheveled, and sweat trickled down his forehead. Eugênia saw her husband's face screw up with annoyance, but instead of attacking her as Eugênia had expected, Aristeu buttoned up his trousers and walked toward the door.

"Be prepared tomorrow," her husband ordered her, and Eugênia only started breathing again when she could no longer hear the sound of boots on the floor.

As she lay on the bloodstained sheet, an unexpected smile appeared on her lips. She did it. She'd gotten rid of her husband, at least for one night.

The pain from her freshly wounded hand was small compared to the feeling of victory Eugênia felt in that moment. On the floor, the lace with the desperately stitched words *fear* and *hatred* was stained, but her honor was not.

Though she was exhausted, Eugênia couldn't sleep for the rest of what was her wedding night. Her mind raced, emboldened with the mission to perfect her plan to avoid Aristeu, night after night, as she'd just done. She had to find a way out. She needed to escape that nightmare, and the only people she could trust were us, the Flores lacemakers.

9

Bom Retiro, 1918

Weeks after the wedding, a messenger from Fazenda Caviúna knocked on our door to deliver a package that had been sent to us by Mrs. Eugênia Medeiros Galvão. Inside was a table runner and six dainty napkins. According to the messenger, "The missus said it's a present for Miss Inês, and not for sale." My aunt balked at such a proviso but soon discovered a way to find fault with the set.

"No one would buy it anyway. Look, this one's stained. It's been washed, but you can still see it. Not to mention all the dust they picked up on the road. They're practically another color."

"What color, Aunt Firmina?" Cândida wanted to know, but my aunt didn't bother to come up with a bird bearing a resemblance to the grimy tone of the lace pieces.

"The color of dirt," she replied impatiently. Not wanting to leave my sister without the information that meant so much to her, I whispered in her ear:

"They're kind of orange, like a campo oriole's chest."

As soon as I laid eyes on the lace, I noticed there was a message, and I offered to wash the pieces.

"Good idea, Inês. Put it to soak in vinegar," my mother advised. I volunteered to do the task the next day but took the pieces back to my room to decipher them later. As soon as Cândida fell asleep, I took the set out of its wrapping and spent the night poring over the pieces.

On the table runner and the six napkins, Eugênia recounted her recent hardships and explained that, since arriving at Fazenda Caviúna several weeks ago, she'd been forbidden to go out. She lived like a prisoner, locked inside the main house, and the only activity her husband allowed her was making lace.

"That way he keeps me still and my head down, the way he likes," she explained to me, through her code.

Those first days of marriage she devoted herself to her work like never before. Making lace was Eugênia's way of keeping her mind sharp, and, while her fingers moved the needle up and down through the fabric, she fleshed out her plan.

On each napkin, Eugênia had stitched part of her new routine. The first was entirely devoted to Aristeu's temperament, which, despite his reserved appearance, could, according to her, turn quite violent.

On another, in a less bitter tone, Eugênia spoke of the children. Smart and sensitive, the little orphans also feared their father, like everyone else there, but they had lived with him for so long that they developed an instinct to keep their distance. Luckily, Aristeu had no patience for his children, and their relationship boiled down to polite greetings: "Good morning, Father, sir," "Excuse me, Father, sir," to which Aristeu would reply with a nod, which meant that the children should leave. Once these formalities were completed, the little ones went outside to their world of play, free to frolic in the fields, with almost no contact with their father.

Aristeu wasn't harsh or mean to his children, Eugênia emphasized on the napkin. He just never saw them. "As would have happened to me, if I'd behaved like the wife he thought he found when he went to my father's house to negotiate for me." Not that the sheriff had received any money in kind for Eugênia, but he had allowed himself to be seduced by the prestige of having grandchildren who were heirs to Caviúna.

The third napkin was dedicated to her parents, whom, according to the message, Eugênia would never forgive for having given her away without a single regret to a vicious predator like Aristeu.

On another, Eugênia's story took on a lighter tone. It was the part dedicated to the longing she felt for us and our afternoons making lace together. According to her, the memories of our friendship were the only ones that comforted her during her endless days. She'd clung to lacemaking to survive. She worked from the time she woke up until her last prayers before going to sleep. As she worked, her mind became free and traveled to the house with the blue windows, where she could almost hear the rhythm of her companions' breath. In her solitude, even Tia Firmina's complaints seemed welcoming.

If the Colonel had asked any inhabitant of Bom Retiro who knew Eugênia reasonably well, or if he'd at least asked the opinion of the bride herself, he would certainly have chosen another girl from the city more suited to the role of wife. But, oblivious to this detail and blinded by his own arrogance, which prevented him from believing women like Eugênia existed in the world—women who would never be cogs or mold themselves into preexisting machines—Aristeu decided on a second marriage with the sheriff's daughter, thinking it was what was best for him, never imagining the extent of his error.

To punish Eugênia, who wouldn't bend to his demands, he denied all of her requests. Even the most banal ones. My friend was not allowed, for example, to go into town to shop or visit her parents. Aristeu felt wronged. He had entered that marriage in search of peace, and his wife's stubbornness had only brought him vexation.

Somewhere, hidden inside his heart, her husband longed for his life as a widower, and my friend took pride in provoking that feeling in him. "That's my small victory, small like our seed stitch, at first almost invisible, but, in sufficient quantity, fills the entire design," she said on one of the napkins.

In her most impactful account, made with smaller stitches, close together, so they'd all fit, Eugênia talked about the fateful night, after delaying it with small ruses she'd devised to keep Aristeu away, her husband finally took her for himself.

After her husband's first attempt, when Eugênia had stabbed herself to make it look as though the marriage had been consummated—verified and commented on by the servants of the house the following morning, as her husband had predicted—Eugênia had managed, one way or another, to remain unharmed in the nights that followed.

One night, she dragged over the heavy rosewood chest of drawers to block the door, though she knew it wouldn't be enough of an obstacle if Aristeu really wanted to enter. Even so, she was betting her trick might at least embarrass him—the door blocked by the piece of furniture would show Aristeu just how much he was unwanted.

Like Scheherazade avoiding certain death after her marriage to the king, Eugênia avoided her husband. At dinner, she would discreetly keep track of how much wine he was drinking and pour him a little more, hoping it would be enough to make him drowsy and put him quickly to sleep, in which he would lose the ardor for his virgin wife's body along with consciousness.

One night, however, when she was already in bed, eyes lit up like two stars in the darkness, scissors within reach—a habit she'd acquired since Aristeu's first attempt—Eugênia heard footsteps getting closer and closer in the hallway, and then the high-pitched screech of metal against metal as the doorknob turned. Aristeu pushed the door, which tapped against the chest of drawers. Eugênia prayed for a miracle, cringing in anticipation of watching the bedroom door open, as all it would take was one firm kick from her husband to dislodge the piece of furniture.

She prayed to Saint Agatha with such faith that her prayer was answered. The small crack that had opened at Aristeu's first push was soon shut, and a few minutes later Eugênia could no longer hear her husband's footsteps in the corridor.

The next morning, however, when she returned to her room after breakfast, where she'd enjoyed the happy company of the children, the rosewood chest of drawers had been removed, along with the bedside table and the reading chair. The room was practically empty, just the bed and a chair. The items on her vanity were gone, and the clothes she'd kept in the dresser drawers were now arranged inside an armoire that was fastened to the wall and impossible to move.

When Dorina came to serve her tea that afternoon, as the lady of the house had refused lunch that day, the maid told her what happened. Unfortunately the furniture was infested with termites.

"The master had it burned as soon as the lady woke up. Such a shame. Such a fine piece of furniture."

"Termites don't eat rosewood," Eugênia replied calmly, taking a sip of tea, and Dorina thought it best to change the subject. It was unwise to contradict her two bosses on the same topic.

Later, at dinner, Aristeu was more talkative than usual and, at one point, even said:

"Termites are treacherous beasts. They look harmless, but they're foul little devils." He said it in a teaching tone, addressing the children. "They toil away, hidden from our sight, then catch us by surprise. That's why we must be firm and quick with those cursed things. Before they eat everything inside and turn the whole house to sawdust."

With no furniture in the bedroom to serve as a barricade, Eugênia knew there would be no way to stop Aristeu from making a visit. As she listened to him talk about termites, she understood the consummation would likely take place that very night. This time Aristeu was met with no resistance. Not at the door, nor from his wife.

During the act, Eugênia lay motionless on the bed, with her lifeless hands at her sides like a corpse. Dead, as she'd predicted on her wedding veil. Her husband said nothing, he just lay on top of her and relieved himself of his pent-up desire.

Eugênia allowed herself to be violated without making a sound, like a rag doll arranged in various positions. She allowed her husband to manipulate her arms, legs, and body as if they weren't her own.

The act did not last long, so great were her husband's desire and expectations, and Eugênia endured the pain, shame, and revolt. She seemed absent, but she wasn't. She felt each thrust, the blood seeping between her legs, as she looked up at the ceiling, imagining herself in another place, another time, another body.

When Aristeu finally got up, Eugênia noticed her husband searching for her gaze, now empty, and, not finding it, he ordered, before leaving: "That sheet had better be white by first thing tomorrow."

Her husband would never allow word to travel among the servants that his wife had kept herself pure so long after their wedding day.

As soon as Aristeu was gone, Eugênia washed the blood of her virginity in a tub of water and spread the sheet over the back of the only chair in the room so that the fabric would dry before dawn. The next day, when Dorina went in to wake her, there was no sign of what had happened the night before.

I finished reading Eugênia's story with a flushed face and let the napkin rest for a few moments on my lap so I could gather my thoughts. I wasn't in the habit of thinking too much about what men and women did in the privacy of marriage, but I had always been puzzled by my failure to understand how the same act could be one person's nightmare and another's desire.

Shaken by what I had just read, I had still one last piece to decipher, and that would be the most surprising of all.

The lace table runner Eugênia made had a different purpose from the napkins. While the napkins talked about the past, the runner bore a proposal for the future. On it, Eugênia explained in detail the plan she'd devised.

The idea of running away from her husband had first come to her on the day her father announced the marriage to her in the parlor of her old house. Her desire to escape—which at the time some may have deemed an overreaction, the aimless fantasy of a skittish bride—had become an urgent need for Eugênia after the wedding. Even if she went down the "wrong path," as people said, even if she had to beg on church steps, nothing would be worse than living there, a prisoner, unable to leave, her body violated every night, the only exception being the week of her period.

After that first time, Eugênia thought her husband would leave her alone for a while. But, strangely, the paralysis and distance Eugênia had shown during the act only whetted Aristeu's appetite. She suspected her husband wanted to get some kind of reaction out of her, whatever it was, and that's why he didn't give up.

Some occasions, her husband pretended not to care about Eugênia's stiffness and acted like he was performing a mechanical task. Others, he would say something nice, almost tender: "Are you cold? I'll close the window." Still others, Eugênia felt that rage ruled every inch of Aristeu's body, moving frantically on top of her as if the intensity of his desire might pull her from her stupor.

There were also nights her husband was quiet, almost sad, and it was only on those nights that the two seemed to share some kind of communion. Two zombies, two unfortunate souls wandering in search of what they wanted so much but would never have. Once, Aristeu even laid his face on Eugênia's shoulder, as if losing himself for a moment, and smelled her hair, which she pretended not to notice.

Little by little, her husband's frequent visits began to shape Eugênia's body. She didn't feel the same physical pain during the act, which made her even more melancholy. Her body no longer considered Aristeu an invader, but her soul resisted: it would never belong to that place or that husband fate had imposed on her.

Taking her own life never occurred to Eugênia. She loved herself as she would never love anyone else, and, for that very reason, she would do anything to save herself.

Her plan was spelled out in detail on the table runner she'd sent me. Since her husband didn't allow her to have contact outside Caviúna, we'd have to communicate only through lace. In a month's time, Aristeu would take a trip, creating an opportunity for me to deliver her share of the money from the lace she'd been making. Adding these new items to her work from before the wedding, for which she was entitled to a share, would total a few thousand réis, enough to open the doors for her freedom.

Eugênia had noticed it was Vitorina's younger brother who delivered goods to Fazenda Caviúna every fortnight, and if I could manage to join him on his next delivery, which would coincide with her husband's trip, everything would begin to take shape.

Until then, she planned to make new pieces. It was ironic that lacemaking was one of the few activities her husband allowed her, never imagining it would be from that work, which he considered a woman's pastime, that his wife would obtain her freedom.

Money in hand, Eugênia would arrange transport to cross the Sertão, and, upon reaching the capital, she would be able to support herself for a while until she found someone who sympathized with her story and could give her a hand.

The table runner didn't go over all the details, but it did give me the date for our meeting. My mission would be to find a way to get to the ranch on the day of the grocery delivery. Then, with her husband away, we could figure out what still needed to be arranged. As far as Aristeu, we could make no mistakes. Eugênia knew that the moment she left through the gates of Fazenda Caviúna, her only way out would be to disappear into the world.

10

Lately Alice was a little tired of men. She knew thinking about them that way was a shallow generalization, like when people talk about women—she knew of course it was "not all men." But she felt unable to control her irritation when talking to what her generation called a white, middle-class, heteronormative male. True, she found their bodies attractive. But the exhaustion she felt just thinking how much she would have to explain, forgive, and put up with was enough to make her want to avoid any involvement.

It was remarkable to watch them behave like newborns who had to be taught everything: that no, it wasn't a woman's natural instinct to take their dishes to the sink for them; yes, women were more interested in sex than they thought; yes, pubic hair was part of the female anatomy, and if they had a problem with that, they should shave their own pubes instead of policing ours. If they hadn't learned those lessons by then, why should it be up to Alice to teach them?

At eighteen, Alice was convinced that most men would go down an unredeemable path. Some were more attentive; she could admit that. But even they rarely understood the extra weight their sisters, female friends, and coworkers carried around on their backs. The people who benefit from privilege can't see what things are really like.

Then Alice met Sofia, who offered her not just friendship, but a previously unexplored option for romance. She didn't think much about it, and, despite not having changed their social media statuses to *in a relationship*, Sofia had been her most stable relationship in months.

"I don't know how you can live like this," said Sofia as she entered her bedroom, starting to take stock.

Alice smiled, knowing her room would be tidy in a matter of minutes. All she had to do was sit there. Alice realized immediately she was thinking like a white, middle-class, heteronormative male—it was unfair of her to just lie there while Sofia picked up her clothes from the floor. "Let me help."

Maybe it wasn't even a question of gender.

Alice was messy and Sofia was extremely organized, the type who can't sleep if there are dirty dishes in the sink. Knowing Sofia, Alice let her have some fun straightening her notebooks and organizing her drawers. She considered this permission an act of love—clutter didn't bother her, and because she was competitive by nature, if someone criticized her mess, she'd usually say something like: "And whose room is it? Mine? That's right, you can go now."

"What about these?" asked Sofia, holding a stack of papers. "Can I throw them away?" She started to list off the contents of the pile: an overdue bill, movie ticket, gum wrapper . . .

"Uh-huh," Alice agreed absentmindedly.

"You didn't even look, Alice. And these empty envelopes? Are you saving them for something?"

Alice sighed and took the papers Sofia was holding out. She sorted through them, putting aside what was useless—almost everything. "Trash, trash, trash." Until she saw the yellowed piece of paper that had come with the veil given to her by her aunt from Pernambuco.

"What's this?" Sofia was curious.

"It came with that veil." She pointed to the piece of lace strewn across the back of her desk chair.

"Is it to keep or throw away?" was all Sofia wanted to know, anxious to tie up the plastic bag she was stuffing with what they were throwing out.

Alice was unsure, which made Sofia a little impatient, so she decided to assess the importance of the note herself.

"Let me see it."

As soon as she saw what was written, Sofia looked back at the veil, intrigued. "It's a code." Alice didn't understand right away, so Sofia elaborated: "Each symbol is a letter—look."

Sofia worked in software development, as a systems analyst; she had a talent for finding patterns in the world.

"And it came with that veil?" she asked, and without waiting for Alice to answer, she took the lace and laid it out on the bed.

"It starts here. This stitch, if we look for a similar symbol, is an *E*. That one, a *U*," she said, concentrating hard.

She checked the paper in her hands once more and began to decode the message.

"*I, Eugênia . . .*"

Alice laughed, skeptical, sure it was a coincidence.

"Stop it, Sofia. You're just messing with me."

"Why would I make up something like this? If you don't want to believe me, then don't. Check for yourself, and see if I'm not right," Sofia dared Alice, tying up the garbage bag and putting the paper back on the table.

Still skeptical, Alice picked up the veil, which softened Sofia, and made her continue.

"If it wasn't a code, it wouldn't have patterns." Sofia sat down beside Alice so she could show her what she meant. "This sequence of stitches here, for example, is repeated in several places. *Eugênia* at the beginning. *Eugênia* at the end, like a signature, see?"

Alice followed Sofia's fingers, which moved quickly over the lace, and she had to agree her girlfriend was right. The stitches formed words, which formed sentences. The veil was a letter.

"Who's Eugênia?" Sophie asked, curious. "Is that your aunt?" Alice shook her head. Her aunt was named Helena and had only given her the veil. She'd said it once belonged to a relative, but Alice didn't know who. Maybe her great-grandmother, or her great-great-grandmother?

"I've never heard of Eugênia. But I didn't have much contact with that side of the family, either. My grandma and my mom didn't get along," she said. "What else does it say there?" she asked, curious to know more.

Sofia took the paper and continued deciphering the message and showed Alice how.

"This is *A*, see? This is *O*."

"Let me try." Alice perked up, and, as she checked the code, she read the words in lace aloud: "I find myself prisoner of a nightmare from which I intend to escape."

The two of them looked at each other, as if they'd just seen a twist in a movie they weren't expecting. Lying side by side on the bed, they spent the next few hours reading that story from another time and with a tragic ending.

◆ ◆ ◆

"Do you think she made it?" Sofia asked when they finished reading. "Your aunt or your mom should know."

"My mom isn't talking to me this week, did you forget?"

Sofia rolled her eyes and got up. "I'm going to get going before the whole woe-is-me act gets started."

"Hey, don't go. Sleep over, Sofí," Alice said, a strategy that didn't usually work with her girlfriend.

"I can't. I have to finish a job. If I show up tomorrow wearing the same clothes, people will crack jokes, and it'll piss me off. I'd rather not."

"You can say you had a great night," Alice suggested charmingly. "Or wear some of my clothes."

"Do you have anything that's a size large?"

Alice pouted, and Sofia put the matter to rest.

"We'll see each other tomorrow, then."

As she escorted Sofia to the door, Alice walked past her mother, who was stretched out on the living room sofa in bare feet, drinking a glass of Malbec, her face illuminated by her laptop screen. From the grin tugging at the corner of her mouth and her flushed cheeks, Vera was definitely chatting with someone on her dating app.

As soon as she said goodbye to Sofia at the elevator, Alice went into the living room and asked: "Mom? What was my great-great-grandmother's name again?"

"Huh?"

"My great-great-grandmother, your mother's grandmother. Was it Eugênia?"

"Hold on, Alice," replied Vera impatiently. "I'm in the middle of a conversation here."

"Is it that hard to answer? It just takes a second."

Her mother looked at her, surprised. It was rare for her daughter to ask anything about their family. Although Vera found Alice's behavior abnormally positive and mature, her timing was atrocious. She didn't want to interrupt the flow of conversation with the interesting engineer, who "liked hiking on weekends, loved to travel, and preferred cabernet."

"Where's all this coming from?" asked her mother, speaking slowly, her attention divided between her daughter and the chat, giving her time to type one more sentence. *My daughter is asking me something. One minute. Don't go anywhere, okay?! Ha ha.*

"I'm just curious, that's all. Can't I be curious?"

"Carmelita," Vera replied without taking her eyes off the computer screen. *Hey, I'm back. All taken care of. So . . . how about we meet up in person?*

"Carmelita? And there was no Eugênia in the family?" Alice insisted.

"Oh, I don't know, Alice. Maybe there was. How should I know?" Vera snarled back, irritated. "I didn't even know my own grandmother. Leave me alone, go on."

Alice had just spent three hours in her room with Sofia, doing who knows what, and now here she was demanding to know about something she'd never been interested in before, right when she was enjoying herself. It was Vera's turn. Equal rights in the house. That was the deal.

While she and the engineer tried to decide where to go for their first date—maybe that Italian restaurant that just opened, they could meet in the middle—Vera was still searching her childhood memories and things her mother had told her for some mention of the name Eugênia. She did this to get rid of her daughter, who was stubbornly still standing in front of her.

Her mother, Celina, didn't talk much about her family in Pernambuco. She'd had a falling-out with her mother when her father committed suicide. From what she understood, her mom had blamed her own mother for her father's death in a way Vera had never understood.

To forget the pain, Celina had moved to Rio at the age of seventeen and created a new life there, as if she were the first of her bloodline. Even though she knew as a child there was this hole in Celina's past, Vera never felt the urge to find out more, and, as a teenager, she'd come up with the story that her grandfather had taken his own life when he uncovered his wife's betrayal. Only a drama of that magnitude could justify a daughter disowning her mother, instead of supporting her as a widow.

If Vera had ever heard the name of a more distant ancestor, it was when Alice had had to draw her family tree for a school project. She remembered her mother had uttered the few names she knew by heart, with some hesitation, as if they were forbidden.

Alice's father's side was also full of holes, and ever since Alice had drawn that incomplete tree, she'd felt like a fruit that doesn't grow from the branches, but that sprouts straight from the ground—a pineapple, a watermelon, a strawberry.

At that point, Vera had already moved on from her daughter's question. *I have a confession to make. I lied about my age on my profile. I lowered it a little bit, hope that's no problem for you.*

She tried to continue the conversation, but her daughter's inquisitive presence was bothering her and made her lose her cool. She wanted Alice to go back to her room and leave her alone.

Do your children live with you? My daughter is eighteen, but sometimes she acts like a child. This new generation can't cut the umbilical cord, don't you think? At her age I wanted to get as far away from home as possible.

Realizing Vera was absorbed again by her computer screen, now with no chance of getting her back, Alice gave up.

"Forget about it. Just don't say we never talk." Before she left the room, Alice tried one last time to provoke her: "You can keep having your little chat, it'll never come to anything."

The rude comment made Vera lose her temper, and she pushed her laptop aside. She hadn't gone through a traumatic, eighteen-hour labor to give birth to that girl just to have to listen to her abuse. For her, there was no greater ingratitude than that of children. Always thinking they come first.

"Watch your tongue, girl. Who do you think you are, judging me? Go find your own place to live and pay your own bills before you speak to me in that tone."

"I'm counting down the days, that's for sure!" Alice shouted from the hallway and slammed the bedroom door.

"Same for me!" Vera shouted back, downing the last of the Malbec in her glass and returning to the chat window. *Hey, sorry, it was the doorbell. Was I ever married? Yes, but that's in the past, now I'm more focused on the future.*

11

Tia Firmina was the only one surprised that Eugênia wanted to be paid for the pieces she'd made during her last months as an unmarried woman.

"That girl never cared about money. Now she's rich and suddenly she's counting her pennies?"

"She's within her rights, Firmina," my mother said. "It's only fair to be paid for the work you've done."

"She should donate the money to the poor, at least. Give it to charity."

"That's precisely what Eugênia intends to do, Tia," I lied, trying to keep the discussion from going on any longer.

"Well, if it's for charity, we could sell them at the church bazaar," Tia Firmina suggested. "Then Madame wouldn't even have to go to the trouble of deciding who will receive her alms."

"It just so happens she already knows who she wants to give the money to," I said, lying for the second time to cover up my friend's true motivations. "Eugênia's going to help some needy families at the ranch. That's why she asked us to send the money directly to her."

"And how do you know so much about Eugênia's intentions, Inês?" asked Tia Firmina. "That man who came here to deliver the package barely even said hello."

"We talked about it when I saw her at the wedding," I said, lying for the third time, and my aunt finally seemed satisfied, but not without getting in one last complaint:

"Instead of taking care of the house and her husband, Eugênia's decided to make more lace than when she worked with us. What is with young people these days?"

After a few weeks, all the lace made by Eugênia, both the older pieces and the new ones, had been sold. The man in the dark suit took most of it, making payment in advance, and, as usual, the rest were sent to other nearby ranches. This kind of trade with other towns was only possible thanks to Vitorina's brothers. They took our work along with their deliveries to Triunfo, Serra Talhada, Santa Cruz da Baixa Verde, and Quixabá and always returned with a fat envelope for us.

Eugênia had been working hard, and she was the lacemaker with the most pieces up for sale. Our prices weren't cheap—our fame had spread to other states—and by then we were also sending out orders independently through the mail, without the man in the dark suit as middleman. Tia Firmina had even opened an account at the bank branch in Triunfo, and that was where she deposited the Floreses' savings.

Once I found myself in possession of a good sum of money to send to my friend, I asked Vitorina when her brothers would make the next delivery to Caviúna.

"You'll have to ask them. If I kept track of their comings and goings, I'd never have time to make lace."

"Why don't you go to the store with Vitorina and find out?" my mother suggested, with a cheeky look I'd never seen before. "While you're there get some rice. We're running low."

I admit, it took me a while to realize my mother had started to get her hopes up about my love life. Ever since I'd danced with Odoniel at Eugênia's wedding, she'd been sending me to the store, more frequently than was necessary to keep our larder stocked, secretly hoping we'd grow to have feelings for one another.

Odoniel was stacking bags of beans when we arrived. Before he even had time to greet us, Vitorina was already at the door at the back of the store that led into the family home.

"You go ahead, Inês. We'll talk later," she said, leaving us alone. "If I don't go in and get my mother's blessing, she'll never relax. All she has to do is hear my voice, and she'll start calling for me, and if I don't tend to her first, she'll say I don't pay her enough attention."

"Do you need something, Inês?" asked Odoniel as soon as Vitorina had disappeared behind the door.

"I do, actually."

"Beans? Potatoes? Did you see how big these pumpkins are?"

I hesitated briefly, then explained: "Actually, I need a favor."

A little taken aback, he listened. Although Odoniel had always been very helpful to me, I felt embarrassed making such an unusual request.

"I was thinking of visiting Eugênia at the ranch," I began, trying to ascertain Odoniel's reaction as I explained my intentions. "We haven't seen each other for some time, and Vitorina mentioned that one of you is going to Caviúna soon. So, I thought . . ."

Maybe because I felt guilty for getting Odoniel involved, I couldn't finish my sentence. Instead, I hoped he would understand what I was asking of him, which is precisely what happened.

"You can come with me," he offered with a smile, and my embarrassment melted away immediately. It was just a visit between friends, not a crime. "I have a delivery scheduled there tomorrow, in fact," he said, already starting to plan our trip. "I usually leave at six. I can stop by your house around that time. Does that suit you?"

"It's perfect," I replied, smiling back at him. I had the impression Odoniel and I had something in common: he was the type of person you could always count on.

One of the teachings their father had passed on to all his children, including Vitorina, as far as I could tell, was "The secret to keeping your clientele is to make life easier for whoever walks through that door. Do that and there will always be cash in the register."

Satisfied with our plans to go to Caviúna and having nothing else to do there, I thanked him and went inside the house to say hello to Hildinha.

Later, over dinner with my family, the news that I was going to visit Eugênia the next day caused an uproar in the house with the blue windows. Tia Firmina thought it was outlandish to travel all that way on a dirt road just to visit someone who'd be at the procession of Saint Agatha in a few weeks.

My mother, excited I was getting closer to Odoniel, asked me three times if I didn't want her to iron a dress or to lend me a hat. Cândida, on the other hand, made me promise I would observe every detail of the Fazenda, so I could tell her all about it later. Her requests were very specific: she wanted to know if the garden smelled of jasmine or manacá, if the kitchen smelled like stewed meat or caramel, and, of course, what birdsongs I heard on the property.

There was so much excitement I don't think any of us slept that night. My mother with the hope of having grandchildren, Cândida eager for descriptions that would fill her imagination, and my aunt with a tightness in her chest she'd felt before. It was only later that I would understand the extent of those fears.

When I went downstairs in the middle of the night, it smelled of coffee, and everyone in the house was up. The three of them were busy making cajá compote. My mother stirred the fruit softening over the flame, with a long wooden spoon; Cândida counted out the star anise they'd use to finish the recipe; and Tia Firmina washed the bowls into which they would pour the jam.

"Go back to bed, Inês. You need to be fresh tomorrow," said my mother, again in that jovial tone motivated by her hopes of a growing family. The arrival of a new generation would bring joy to the house and would even be cause to make those roof repairs they'd been putting off forever.

As soon as the sun was up and we were seated around the kitchen table and eating the still-warm jam, we heard the sound of Odoniel's truck approaching. It smelled of onions and cumin, and since that day, whenever I've added one of those two seasonings to any recipe, memories of that morning come rushing back.

During the trip, I didn't have to try to keep the conversation going. Odoniel took it upon himself to liven up our time on the road and told all kinds of stories, some of events witnessed by him, others he'd only heard secondhand during his travels around the region. I don't know if he was doing it for me or because it was his habit to try to make everyone's life easier, as his father had taught them, but as he drove along he pointed out dozens of landmarks he considered of interest: Colonel So-and-so's farm, a ditch where a river had dried up half a century ago, a bend said to be haunted by a ghost, waiting in ambush.

"Well, if it ain't the ghost himself!" he shouted unexpectedly, and I jumped and looked to where he was pointing. There was only a cross with a scarf tied around it, dancing in the breeze.

"Sorry, Inês, I couldn't resist," Odoniel confessed, laughing. "I hope you'll forgive me."

I admit I was upset—not with him, but with my own self, for having fallen for the joke. But I said it was no problem, and we laughed together. Odoniel was as delightful to be around as his sister, with that same welcoming "come back anytime" feeling, without judgment, open to others.

It was only after an hour on the road that he asked me a more personal question: "Do you ever feel like leaving Bom Retiro, Inês?"

Unlike my friends, who were always making plans for the future, I'd never thought much beyond the next morning.

"I don't feel the need, urgency, or obligation to go anywhere in particular," I replied. "If life takes me away from here, so be it. But, on the other hand, if it's my fate to spend a hundred years in Bom Retiro, I don't see a problem with that, either."

"So, you're going to live to a hundred?" he joked, and I teased him back.

"The longevity of the Flores women is famous around these parts," I said. Then, in a lighthearted tone, since I regarded the legend about my family with good humor, I added: "Unlike the men."

Odoniel smiled in surprise and admiration, perhaps thinking I was sensible for not letting myself be rattled by other people's opinions.

"I'm like thread on a spool," I added. "Which could be turned into lace or forgotten in the sewing basket. I don't feel tied to any one place. Not this one, where I was born, or any other."

"You're a free woman, then," Odoniel said, pretending to understand.

"I think so."

His words made me reflect. Deep down, I didn't want this or that. I just waited, calmly, for what each moment offered me, and, in some way, that was a kind of freedom, because I wasn't even a prisoner of my own desire.

Around my waist, underneath my cotton skirt, I felt the silk handkerchief I'd used to wrap Eugênia's money. From time to time, especially after we lurched over a pothole, I'd have the urge to reach for the bundle to make sure it hadn't magically disappeared.

I'd agreed to go along with Eugênia's plan without judging whether what my friend was doing was prudent or not. At the time, I thought that decision wasn't up to me—up to then, I'd always believed helping others was what good people, like me, did.

Shortly after our arrival at Caviúna, Eugênia appeared in the kitchen wearing an elegant broderie anglaise dress and greeted us perfunctorily, as befitted a lady of her position. We weren't there as visitors, and it was safer if none of the servants caught on that the lady of the house was with an old friend. I greeted her as if we didn't know each other. There, I was just the shopkeeper's companion, perhaps his fiancée or his sister. I'll admit the first hypothesis put me in a bit of a tizzy, but I tried to control my unexpected unease and concentrate on my objective.

"This leather is of very good quality," said Eugênia as she inspected the newly arrived goods, running her hand over some bags Odoniel had brought.

"Isn't it, Dona Eugênia?" Now his younger sister's friend was called "Dona." It was appropriate. "They're from Bahia."

Having rejected the title of Senhora da Caviúna with all her might since arriving at the ranch, Eugênia did not hold the command of the house one might expect. At first, the Colonel's maids, still hoping to please their new mistress and adapt to her wishes, presented themselves respectfully, ready to receive instructions from Eugênia, who dismissed them, alleging illness or other affairs.

To show off their cooking and housekeeping skills, the women spent the first few weeks offering cake to the mistress at all times of the day and taking greater care than ever in polishing the silverware. But, little by little, realizing that the girl barely touched their food and that she wasn't interested in how the table was set or how the dishes shone, they naturally went back to their old ways, to which the master was already accustomed.

Everyone there, especially Dorina, had experienced a certain frustration at not seeing their efforts acknowledged by the new wife, but was convinced there was some upside to the mistress's disinterest in the running of the house. They would be free as in the master's widowed days, with no one giving them orders or criticizing the seasoning.

Ever since the late mistress had fallen ill, the house had run on its own, and Dorina and her helpers decided it was a blessing that God had given them a mistress so indifferent to domestic tasks, who was only interested in making money. This was a point in Eugênia's favor with the maids, who admired her commitment and fervor to working without having to.

"She doesn't even look like a rich girl. She's even getting a hunchback from leaning over that pillow so much," said Dorina.

They began to treat her with the deference of a guest and soon understood that the mistress wasn't one for conversation. Accustomed to an almost-invisible lady, Dorina was astonished to see Eugênia enter the kitchen, wanting to check the goods that had come from Bom Retiro.

"Don't worry, we'll arrange everything, madam."

"I want to help, Dorina. I woke up refreshed today."

The kitchen was spacious, and, through a large window, you could see an open field, where the Colonel's children were playing leapfrog. As soon as they noticed movement at the back of the house, the two children took off running across the yard and soon burst into the kitchen. They hugged Eugênia, spinning their stepmother in a pirouette, and, without pausing, snatched two cocadas from the counter.

"Be careful not to fall and scrape your knees!" Eugênia said, sounding motherly, but the little ones barely heard her, disappearing gleefully through the other door, taking a bite of the coconut sweets. "My God, what a commotion," she said.

Eugênia stood there for a while with a contented look on her face, savoring the newly received embrace from her stepchildren. Despite everything she'd told me on her napkins, my friend still managed to smile.

After inspecting what Odoniel had brought, Eugênia exchanged a knowing look with me and gestured with her head for me to accompany her inside the house, saying, in a louder voice, so everyone could hear, that she had some items for donation that might be of interest to "the young lady."

As we walked toward the main parlor, the wood creaked under our feet. I remembered Cândida, who'd asked me to memorize the smells and sounds of Caviúna. The classical furniture arrangement, the French porcelain, and the landscape paintings of other countries wouldn't have interested my sister. Later I would have to describe other sensations to her: the smell of lavender the sofa cushions gave off when I sat down and the squawk of a crow I heard in the distance.

The room was light and airy, and the curtains danced in the cool breeze blowing at that hour. Eugênia said her late mother-in-law had decorated the house to try to make herself feel like she was in the capital. She hated the countryside, and her greatest joy was spending her winters in Recife. She'd even visited Rio de Janeiro during the Portuguese Empire, and apparently she'd met Pedro II himself at a soirée.

In times past, that overly elegant parlor had made her mother-in-law believe she was somewhere else. Even if for different reasons, Eugênia shared a similar desire, though her mother-in-law, who was rich from birth and widowed young, had not been taken prisoner by her husband.

With the power only money provides, Aristeu's mother had asserted her will by force in the region. There were countless stories about her cruelty to enslaved people, and it was even said she'd died of grief when slavery was abolished. Aristeu had certainly inherited his mother's heart of stone.

During the time we spent together that day, Eugênia kept a formal attitude as she didn't consider it prudent to express how close we were. Being caught in friendly conversation with the store delivery girl might arouse further distrust, and to keep up appearances, to protect me from accusations of being her accomplice in the future, she thought it wiser for us to give a wide berth.

As we approached the window, I admired the vast field before us for a few moments. On one side, never-ending rows of sugarcane. On the other, a huge pasture for cattle. The two riches that had made the Medeiros Galvão fortune.

"Pretty," I said, and Eugênia sighed.

"All I see is a desert. A forgotten land, frozen in time. Women in Recife and Rio de Janeiro aren't treated like cattle. Do you remember that newspaper Vitorina showed us?"

She was referring to a copy of a periodical published in Recife, which had found its way into Vitorina's hands, brought by a peddler who used to do business with her father. It was called *Ave Libertas*, from the Latin for "hail freedom," and was written and managed entirely by women. When she saw what it was about, thinking that the content might interest us, Vitorina had stolen the paper from her father's desk and hidden it for one of our lacemaking afternoons.

Vitorina was always the one who brought the outside world into our small circle. When she opened the paper proudly on the table, we gathered around the already-yellowed copy, eager to learn more.

"It was wrapped around a piece of beef jerky, can you imagine?" she explained and then asked me to read the main article aloud.

From the letters printed on that crumpled page, we came to understand that Ave Libertas was a group of ladies who'd played an important role in the struggle for the abolition of slavery, raising funds to buy enslaved people and then setting them free. Now, a few decades later, they were engaged in another equally noble pursuit: helping to prepare freedmen to take on a new role in society and teaching them to read. The group also fought to change laws that would benefit women, such as a woman's right to vote and something we'd never heard of: divorce.

"What is divorce, Inês?" asked Cândida when she heard that word unknown to everyone there. I read on a little further to try to figure it out.

"From what it says here, it sounds like the undoing of a marriage."

"But what God has joined together, let no man put asunder!" said Tia Firmina, indignant. "It's in the sacred text."

"Are you sure this is real, dear?" asked my mother, who also doubted such a thing existed.

"That's what's written here, Mama: *Recently, it was decided that husbands and wives can live separately, in cases of adultery, abuse, or abandonment.*"

"Oh my God. The world is lost," said Tia Firmina, making the sign of the cross three times.

Even so, I went on reading, *the union cannot be completely dissolved. Husband and wife receive authorization to live separately but continue to be united in marriage.* "From what it says here, it seems there's a proposal for a new law that, if passed, would allow a marriage to actually cease to be valid. A divorce law."

"So, this divorce is a 'de-marriage,'" Cândida concluded.

"And will these people be able to marry other people?" asked Vitorina, intrigued by the possibility.

"What a preposterous thought," grumbled Tia Firmina. "Does it say if anyone asked God if He agrees to this de-marriage? I bet not."

At the bottom of the article was a photo of Maria Amélia de Queirós, a lady of the upper class, with strong features, her hair in a bun and a string of large pearls around her neck. We spent some time admiring the picture of that woman who occupied a position that was unthinkable to us, capable of making her ideas reach miles away, all the way from Recife to Bom Retiro. Ideas like changing existing laws and allowing marriages to be undone.

Ironically, back then, Eugênia thought it was a waste to fight for such a cause. My friend still believed she'd find her one true love whose name started with the letter *S*, someone she'd never have the need to leave or divorce, or "whatever that nonsense is called."

Months later, however, her memory of that article in *Ave Libertas* gave Eugênia new hope, as she clung to the idea she could be like those women. In a big city like Recife, everything was different, you just had to get there.

With the money from the lace, still wrapped in the silk scarf around my waist, Eugênia would rent a room in the capital and go knocking on the magazine's door. The address was at the bottom of the page, Eugênia remembered. I just had to ask Vitorina to show it to me again, translate it into code, and send it in a lace handkerchief.

"Those women are fighting for the good of other women, Inês. Many of them were in situations like mine. They won't turn me away."

To support herself in her new life, Eugênia was counting on selling her lace and said she was eternally grateful to Vitorina for having taught her a trade that would guarantee her survival and freedom.

Eugênia had dreamed for so long about that plan that she had it down to the last detail. To me, the escape plot seemed a bit fanciful, like something in one of the novels Eugênia had always liked to read, but my friend was so sure of the success of her undertaking that she didn't doubt it for a single moment.

While explaining to me what our next steps would be, Eugênia seemed to tell a story about something she'd already done, and not a plan to be carried out. Leaning against the window frame, under the gaze of her slave-owning mother-in-law immortalized in an oil painting, she didn't see the green countryside, but the blue sea at Boa Viagem beach. She was no longer in the big house, her husband's fiefdom, but in a rented room, small but dignified, from where she could fly wherever she wanted, free as the birds my sister cared for.

Eugênia also told me that, during one of her husband's recent trips to Triunfo on business, she'd used his absence to search his office, and there she had found a map of the capital with a detailed chart of its streets. From that day on, whenever Aristeu went riding, Eugênia memorized the map with the aim of absorbing it as if she had been born near the sea and not in the Sertão. Her eyes roamed the printed layout with hundreds of lines, trying to choose the street where she would live. She made up routes, shortcuts, and neighbors, and houses, trees, and people began to appear before her.

"For everything to go as planned, I need you, Inês," Eugênia assured me vehemently. "I'll never make it without help."

I admit I didn't feel able to judge her plan, since I'd never left my hometown, but I knew my friend's determination and knew she would do it with or without my support. What's more, I was confident in Eugênia's power to make her dreams a reality and bring her goals to life.

But even if Eugênia's escape went exactly as she imagined, her choice would still entail a lot of suffering. If she was successful, she'd have to endure the risks of the trip, the lack of money, the longing for her family, and the loneliness of the capital, among a host of other misfortunes I couldn't even imagine. If she failed, however, Eugênia would have to face her husband's wrath, which would be ruthless.

"What if the Colonel finds out?" I asked fearfully.

"He won't." And, after reflecting for a moment, she explained to me the reason for her certainty. "From now on, we'll only communicate through the lace. And you'll promise me you'll keep my secret as if your life depended on it."

"From my mouth, no one will ever know," I assured her, but still I pondered. "But the Colonel might find out from someone else."

Eugênia didn't even want to hear that hypothesis. She trusted her husband's arrogance would help keep him in the dark. Aristeu was a slave to his pride. On the couple's wedding night, the same night she'd stabbed her hand with the sewing scissors, her husband had been more concerned about what the servants would think the next day than about taking her as his wife. When he was in front of guests or important figures, he'd say things like "I am not the man to allow this or that, you know me well." Eugênia knew Aristeu thought highly of himself. Always wary, jealously guarding his public image. Being abandoned by a runaway wife was a possibility that would never cross his mind.

The storm would come after. As soon as he'd noticed his wife's absence, Aristeu would hunt her down wherever he went, motivated by shame and unmeasurable hatred. And that was why Eugênia had to escape as fast as she could to the farthest place the lace money could get her. Her husband would certainly rather see her six feet underground or locked up in an attic for the rest of her life than let her go and be free.

"By the time Aristeu realizes what I've done, I have to be out of his reach. That's why I need you, Inês. You're a Flores."

I didn't understand what my name had to do with it, but Eugênia soon explained: "You don't have a father or older brother watching your every move. You can send a message by post to Recife and hire transport without having to contend with anyone. And when I'm long gone, Aristeu won't make any connection between my disappearance and you or your family. He doesn't know the code. For all intents and purposes, I never left this damned house, nor did I send any correspondence. And when you hear of my disappearance," she continued her instructions, "you'll feign surprise. You'll say you never imagined I was capable of such folly. 'Running away like that, how mad, where was Eugênia's head, Colonel?! If she contacts us, we'll let you know right away. But she'll be back sooner or later, regretting her wrongdoing. Eugênia was always impulsive like that, but she soon regrets it, you'll see.' That's what you're going to say."

I pretended to understand, and she sighed. "I just feel sorry for the children, who will have to stay here," Eugênia added, looking out at the field and perhaps already seeing the ocean. "My only consolation is that Aristeu doesn't mistreat them the way he mistreats me. They have that advantage." And after another sigh she added: "It's that reason alone that I leave with a clear conscience."

"And when will you run away?" I asked reticently.

"Before I start to grow a belly."

The possibility of having a child who resembled, even slightly, that man who'd stolen her future made Eugênia sick. Her hatred for Aristeu was so great that she was incapable of factoring in that the baby would be a sibling to those two children she loved so much, as well as her own child. Whenever her mind wandered and she accidentally pictured herself with a baby in her arms, she saw herself holding a miniature Aristeu, disturbing and monstrous, with the features of the man who'd forced himself on her so many times, without respite or pity.

Though at first she'd been afraid of her husband, now her feelings for him were of gnawing disgust. When they met for dinner, or when they had visitors at the ranch, Eugênia was constantly irritated. The way he continually cleared his throat, the way his lips curled down when he read, and even the smell of mungunzá he loved so much provoked her anger. Eugênia knew she would never again be able to enjoy a bowl of that sweet corn mush without thinking of her husband, and she hated him even more for having spoiled that pleasure for her, too.

"That good-for-nothing even took that away from me!" she said angrily, then composed herself. She still had some instructions to give me.

"The first step is to send a letter to Maria Amélia de Queirós, the lady who signed that newspaper article. Talk about needing help, which will be requested shortly, but without any details. Don't give my name, or Aristeu's, or the ranch. Choose ambiguous words. That way, no one will be able to identify what it's about, in case the letter is intercepted. Ah! And send the code separately, in another envelope, asking Maria Amélia to keep it and wait. Then we'll send her a mantilla veil as a present, and it will contain my whole sad story, in detail."

With that, Eugênia got up and took a beautiful piece of lace from a drawer in the sideboard.

"It's all here." She started to show me in the veil. "*I, Eugênia Medeiros Galvão, formerly known as Eugênia Damásio Lima, find myself a prisoner of a nightmare from which I intend to escape.* I want to do it on the Feast of Saint Agatha," she confessed to me.

"But that's in February." I was on alert. The date was very close.

"If we're efficient, there will be time to arrange everything. An important figure like Aristeu can't miss the procession, and he'll have to appear alongside his family. It will be my only chance, Inês. As often as that good-for-nothing climbs in my bed, I'll be pregnant this year, which will make my escape incredibly difficult. Look at my hands, raw from the needle. I haven't stopped making lace a single minute. I work until my eyes burn. I lose track of whether it's day or night. All so that I can achieve my freedom."

"Doesn't the Colonel find your devotion to lacework strange?"

"Nothing of the sort. That fool finds it convenient. A lacemaker is always silent and keeps her head down. A lacemaker doesn't stand up to anyone, she doesn't make threats. That's how he wants me: hunched over and silent. But Aristeu can't imagine what's coming."

Although I was worried the plan wouldn't work out, I assured my friend I would try to do everything she asked of me. As soon as I got back to town, I would go see Vitorina, pretending to be curious to take another look at the magazine, so I could memorize the address.

"And remember not to write it down. Recite it in your head until you get home and then embroider it on a handkerchief."

With the address, I could send the veil with the request for help to Recife. Eugênia also wanted me to book transport for the day of the festival to take her along the back roads from Bom Retiro to Pesqueira, a town outside the Pajeú River valley and located halfway to the capital.

"Pesqueira is far enough away that I can arrange transport myself, without being recognized as the wife of Colonel Aristeu Medeiros Galvão. If I stop in Monteiro or Camaleão, it's riskier. Aristeu has so many acquaintances there. Oh, Inês!" Eugênia remembered something else. "Arrange the trip like it was for you. Preferably with an out-of-town driver. No one will question it."

"Because I'm a Flores," I added, and she said:

"The curse that has befallen your family is actually a blessing. If I was lucky enough to have your last name, Aristeu would have kicked the bucket by now."

"There's no curse, Eugênia," I said, repeating what I heard at home, but Eugênia didn't pay attention, taking the rest of the lace out of the big drawer.

"I made these here to be sold," she explained. "With the money, you can pay for the transportation. What about the others I sent you? Did you manage to sell them?"

I nodded and took the silk scarf from my waist. Eugênia got excited, something I hadn't witnessed for a long time, and when she took that bundle of cash from my hands, she immediately hid it in the fold of a tablecloth she was working on.

"It's forty thousand réis," I told her. "We had a lot of demand last month, and your lace was perfect. They sold before Vitorina's and even Tia Firmina's."

"I bet that made the old biddy hot under the collar," Eugênia joked. "Forty thousand réis will be enough to pay for my accommodation and food during the journey. Any change of plans, I'll message you in the lace."

Eugênia looked at the clock on the wall, calculating that our conversation had already taken up too much time.

"I don't think we'll have another opportunity to meet until the Feast of Saint Agatha, my friend. I'm a prisoner of this place. A fate I never imagined for myself," she concluded, with regret.

I gave Eugênia a sympathetic look, and she tried hard to push aside the melancholy that had washed over her. She wiped away a tear and assured me she would not let herself get down. Her nightmare was nearing its end.

"Aristeu takes me for a plaything. But, while he sleeps peacefully, we're moving in on him. Let's go now. Our conversation has stretched on too long."

I left Caviúna thinking about the instructions Eugênia had given me. Without me noticing, something on my face, perhaps my frown or pursed lips, indicated my distress, because in the first few minutes of the trip Odoniel asked me:

"Did something happen, Inês? You look worried."

"No," I lied, so he wouldn't suspect my meeting with Eugênia had had the power to alter my behavior. "I'm tired from the journey, that's all." After a pause, I asked him: "How long does it take to get from here to Pesqueira?"

Odoniel found the question strange and joked, "Well, well. Changed your mind about seeing new places? Taken a shine to life on the road? It was my company, I bet."

His comment made me flinch. My sudden curiosity called me into question. Faced with my silence, Odoniel seemed to regret the joke and gave me the information I needed.

"Two days by wagon. Or a day by car or truck. There's a carriage that usually makes the trip to whoever pays the price. Just tell the driver to put Bom Retiro on the route. Do you need to send an order there?" he asked, just to understand what exactly I needed. "It might be cheaper to send it by post, if the customer isn't in a hurry, of course."

I let him believe that assumption.

"Yes, it's for an order, but it's not confirmed yet. Just in case, it would be useful to have the contact of that carriage driver. Do you know how I might talk to that man?" I asked, like I was hinting at a remote, future possibility.

He smiled, happy to be able to help me once more, and promised to take me to speak to the driver as soon as he made an appearance in Bom Retiro. According to him, the man usually stopped at the store when he was passing through.

The rest of the trip was filled with the noise of the truck's engine and Odoniel pointing out the occasional curiosity on the roadside.

"That's where they killed a prefect, back during the time of the Empire. They set up an ambush behind that peppertree, see? And that ficus over there at the top of the hill, see? It's the biggest one in the whole region."

I nodded, feigning interest, though I hadn't actually seen the tree. Still, I was secretly grateful for that happy, carefree voice to lull me along, giving me the childlike confidence that everything was going to be all right.

12

Tia Firmina prayed the Apostles' Creed, knowing full well it would never be enough. And I prayed the Our Father, the novenas, and the rosary, knowing they wouldn't be enough. Tia Firmina had kept herself pure her whole life, a devout virgin, but it was too little to alleviate the ills her family was yet to suffer.

Unbeknownst to us, that woman with the wrinkled face was engaged in constant bargaining with the divine, trying to purge us of the sin we carried in our bloodline, a secret of which she was the only guardian.

Tia Firmina had spent her life plagued by the feeling she had to keep silent about the story of the gypsy woman who'd loved her grandfather and to whom he'd sworn his love, but whom he'd abandoned with a child in her womb.

My great-grandfather had put an end to their romance as soon as he found out there was a baby on the way. A man like him couldn't have bastard children with gypsies, only with "young ladies from good families." At the time, the young man was already engaged to Das Dores, the daughter of a functionary at town hall.

When the pregnant young woman asked him to take responsibility for the child, my great-grandfather pushed her away. He'd never promised her anything, nor had he sworn his love to her, was she mad? Wanting a commitment, demanding a life together?

The gypsy listened to him hurl those insults and, in the darkness of her grief, had sworn revenge. The day after he broke things off, she took off her colorful clothes and pulled back her hair, which she always wore down, braiding it tight, to blend in more easily with the residents of Bom Retiro. She wanted to approach the girl who was betrothed to her lover and beg her for mercy. She would ask Das Dores to move on with her life and leave the father of her child to her. She was sure that Das Dores, disappointed by her groom's betrayal and touched by the impending birth of an innocent child, would take pity on her situation and back out from the marriage.

Das Dores would be better off. She deserved a man more worthy of her purity. Certainly she'd have a better future without a groom like that, even if the gypsy wasn't able to use her divinatory arts to prophesy that exact outcome. Those with ties to the occult know that clairvoyance can be blurred when matters of the heart are intertwined with the desires of the one making predictions.

Tears flowing, the gypsy showed Das Dores her rounded belly and appealed to the young woman's kind heart, certain she would put an end to their engagement immediately. But Das Dores, out of fear or naivete, hadn't completely believed the words of this stranger who approached her on her way back from the market. She'd been taught not to trust gypsies.

Das Dores was not a mean-spirited young woman—quite the contrary, she was charitable to the servants in her house and fulfilled her religious duties. But this strange woman with bloodshot eyes had appeared out of the blue, tugging at her sleeve hungrily and with an intensity that bordered on theatrics. It gave her goose bumps just to recall it.

But Das Dores also found it impossible to imagine her fiancé, such a discreet young man, ever getting involved with that kind of woman, who danced round and round, slept under the stars, and wandered the globe with no fixed abode.

Still trembling, Das Dores told her fiancé what happened. He not only denied the accusations but was offended Das Dores had even listened to her.

"If that crazy girl shows up again, don't look her in the eye. You know those people have the gift of bewitching. They're master manipulators. I'm going right now to find that madwoman, and I'll make her answer for all this slanderous nonsense she's said about me."

"But how do you know her, dear?"

"From nowhere at all. I don't cross paths with people like that. She must have seen our names on the wedding banns posted on the church door and decided to defraud us. It's clearly a ruse. Those gypsies think they're clever, but they don't know who they're messing with. I'll gather a couple of men and drive the whole band away from here."

Part of Das Dores's heart believed the pregnant girl's tears, while another told her it was unwise to believe a stranger instead of trusting her future husband.

"She looked so sad, dear," she even argued with her fiancé.

"Crocodile tears, false like everything else about those people. Das Dores, my child, you are very naive. Malicious people will have a field day with you, taking advantage of your kindness. Anything is possible with a gypsy. Have you not heard what they're capable of? Sorcery, spells. They're a pack of criminals."

Das Dores brought the rosary she was holding to her lips, startled by what he was saying. The next day, the groom did as promised. He rounded up a group of men with the help of some landowners in the region who considered themselves responsible for keeping order in the Pajeú valley and drove the gypsies out from their camp on the outskirts of town. The chase went on for leagues and only stopped when the gypsies, under fire, crossed the border into Paraíba.

So it was to everyone's shock and surprise when, months later, the gypsy woman reappeared at the wedding, this time without her round belly. As soon as she recognized the woman among the guests, walking toward her, Das Dores instinctively got behind her husband.

"Don't be afraid," said the gypsy calmly, reading the fear in my great-grandmother's eyes. "I just came to pay my respects to the bride and groom. And to tell you that my son didn't survive his mother's grief. My sadness dried up all my milk, and the boy lasted only seven days. And so I've come to warn you that seven generations of this family will be unhappy in love, starting with you."

And with that, she turned to look at Das Dores, who was shaking with wide-eyed terror, and left, oblivious to the abuse her former lover hurled at her.

The bride's cousins rushed to comfort her, and the consensus was that there was nothing to fear. Better to just forget what happened, that's how those nomadic people survived, inflicting fear on good people.

"A band of thieves, my child," said the groom. "Let's go back to the party, let's bring out the cake, let's start the music again."

And so the incident lay dormant, locked away in a corner of the family's memory, though it still seethed like an open wound in Das Dores's heart. Until one day, barely a year after their wedding, her husband was bitten by a green racer snake while he was resting under a jurema tree, and there was no time to save him from the poison that flooded through his veins.

Das Dores was a pregnant widow before the age of twenty. In her womb, the first child born under the gypsy's curse, little Lindalva.

"Well, the gypsy did say they wouldn't be happy," the townsfolk said.

After the death of her husband, Das Dores retreated into her grief, blaming herself for the tragedy. If she'd listened to the gypsy's plea, this disaster could have been averted. Her body, already thin, grew so frail many thought she'd die of heartbreak before she even gave birth.

She was so skinny that, when she went out into the street, just to go to Mass on Sundays, no one would ever guess she was pregnant. The pregnant gypsy's tears would haunt her for the rest of her days. For hundreds of nights, until her old age, Das Dores dreamed of the bastard baby who died on the seventh day.

Just three months after her husband's death, the birth of a daughter with rosy cheeks and fussy cries brought her new hope. Lindalva grew up healthy, turning into a beautiful and much-courted young woman. But, like her mother, she was also widowed early. Watching her daughter suffer as she did, Das Dores understood everything. She understood the gypsy had passed on to the women in her family her same fate: to grow old alone. And for the men, as revenge for being abandoned, their fate was death.

Tia Firmina had heard the story as a child. Playing quietly in a corner, she heard her grandmother Das Dores whispering to her mother, Lindalva. At the time, they thought the girl wasn't paying attention to what the adults were discussing. But little Firmina, who had always been so clever, heard every word of that conversation and never forgot it.

Her father had just died, after falling from a horse, and Das Dores confessed her suspicions to her widowed daughter, suggesting that her son-in-law's death might be linked to the death of the girl's father: both victims of a curse pronounced on her wedding day.

Lindalva, who'd never even heard of this curse, listened in disbelief to her mother's story. She burst into mournful sobs, unable to accept that her husband had died for the sins of a father she'd never even known.

"We could have warned him, Mama," she said, sobbing. "Why didn't you tell me sooner?"

"I didn't believe it myself, dear. When your father died, I clung to the idea that it was just a terrible stroke of bad luck. But now with your husband's accident, so young. I worry about what will happen when Firmina and Carmelita get married. I'm certain this curse is real. The death of my son-in-law has erased all doubt. We must protect your daughters. Maybe a faith healer? A Mass? Firmina and Carmelita don't deserve this fate. What if it's not just husbands who die? What if they are also in danger?"

The young widow's eyes widened just imagining the possibility.

"Enough, Mama. Enough!" Lindalva ordered her firmly, wiping away her tears. "God is greater than this heathen spell. Magic loses its power when we stop believing in it. I'll have a Mass said every month for the soul of this woman who wished us so much harm, and that way we'll be protected."

Das Dores had been reticent, doubting whether a special Mass would make any difference. She still remembered the gypsy's eyes, which she was sure emanated a power bigger than anything they knew. But, trusting her daughter's instinct and faith, she agreed to leave it in God's hands. They swore they would never repeat the story to anyone lest it grow stronger. And if they heard anyone mention it, they would vehemently deny it.

They also decided to put the name Flores, as people already called them, on the girls' birth certificates and on those of future generations, so they might deceive the occult, which would look for them by their old name: Oliveira.

Playing in her corner, however, little Firmina listened to the whole story and took to heart her elders' claim that only God could prevent the deaths caused by the family's sin. From that day on, Firmina began to show an unusual interest for her age in church affairs. She offered to help at Mass, asked about the fundamentals of the catechism, and read the Bible as if it were a book of children's stories. Her mother never suspected the true reason behind her daughter's sudden devotion, but welcomed it, secretly thinking that if Firmina led the celibate life of a nun, she would have a better chance of being happy. The family would gain points with the divine, and their descendants would be even more protected.

My mother, Carmelita, never knew a thing. Her older sister never revealed to her what she'd heard as a child, sticking to her mother's belief that magic loses its power when no one speaks of it. Still, Lindalva hung a sacramental medal from the headboard of her youngest daughter's bed to protect her against harm.

All her life, Firmina had questioned whether she'd really heard that conversation. Sometimes she doubted herself. Could it have been a childish dream or fantasy? But she was convinced every time she noticed the despair in her mother's eyes when her youngest, Carmelita, already a teenager, talked about boys and marriage.

"You're still too young for that," Lindalva would say, putting a stop to the conversation, even when all the girls in Carmelita's circle of friends were already married and had children.

Firmina agreed, chiming in: "Will you have the heart to abandon us?"

"My husband can live here after the wedding. It's a big house," replied my mother, trying to reason with her older sister, who had other worries on her mind.

Rumors circulated here and there that the daughters of the widow Lindalva, granddaughters of the widow Das Dores, hadn't yet married because of a curse, but it only really gained traction when my mother, Carmelita, lost her son and then, a few years later, watched her husband, my father, die of malaria, leaving behind two young daughters. That was when the black cloud that followed our family formed.

As for Tia Firmina, after the death of her brother-in-law and nephew, she clung even harder to the saints, since the Masses said for the gypsy's soul hadn't been enough to spare Carmelita. Praying in silence at her brother-in-law's wake, Tia Firmina blamed herself. If she'd warned her younger sister, she could have spared her. She'd witnessed how her blood relatives—grandmother, mother, and sister—had all suffered more than they deserved. She didn't think it was fair to me, or to Cândida, or to our daughters, or to our daughters' daughters, that those tragedies continued to happen.

When Das Dores and Lindalva died, Tia Firmina became the only one to know the truth about the curse, which she pretended not to believe. While I, my mother, and Cândida laughed at what we considered a hare-brained tale, Tia Firmina prayed a Salve Regina every night for each future generation, hoping the day would come when she would see Our Lord Jesus Christ overpower the grief of a woman jilted more than half a century before.

It was precisely because of her fear of what unfortunate fate lay in wait for us that my aunt grew more alert than usual when she saw me getting closer with Odoniel. Never imagining my conversations with the young man and my frequent visits to the market were all to try to help Eugênia, Tia Firmina began to disparage Odoniel and even Vitorina.

"Merchants are not good people. They're always trying to deceive us, exaggerating the quality of their wares, putting extra weight on the scale. It's in their nature, they refuse to take a loss. They find some way to make average look good and good look great. That's why I say: don't let yourselves be fooled by a merchant, girls," she advised us.

The message was directed at me, with the good intention of saving me from early widowhood and saving the life of a boy whom she was actually fond of, always so polite when he waited on her at the store. She never revealed that, in her heart, she'd always believed in the curse she so vehemently denied. She'd sworn she would take that secret she overheard as a child to the grave, because, as her grandmother had said, only silence can annihilate the power of Evil.

Suddenly interested in my every move, Tia Firmina started asking me more questions than usual. She found my going out for no reason strange, my trips to the post office, my sudden interest in the amount of money earned from the sale of some lace. Feeling a growing distrust, she began to follow me. As soon as she'd noticed I was getting ready to go out into the street, there she'd come, saying that she'd forgotten to place the flowers on the altar. "I need to stop by the church. Wait, Inês, I'll go with you."

She also began to gossip with our neighbors, who always had their finger on everyone's whereabouts, inquiring if one of them had, by chance, happened to cross paths with me. She'd drop my name in casual conversation, pretending she had no intention of finding out anything specific, hoping someone would absentmindedly reveal to her some wrongdoing of mine.

On one of these occasions, Eugênia's mother said she'd seen me dealing with a man who took passengers to other cities. My aunt felt her blood boil when she heard that. To keep my reputation intact, she replied there was nothing strange at all about it. In fact, I was arranging for the transport of some of our lace to the coast—at her request, even. The neighbors didn't suspect a thing, but Tia Firmina left the church with a troubled mind, wondering what her niece might want with a man like that.

Only one answer came to mind: running away for love. She was so vexed she added thirty Our Fathers and twelve Hail Marys to her nightly prayers and made endless pledges to multiple saints. She was convinced I was preparing to elope with Odoniel and that my fate would be even sadder than all the other Flores women's. When I inevitably became a widow, I would be alone and far from home.

Her mission from that moment on was to prevent tragedy from catching up with me. She hadn't been able to save her father, nephew, or brother-in-law, but she would save me and Odoniel. Steadfast in her purpose, she wouldn't rest until she found a way to intercept the driver. She introduced herself as a relative of the young lady who'd come to speak with him the other day. She asked after our arrangement and found out that I'd scheduled a journey to Pesqueira for the fifth of February, the Feast of Saint Agatha, departing from a point on the road outside the city.

Her heart almost bursting out of her chest, Tia Firmina politely thanked the man, as if she already knew everything, and returned home in a state of panic, already devising ways to prevent Odoniel and me from succeeding in our plan.

Over the next few days, she refused to get out of bed, she was so weak. The weight of those two great secrets was too much for her weary soul.

But God only gives the burden to those who can carry it, she believed. After much thought on the matter, asking for divine guidance in her prayers, she'd convinced herself she could never confront me directly. Young people in love are deaf to the pleas of experience. She even thought I might move my escape plan forward if I felt threatened. She needed to proceed with caution.

She then withdrew part of our savings, as the bank account was in her name, and decided to sacrifice part of what we'd saved to prevent my misfortune. It was a difficult decision, since the money belonged to everyone, but a necessary one. After leaving the bank, she went looking for the driver once more and canceled the arrangement. She told him she'd come at my request. The man grumbled, claiming he'd already spent part of the fare, and he couldn't refund it. But Tia Firmina assured him he'd not incur any loss, quite the contrary; she would pay him extra for the inconvenience. Accustomed to last-minute deals, the man was pleased with the double payment, and he crossed Bom Retiro off his itinerary for the fifth of February. It was better, really, as he could avoid the crowds, and he forgot all about the matter over a shot of the cachaça Odoniel had recommended to him when he stopped by the store earlier.

The next morning, the improvement in Tia Firmina's health was startling. Successfully sparing me from widowhood, she went back to her routine even more energetically than before, unaware she'd interfered in someone else's fate.

Tia Firmina also considered it more prudent to leave me believing everything was still arranged. It was better that I find out my plan had failed on the appointed day, so there would be no time to find alternatives. At the end of the Feast of Saint Agatha, she would assume her role, confess to having canceled the ride, for my own sake. She would still evoke the power of Our Lord Jesus Christ, who had sown the premonition she'd felt that something was wrong, as the only reason I hadn't lost my way.

In the days leading up to the procession, Tia Firmina couldn't wipe the grin from her face, which we figured was because of the approaching festivities. But the truth was my aunt was proud of herself, though she knew pride was a grave sin. Somehow, she'd managed to outsmart the gypsy's curse. She was the first descendant of the cursed Flores bloodline to achieve this feat.

13

Recife, 2010

Before Alice had even spotted her, Tia Helena was waving at the group of passengers coming through the arrivals door at Guararapes Airport. Alice had assured her aunt she didn't need to pick her up. It would be much easier to just get a taxi, but Tia Helena insisted: "How could any-one do a thing like that? If you don't show your guests a good welcome, they won't come back."

"A Flores woman returning to her homeland!" she proclaimed when she saw Alice, who smiled back at her, a little embarrassed. Though Alice was grateful for the welcome, she felt obligated to correct her: her legal name was not Flores.

"But I'm not a Flores, Tia. My name is Ribeiro."

Only her father's name was on her birth certificate, a man she, ironically, barely knew and who had moved to the United States when she was still a baby.

For the first few years after the divorce, her father would still travel back to Brazil to see her. Once she got a little older, Alice started to make the trip to Dallas by herself. She made this journey a few times, and those adventures were some of her most thrilling childhood memories. Being taken by the hand by the stewardess tasked with delivering her to her father on another hemisphere. She used to get special food on the flight, and they would give her a coloring book with pictures of little airplanes and a box of crayons. She had good memories of those times abroad, where she got lots of presents and heard people speaking a different language. But when her father remarried, to a Colombian woman he met there, and then had two more children, her American siblings, the daughter who lived in Brazil was no longer his priority, and their visits and meetings became less and less frequent.

Vera was overwhelmed, disgruntled by the unequal division of labor between her and her ex-husband, and took it out on her daughter, even if unconsciously. Now, as an adult, Alice sympathized with and even admired Vera's efforts to raise and educate her without a partner. But deep down she couldn't forgive her mother's constant resentment for having only fulfilled her role as a mother. After all, she hadn't asked to be born.

On the car radio, there was a discussion about a mother who was unable to regain custody of her child. Lílian, 27, accused her ex-husband, Alberto, 50, of domestic violence while they were married. Alberto, in turn, alleged abandonment and kidnapping of a minor by his wife.

"I had to run away and report him before he killed me," she explained to the host of the radio program. "I couldn't leave my son in that house."

Her ex-husband was a successful businessman, and she was a former model. They met at an event he sponsored. It was love at first sight, and a marriage proposal soon followed. Lílian was treated by her husband like a princess—Alberto was the man she'd always dreamed of, opening car doors for her and leaving her love notes hidden around the house.

That is, until the first time he shoved her, over something trivial. Alberto had tried to start a conversation while Lílian was watching TV and she didn't pay him the attention he thought he deserved. "Hey, are you deaf or what?" he said, shaking her out of the blue.

"What? Sorry. I was distracted. What is it, love? You were saying . . ."

Then came the manipulation and the gaslighting.

"Do you really need to go to that gym? Why don't you buy a tread-mill to have here at home? Much more practical. Besides, I love you just the way you are. Who are you trying to look good for? Just me, I hope."

"Of course it's for you, love. But you're right. Having a treadmill at home is a great idea. I won't have to fight traffic to get to the gym."

"Your friend's birthday? Isn't she the one who talked about you behind your back? I don't think that bitch deserves your presence."

Her husband used any excuse to pressure his wife into doing what he wanted.

"Good point, love. I'll just say I have a cold."

Alberto also didn't hide his grumpiness when Lílian would leave to go work at an event, even though she was being offered fewer and fewer jobs after turning down so many. Interrogations about her whereabouts became a daily occurrence.

"Isn't the dentist just around the corner? You took so long. Wasn't it just for a cleaning?"

"It was, but she ended up needing to do a root canal."

In those moments, when whatever the previously announced story was failed to perfectly align with what actually happened, Alberto would puff out his chest victoriously, certain that he'd caught his wife in a contradiction and that he was about to reveal her as a liar.

"I think I'll pay that dentist a visit one of these days. I've been meaning to go. From what you say, she sounds good. But she sure is slow."

"She's just thorough, love, but I think it'd be great for you to go see her. We can go together. Want me to make an appointment for you?" If Lílian said no to any of Alberto's requests or he sensed the slightest whiff of annoyance at his reprimands, she was met with jealous arguments, violent fights, and name-calling, and, finally, if she threatened to leave, profuse apologies: "No, please. I'm nothing without you. Forgive me."

After the baby was born, Lílian's body changed, and she was no longer her husband's princess. "You really need to go on a diet, huh?" he'd say, pretending to be joking, as she tried to get the baby to stop crying. "Some breast implants later this year might be nice," he told her when she lifted her blouse to feed her son, an act that bothered him, even though it was just the two of them in their luxury apartment. "Do you really have to do that right here in the living room?"

Before the boy was even one, Lílian was unexpectedly slapped in the face, because Alberto had had "a stressful day trying to provide the good life she enjoyed." And after her son's first birthday party, when all the guests had left, he kicked Lílian repeatedly in the stomach because, according to Alberto, she hadn't "paid enough attention to his family."

"All you do is embarrass me. You barely spoke to my mother. Now, you're going to have to call and apologize," he ordered, and Lílian believed him, no longer able to differentiate between reality and her husband's perspective and not remembering exactly what had happened at the party hours before. Confused and filled with guilt for possibly upsetting her mother-in-law, she obeyed Alberto's order to try to calm him down. She dialed her mother-in-law's number, her abdomen still sore, trying to understand where her Prince Charming from the early days had gone, the one who'd sworn to protect her.

"I'm only doing this for your own good. Don't you think I'd rather be on good terms with my wife? You think I want to be here fighting with you? This argument is ruining my day, too, you know."

That night, Lílian waited for Alberto to go to bed, then she took her son and went to the women's police station, where she showed them her bruises and pressed charges. Humiliated, she went to her mother's house on the outskirts of town and waited. Now, a few months later, the judge found that Lílian had kidnapped the child and granted custody to his father. The matter was still in court, but Lílian couldn't afford lawyers as prestigious as Alberto's.

"I'm afraid he'll attack my son to get revenge on me," she said, her voice cracking, during the interview. "There's got to be justice in this world. You can't separate a mother from her child."

Everything seemed to indicate, however, that Lílian would be kept from her son for a long time. Witnesses claimed that Alberto was affable, a gentleman who'd never been violent. And he was always extremely affectionate with the boy. Lílian, on the other hand, had come from nothing and had used her marriage to gain access to a higher social circle than the one she'd been born into. She was clearly a gold digger. A whore.

Tia Helena was upset by the story and shifted in the driver's seat.

"Wouldn't you rather listen to some music?"

"I want to know how it ends."

"It may never end," her aunt replied, and Alice nodded.

In the apartment with its big windows overlooking Boa Viagem beach, Alice stopped to look out at the sea and feel the salty breeze in her hair. On a shelf in the living room were many photos of Tia Helena on trips, at parties, by the pool.

"I don't know if your mother told you, but Flores wasn't our real name. Maybe that's why she didn't give it to you."

Alice looked surprised to hear that, and her aunt explained:

"Our family used to be called Oliveira. They lived for a long time in a house with a flower garden. Small town, you know how it is. People started calling them 'the Floreses' because of all the flowers, and they wound up using the name on their official documents. They were highly regarded lacemakers and even founded a cooperative in Bom Retiro."

"Was it one of them who made the veil?"

It was a long story, so Tia Helena went to get the bolo de rolo she'd made specially for Alice.

"You have to try my recipe. The one I took to Rio wasn't home-made. Not to brag, but there's none quite as good as mine. I baked it this morning. The secret is to bake extra-thin layers and not leave them in the oven for more than five minutes, so they won't break when rolling."

Alice accompanied her aunt to the well-equipped kitchen—she could wait a little longer to talk about the veil, the reason she was there.

After she and Sofia had decoded the hidden message, she'd become obsessed with finding out more about Eugênia's story, and the best way to find out was to accept her aunt's invitation to come visit her in Pernambuco on a long holiday weekend. She'd chosen the Feast of Corpus Christi.

"And? Do you like the cake?" Tia Helena asked, already knowing Alice's answer.

"It's wonderful, Tia. I'm speechless," said Alice, licking her fingertips smeared with guava paste.

She felt more comfortable there than she did in her own home. The breeze that blew through the living room felt like an invisible guest, rustling papers and tousling her hair, like Saci, the mischievous mythical being, playing pranks.

As soon as they finished eating, Tia Helena asked Alice if she wanted to look at some old family photos. She kept the albums at the very top of an armoire. Alice offered to climb up to get them for her aunt, but Helena wouldn't allow it.

"It's the kind of thing only the person who put it there can find, my dear. But you can hold the ladder for me. Steady, now, Alice."

"Don't worry," Alice reassured her, gripping the aluminum frame of the ladder they'd brought together from the laundry room.

Up top, Tia Helena craned her neck, pushing aside some folders and shopping bags until she found what she was looking for.

"Here it is," she said, pulling out a cardboard box. "Help me out here, darling, it's heavy."

After taking the box down, they sat down on the patchwork quilt that covered the bed in the room where Alice would sleep that night. Tia Helena waited a moment to catch her breath.

"When I got your message asking if you could visit me for the weekend, I figured you'd cracked the code. You were fast and very smart."

Alice's body twitched; she wasn't used to receiving compliments. She was raised on a battlefield.

"Actually, I wasn't the one who figured it out," Alice clarified, so as not to take Sofia's credit. "It was a friend."

"Then, you choose your friends well. A quality that runs in our blood. Your ancestors also chose their friends well. Friends are sisters that life gives us."

Alice smiled in agreement.

"I, for one, don't think I'd ever have figured it out on my own." Tia Helena went on. "It was my cousin Celina, your grandmother, who showed me the code and taught me the secret. Gee, that was more than forty years ago now. I'd stay up all night holding that little piece of paper, reading each passage carefully. When I passed the veil on to you, I wanted to test you. I was curious if you'd figure it out for yourself. But if you hadn't, I'd have told you anyway. I'm not sure when, maybe right before I died," she confessed with laughter. "There are no rules to this tradition. We have to do what we feel is right. Like you did, coming all this way."

"Who is Eugênia, Tia?" Alice asked the question that had been plaguing her for weeks. "Is she one of our relatives?"

"No," Tia Helena replied, to her niece's surprise, who looked at her, confused.

"No?"

"Eugênia was the daughter of the town sheriff and was part of the group of lacemakers who used to meet at our ancestors' house. She wasn't a member of the family, but she was a very good friend of the Flores women of Bom Retiro. Here they are, look," she said, pointing to a yellowed photo of women holding up a variety of lace items for the camera. They were all dressed in black, like widows. "This is your great-grandmother, and this is her sister. Here, your great-great-grandmother Carmelita and her sister, Firmina. Oh! This one in the corner is a local girl, a friend of the Floreses, Vitorina. She's still alive, can you believe it?"

"Wow!" Alice exclaimed. "She must be what . . . a hundred years old?"

"Older than that, I think."

Intrigued, Alice brought her face a little closer to the photo to better examine the features of those women from last century. She was also looking for some trait that resembled her or Vera or her grandmother, but she couldn't find any. As happens in old photos, no one was smiling, and they all looked much older than they really were.

At one point, Alice's gaze landed on the only girl who hadn't been identified yet by her aunt. She was the best dressed of the group and was in the center of the photo, seeming to stare right into the lens.

"That must be Eugênia," Alice said, having deduced it by elimination. "The girl who made the lace veil to get away from her husband."

Alice knew Eugênia's story as far as the last part revealed by the veil.

"Yes. The code was created so the lacemakers could communicate without the danger of being discovered. As you already know, Eugênia was in a difficult situation. She was terrified of her husband, who was a very powerful man and ruled the entire region."

Tia Helena paused before she went on.

"The plan described in the veil was put into practice, but things didn't go as planned."

Then she opened another box, which contained some newspaper clippings.

"Your great-grandmother kept some newspapers from back then and other pieces of lace that contained messages. Just look at these angel wings, how wonderful. They have a message, see?"

Alice studied the lace.

Don't go, she quickly deciphered, proud of having already memorized the code and of being part of that fellowship of women, a sisterhood. The lacemakers in her family had found a way to defend themselves, at a time when women had no voice. Or when they had even less of a voice than they do now. Like Lílian, fighting for custody of her son.

Unlike the lacemakers in the photo, the woman she'd heard inter-
viewed on the radio at least had the right, a right attained by those who
came before her, to make some noise. She could publicly denounce
Alberto and take him to court, even if there was no guarantee she'd be
able to regain custody of her son.

"I'm curious, Tia. About several things, actually," Alice said. "Why
did *I* get the veil? You'd never even met me."

Tia Helena smiled, because perhaps she'd asked that same question
herself once, to the person who'd given her the veil.

"We didn't need to know each other, Alice. We're connected like the
threads in a piece of lace. Eugênia's story must be told and remembered
so we don't forget her. It's symbolic, I know, but it's these kinds of small
gestures that remind us we must always seek freedom and that even in
defeat there is victory, because there was a struggle. Like that girl we
heard on the radio today."

Alice nodded, understanding what her aunt meant. One mother
fighting for custody of her child made other mothers want to fight, too.
Even if Lílian didn't win her own battle, she would inspire other women
in a similar situation.

"Was my great-grandmother involved in Eugênia's plan?" Alice
asked.

"She did what she could," Tia Helena replied. "In spite of the lim-
itations. After many years, she was the one who decided to start the
tradition of passing the veil on to younger generations. I have to admit,
since I didn't have any children of my own, at first I didn't know what
to do with it," she said, amused. "And the way the veil came to me was
one of those twists of fate. My cousin Celina, your grandmother, had
the veil, but she decided to move to Rio when she was young, after her
father's suicide. She was so shaken by that tragedy that she just wanted
to leave the past behind, forget she was a Flores. But she didn't have
the heart to break with tradition. So, instead of returning the veil to
her mother, whom she was on the outs with at the time, she passed it
on to me. How about that! And I'm not even a Flores! I'm descended

from Lygia Oliveira, sister of Das Dores, the cursed bride, as legend has it," she added.

Alice was already lost in that intricate family tree she was only learning about now that stretched back over a hundred years before the day she was born.

"I think I'm going to have to write down all these names, so I don't get confused about who's who," Alice joked, and Helena laughed, saying soon she'd have it down. The names would come to mind naturally.

"I went to Rio determined to give the veil to your mother, my niece. But when I saw you with that blue hair of yours, like the windows at the Casa das Flores in Bom Retiro, I knew it had to be yours."

It sounded like a compliment, and Alice thought she could get used to that kind of thing.

"You did the right thing, Tia. My mother would have never cracked the code," she said, sneering. "She'd wear the veil like a scarf, tell her friends it was a family heirloom, but never take one good look at it. Not really."

Tia Helena looked at Alice, not understanding her motivation for criticizing Vera. It was hard to explain. The tension between mother and daughter was the fruit of years of small scraps of resentment sewn together on both sides. One threaded the needle, the other stitched the binding—a patchwork so complex that Alice believed there was no way it could be undone.

"We have no idea what would have happened," Tia Helena replied. "Perhaps Vera would have been able to figure it out another way. You didn't figure it out straightaway, did you? It was your friend."

"Yeah, but at least I'm here. My mother never would have made the trip," Alice insisted, continuing to nitpick, which she immediately regretted. Tia Helena wouldn't understand her resistance to acknowledging anything positive about Vera.

Alice got annoyed whenever someone defended her mother. "You've got to go easy on her," they'd say. "She's from another generation." But Alice couldn't. Being older didn't mean being wiser. Years couldn't erase repeated mistakes. The fragility of the body was not a sign of the strength of the soul. Elderly people who have a hard time carrying groceries home from the supermarket could have committed terrible crimes in their youth.

Alice's theory could even be considered youthful arrogance, and maybe it was, but she had known her mother since she was born and was sure Vera wouldn't have spent more than thirty seconds looking at that veil, even if someone had pointed out the code to her.

"Anyway, I'm glad you came to see where you come from," said Tia Helena, changing the subject. "Your relatives were forced to leave the land of their ancestors and start a new life by the sea, but I'm sure there's a bit of the Sertão in you. Come on." Tia Helena got up, expecting Alice to follow suit, and, when her niece hesitated, she insisted: "Come on, girl, what are you ashamed of?"

Alice obeyed her aunt and stood up beside her.

"Now close your eyes and touch the veil."

Alice felt embarrassed but did what the lady with high cheekbones asked.

"So?" Tia Helena asked her after a few moments. "Did you feel the vibration? Do you feel the Pajeú valley calling you?"

Alice had to hold back her laughter, but out of respect for her aunt, she concentrated, and, as she expected, she felt nothing, apart from the ferocious wind blowing through the apartment, and the smell of the sea.

"And? Do you feel it?"

"I think this veil doesn't like the look of me. It doesn't want to communicate with me," Alice joked, and her aunt said it was just a matter of time.

"I'll leave these photos with you," she said, before leaving the room. It was late. "We can take a trip to Bom Retiro on Saturday. What do you think? I guarantee you that, after almost a hundred years, no one will dare to expel a Flores from there."

14

The guilt over what happened to Eugênia would haunt me for many years, though I knew there was no way I could have foreseen the course of events. While I was making the lace handkerchief with my message to Eugênia—telling her transportation had already been arranged, all she had to do was be at a particular spot on the road, at eight o'clock on the fifth of February, that a carriage driver would take her to Pesqueira— behind my back, Tia Firmina was undoing my best-laid plans, aiming to ensure my happiness and save Odoniel's life, which, in her opinion, was threatened by the curse of the Flores women.

In a week's time, Odoniel would go to the ranch, as he did every fortnight, taking the handkerchief with confirmation of the getaway plan, having no idea what it was. I'd still see Eugênia one last time, at the procession of Saint Agatha, her first visit to town after the wedding, but I wasn't sure I'd have the chance to approach my friend for a final goodbye—I thought it more prudent not to. Eugênia would be under her husband's watch and would certainly be the target of the towns-folks' curiosity, eager to witness the transformation of the sheriff's young daughter into Colonel Aristeu's new wife.

That afternoon, when Vitorina finished her work for the day, I offered to accompany her to the store. I made up a story about needing to go for a little walk to stretch my back when my real intention was to take Odoniel the handkerchief. Tia Firmina, who, without my noticing, had been following my every move, made note.

With my supposed elopement with Odoniel getting closer and closer, Tia Firmina imagined I would need to communicate with him more frequently. Though she was certain that we wouldn't be able to pull off our foolish plan and that we'd spend hours by the side of the road waiting for a truck that would never show up, Tia Firmina remained alert to everything I said and did. After all, Odoniel had easy access to his father's vehicle. In a moment of desperation, realizing our escape had gone awry, his love for me would overtake his responsibility as a son, spurring him to steal the truck, the same one his family's livelihood depended on. Tia Firmina watched over me night and day, searching for any sign of new plots or plans.

On the way to the store, Vitorina told me about her feelings for the schoolmaster, who, according to her, would soon be hers. She just needed to figure out how. No matter how hard she tried, she couldn't seem to motivate the young man to court her, despite all the hints she'd given him. Her mother, Hildinha, now began to complain of various aches and pains and increasingly demanded Vitorina's presence to fetch her compresses and pillows. My friend was weary and hungry for something new.

"I want to have my own life, Inês. I love Mama, but I can't live hers."

Trying to speed things along with the schoolmaster, Vitorina had decided to surprise him with a visit.

"If he won't make a move, I will. Someone has to take the first step."

"But you'd need an excuse to go calling," I said.

It was frowned upon for single girls to visit single men, particularly without a chaperone, as she intended.

"I'll just bring him a piece of cake. A sample of the cheese we just got in. It will look like a delivery. But I need to be alone with him, Inês, otherwise it will never move forward. If someone sees us, even better.

People will start talking, and my father will have to force him to make a commitment," she schemed.

"Before you go setting this trap, you ought to find out if the schoolmaster wants to marry you."

But Vitorina had already decided, without considering the opinion of her future groom, who remained unaware of my friend's plans.

"Does that man even know what he wants, Inês? He's always so lost in thought; all he thinks about are numbers and work. The schoolmaster deserves to have a family, a little fun, a house bigger than that little room he lives in. Why shouldn't he have it all with me?"

The schoolmaster really did seem to be a sad man, and Vitorina did have the power to make anyone's life more colorful, exactly as she'd done for her family when she was born.

When we arrived at the store, Odoniel was tidying a shelf. When he saw me come in, he suspected I was there to talk to him, as was becoming habit, and he grinned. In the last few weeks, we'd been learning each other's ways and feelings, and I already considered him a friend.

I waited for Vitorina to go inside the house to speak to her mother and asked Odoniel if he'd take the handkerchief to Eugênia. I had deliberately not wrapped it, precisely so there would be no questions later, so that it would appear to be just a simple handkerchief.

"Consider it done," he assured me, and I thanked him, trying to push aside the guilt of withholding my true purpose. If it had been a note, I would have never asked Odoniel to deliver it, but it was just a handkerchief that would pose no risk to him.

I walked back home thinking how men might also share some of life's burdens with us, as Odoniel did for me now, and as my father had done for my mother in their years together. I was in the midst of these thoughts when, coming through the small gate that led to the garden of the house with blue windows, I found my aunt waiting for me on the porch with a stern look on her face. I was immediately concerned, thinking something might have happened to my mother or Cândida.

"What happened, Tia?"

She took a while to answer, staring me up and down. There was a storm brewing inside that woman.

"How was the boy? Did you two enjoy yourselves?"

I was surprised by her aggressive, yet tongue-in-cheek tone, but I played it cool, still unsure what she was getting at.

"What boy are you talking about?"

"What boy, Inês?! Oh, come on!" My aunt lost her temper. "The boy from the store you went to visit. I wasn't born yesterday. I know everything."

My heart almost stopped when I heard those words, and for a moment I thought she'd discovered Eugênia's escape plan.

"Such a responsible girl, besotted with the grocer's boy!" she said, and I let out a sigh of relief. Her distrust was about something different.

"There's nothing going on with Odoniel." I was sincere, but Tia Firmina read my nervousness as deceitfulness. It was clear that I was hiding something.

"Don't play the victim, Inês. A girl I raised, going behind my back, preparing to put one over on the family. How do you think your mother will react? And Cândida? How will it look? But you didn't think about them, only about yourself. You're an ingrate."

"You're mistaken, Tia. I barely know the boy."

But she wouldn't listen.

"If you don't shout loud enough, you lose the whole herd. But I know how to shout loud. I won't allow you to get away with this nonsense, running away with that boy."

"What?" I dropped into a chair, stunned by what I'd just heard.

"You should know I've already broken your arrangement with the carriage driver. I refuse to let you sully your honor or bring grief to your mother—she's already suffered so much in this life. I'm here to watch over this family, and you won't destroy it, Inês."

"Tia! How could you?"

"It's done, and I have no regrets. And don't even try to deny it now. I put the pieces together with my God-given intelligence. I've seen all your little outings, that faraway look in your eyes. Always walking on eggshells, putting money aside, calculating your words. And that boy!" she said with a snort, nonplussed. "He could have come here to speak with your mother. But no, you preferred to do everything in secret. And I know why: Hildinha would never allow her youngest son to marry a Flores. They believe in that curse nonsense. And if that's what those people believe, then they don't deserve you. I'm not going to let you run off with that young man, spending the night in sin, running wild on those roads."

As I listened in amazement to my aunt's barrage of delirious accusations, I put my hands to my head, trying to think of what to do next. I'd just sent the handkerchief confirming the arrangements for Eugênia's getaway, which, thanks to my aunt, would no longer take place. I ran to the door to try to get back to the store and keep Odoniel from taking the handkerchief to Caviúna, but my aunt stood in my way, putting the key in the door.

"Don't even think about leaving this house."

"Tia, you don't understand!"

The desperation in my eyes made her even more convinced her theory was correct. She warned me that I would have to kill her before I walked through that door.

"I'm telling the truth. I swear on the soul of my late father and my late brother."

"Don't start calling the dead, they'll hear you and take you with them," Tia Firmina scolded me. "I'm saving your future, you ungrateful girl. You might not understand it now, but one day you'll thank me."

"You know me, Tia. I would never abandon my family."

"Love turns people topsy-turvy, you're not the first," she replied, firmly, and turned her back on me.

Still trying to gather my thoughts amid the despair that gripped me, I looked in disbelief at that woman, who would never be convinced otherwise, so immersed in her fantasy. My mother and Cândida appeared at the door, drawn by the sound of our argument. Cândida ran over to hug me, while my mother tried to find out what had happened.

"Inês will have to pray a lot tonight," Tia Firmina started. "She was very disrespectful to me. She gave me a spiteful answer, one you wouldn't even give an enemy."

"But Inês isn't like that, Firmina," my mother said.

"Well, she has changed quite a bit. Or am I the only one who notices things around here?"

"What did she say to you, Tia?" asked Cândida, but Tia Firmina wouldn't deign to answer.

Sitting there, paralyzed, I wanted to defend myself, but if I refuted Tia Firmina's story, she would be sure to tell them about the carriage ride I'd ordered, which might compromise Eugênia's escape even more.

Cornered, unable to face my mother, I let out a cry of indignation, as if I were trying to free myself of that helpless feeling seizing my chest, and ran to my room—behavior never witnessed by any of those three women, who knew me better than anyone.

"Inês, dear!" my mother pleaded, upset, but I didn't answer her.

"Didn't I say she wasn't acting her normal self?" Tia Firmina boasted. "I'll be spending the night here, in front of the oratory, praying God forgives Inês for her misbehavior," she said in a loud voice, so I could hear her, and so I'd know she would be keeping watch at the door until the next day.

A little while later, Cândida came into the room, where she found me crying on the bed. My mind was still reeling, trying to come up with a way to save Eugênia.

"Do you want me to hold your hand, Inês?"

I accepted the comfort of that little hand, so loved and tiny.

"I can sing, too, if you like," she said, and she chose one of the songs for the Feast of Saint Agatha she'd been rehearsing.

Then, listening to those hymns Cândida chose to try to sing me to sleep, I had an idea. There would still be a chance to let Eugênia know: my friend would be in town for the procession. But, if I went over to speak to her, the Colonel might suspect my involvement later on—even if Eugênia postponed her plans that day, she would certainly try again. I couldn't put my family at risk like that, even though I wanted to help Eugênia.

When I woke up and found Tia Firmina in the same place as the night before, exactly as she'd promised, I acted remorseful.

"Forgive me for yesterday, Tia. I'm ashamed of having disrespected you."

My mother immediately came over to give me a hug, not understanding why I was acting that way, but also suspecting, like Tia Firmina, that it was because I'd fallen in love.

"Whenever you have a problem, you can come to us, Inês," my mother assured me, while my aunt still looked upset.

"I forgive you, if you promise me that such behavior will never be repeated."

"Yes, Tia."

"In any case, I've already told Vitorina not to come this afternoon. All this unpleasantness is just going to get our threads tangled up. No one outside the family enters this house until the procession."

"Don't be ridiculous, Firmina. We have so many pieces to finish," my mother objected, but my aunt stood firm in her decision.

"I know what I'm doing, Carmelita. Believe me."

After breakfast, I offered to help make the angel costume my sister would wear at the festivities. Tia Firmina looked at me suspiciously when I volunteered for the task. But, maybe thinking it was a peace offering or a sign of repentance, she accepted:

"Working on the procession won't redeem you from sin, Inês, but it's a start," she said dryly, handing me the metal frame for the wings, never imagining I would use those wings to convey my message to Eugênia.

My sister was the most important angel at the festivities. Before the procession went out into the streets of Bom Retiro, a child dressed as a cherub was tasked with going up to the altar and crowning the saint, in front of the whole town. That was the high point of the event, one with great expectations—it was a task for someone very small, who not only had to wear a long nightgown but also had to climb a narrow staircase, carrying a heavy metal crown, and fit it perfectly on the little shelf at the top of the saint's image.

Every year, when the chosen child started to climb the steps, people would hold their breath. We watched people's anxious faces, fearful that the angel would lose her balance and the litter decorated with paper flowers would fall to the ground. Ever since Cândida had taken on the role, the tension was so great that when my sister began her climb toward the saint—without anyone's help, as she had insisted—it felt as though time came to a standstill in Bom Retiro. Our clocks might have even fallen slightly behind the rest of the world because of those few tense moments. Even from afar, there was no way Eugênia could ignore the coded message on my sister's wings, which would say *Don't go.*

There was just one problem: the wings already had a lace design, made by Tia Firmina over the course of several weeks, with stars sprinkled around the edges and rays of light slipping between celestial clouds in the center. Unable to change the pattern, I had to rely on Cândida's complicity. Even though I'd promised Eugênia not to tell anyone her secret, I needed help, and no one was more reliable than my sister.

Cândida was not born blind. Her blindness was the result of an accident my father was responsible for. As a baby, she'd had inflammation in her eyes for which the apothecary had prescribed some medicine: two drops, diluted in a liter of water, given every two hours. My father, anxious to ease his daughter's suffering and give her the medicine right away, momentarily forgot the instructions and put the concentrated substance directly into my sister's eyes. One drop in each eye was enough to cloud Cândida's vision forever. My mother used to say her daughter cried so loud that all of Bom Retiro could hear.

My father realized his mistake immediately and despaired.

"We have to rinse her eyes. Quick!" he shouted at me and my mother, holding Cândida under running water from a tap.

My sister soon calmed down, and my father sighed with relief. He hugged his daughter with all the force of his regret. It was as if he'd found her again after having lost her.

"I think she's fine," he said uncertainly, as if trying to convince himself. "She's all right, isn't she, Carmelita? What do you think?"

"It seems so." My mother checked her daughter on her husband's lap. "She's smiling, it must be nothing."

But that same day my mother noticed that little Cândida no longer followed her with her eyes. Only sounds attracted her attention. I was about seven at the time, and I remember my mother asking me if Cândida looked okay. To give her a proper opinion, I showed Cândida my doll, but my sister didn't reach for it like she used to.

Distraught, my mother sent for the apothecary. My father wasn't home at that time, which she thought was opportune, as she didn't want to worry him if it was just an eyelash. Half an hour later, after examining my sister, the apothecary sighed regretfully.

"She'll never see again. Her retinas are burned."

Still smiling, little Cândida waved her little arms when she heard that man's deep voice and stretched her legs with pleasure, babbling happily.

I watched my mother collapse on the floor, like a tree felled at the root, and I feared she had passed from this life without saying goodbye. I backed up against the wall and watched the apothecary go to her, ordering me to stay calm, saying he would handle things.

When I saw my mother there unconscious, arms lifeless, unresponsive, I was flooded by such suffocating fear that I snatched Cândida away. Her warm little body against my chest gave me comfort, even though she was the biggest victim. While I waited for my mother to regain consciousness, Cândida played with my hair, put it in her mouth, and made a funny face. She was such a delight and took such good care of her older sister, I was sure everything would work out.

My father was never the same after the accident. We were all inconsolable at the house with the blue windows, but my father more than anyone, and he began to live inside his guilt. Ironically, our sadness was no match for Cândida's joy, who acted as if nothing had changed, and as the years passed, her tranquility made it so we forgot to lament her fate.

To make up for her not being able to see the world, my father decided to fill the house with sounds. First, he bought clocks, which chimed every hour and played different melodies. He also brought music boxes, some instruments, and many, many birds. He placed them beside his daughter's cradle, saying, "She will never see the colors of the world, but she will hear the most beautiful sounds we can offer her."

After Cândida lost her sight, I lost a little bit of my father. I became the daughter he didn't owe a debt to, the daughter he didn't need to take extra care of, whose unhappiness he didn't need to compensate for.

My mother noticed my sadness when I, innocently, not under-standing the extent of that man's pain, tried to show him a drawing I'd just done. Even though he was well meaning and interested in what I was showing him, he couldn't admire my feat without remembering that Cândida could never draw the same or appreciate the image I had in my hands. The poor man even tried to smile at me, but, within moments, his smile was dragged to some deep place in his soul, over-shadowed by remorse.

Not wanting to provoke even more heartbreak, naturally I dis-tanced myself. When we were side by side, I was quiet, imagining myself as invisible so as not to disturb him and waiting for him to give me a task. I still remember the joy I felt when my father called me, saying, "Inês! Help me with this birdcage. The red tanager likes fruit. And for the orange-winged parrot, a piece of scarlet eggplant. When I'm no longer around, you're the one who'll take care of Cândida's birds. She won't be able to do it all on her own, and it's the only joy our little girl has in life."

"It's okay, Daddy. I will," I assured him, proudly, happy to have some of his attention, even if his aim was to make amends to Cândida.

I admit that, as a child, I felt a little jealous of the attention everyone gave my sister. But my love for Cândida always quashed that feeling. I loved her more than anyone. Since the day she was born, my sister was always like a doll to me.

When my father passed away, it wasn't me, but Cândida, already smitten with those birds, who started to raise and feed them. But, unlike my father, who kept them in cages, she decided to let them go free.

"They'll come back to visit us when they feel like it."

And that's how the birds in the region learned the way to the house with the blue windows and started to make nests in the rafters of our living room. It was like we lived in an aviary. Birds of all sizes flitted around the room at all hours of the day, sang at dawn, fluttered their wings at the change of seasons, and made a deafening noise when the sun went down.

"Cândida, these pests are making a mess of everything!" Tia Firmina complained. "Carmelita, do something."

But my mother wouldn't let us touch my sister's birds.

"It's her only hobby. Leave her alone, Firmina."

"The birdsong is so beautiful, Tia. It calms me down," argued Cândida.

"The damned things make me nervous."

"But they're God's creatures, Tia."

"I'm sure they are, but they were bred to live in the trees, not under my roof."

Cândida was amused and not offended. She loved Tia Firmina as much as her birds, which she cared for like a mother. She named them, could recognize them by the rustling of their wings, checked for eggs in their nests, and worried when a hummingbird didn't appear. It was precisely because of my sister's caring soul that I was sure I could trust her with Eugênia's secret.

"Cândida, come here. I want to show you something on these wings."

Always cognizant of the space in our room, Cândida reached out her hands in the exact direction of the piece in my lap and ran her slender fingers over the relief of the stitches.

"Do you feel it?" I asked, directing her little fingers to a specific spot.

"It's a dewdrop stitch," she identified.

"Yes. Now pretend this stitch is a *D*." She nodded, and I moved on to the next one.

"Now this one. The twist stitch. Think of it like a *T*."

Cândida straightened up, curious, starting to understand the game.

"Are you pretending the stitches are letters?"

"Yes, I'll teach you. There's a stitch for each letter. Can you feel this one? It's the bull's-eye—"

"I know." She cut me off. "A bull's-eye is an *O*," she guessed, enjoying the challenge.

"That's right. You're so clever," I said.

With her trained fingers, Cândida easily recognized the stitches by touch, even the ones that were very similar, like fish scale and tapestry.

"Why are you writing messages in the lace, Inês?"

And, without waiting for an answer, delighted by her own hunch, she ventured the guess that, it seemed, was shared by all the women in that house:

"Is it for your boyfriend? Is it for Odoniel?"

"No," I quickly denied. "Odoniel is just a friend. This message is for Eugênia. She was the one who invented this code, so we could communicate after she moved to the ranch."

Cândida didn't immediately understand. "Why don't you just send her a letter, with words written on paper?"

"We have to do it like this," I tried to explain. "People's lives change a great deal after marriage."

Cândida's face tensed, not understanding.

"Changes for the worse or for the better?"

"In Eugênia's case, for the worse. Unfortunately."

Cândida reflected for a moment, squeezing my hand and suffering silently for Eugênia, whom she loved so much.

"That's why we're never getting married, isn't it, Inês? Our life is good the way it is. Without any young men dying for us."

Normally, I would deny the curse that befell the men in our family, but I stopped myself when I realized that the idea of staying single somehow comforted my sister.

"I need you to do me a very important favor, Cândida," I said, returning to the matter at hand. "I have a message I need to give Eugênia during the procession. A message that no one can read, only her. So I had this idea to make it very visible, putting it where everyone will look: your wings."

Cândida grew excited while I explained.

"I can't change the design already on the lace, made by Tia Firmina, but I made this extra piece, a strip of lace, which you'll wear between the wings for the coronation, understand?"

Cândida nodded and I continued: "You're going to keep this strip of lace hidden, okay? And, when you're about to walk up the aisle, just attach it to a little hook that I'll sew. Later I'll teach you how to do it, and we'll practice together. Do you think you can do that?"

Cândida studied the piece of lace with her hands, calculated the distance between the wings, and said: "It'll be easy, don't worry." And after thinking about it for a moment, she asked me to put a long string on one end so she could find the place to pull more easily.

"And one more thing." I wanted to warn her. "If, by chance, Tia Firmina asks about this extra piece of lace when you come down from the altar . . . ," I began, but Cândida interrupted me:

"I'll say I didn't even notice it. There was no way for a blind child to know," she added, and I wrapped my arms around her fragile body, grateful Cândida existed and had taught me so much.

Since we were little, we were always active participants in the Feast of Saint Agatha. Secretly, my aunt thought her nieces' devotion to the church might offset some of our family's debt with the Almighty. So she was very hopeful when she heard news that the parish priest had chosen Cândida for the day's most important task: crowning Saint Agatha. A very wise decision, in my aunt's opinion, since a blind girl certainly had fewer sins than the others and, therefore, would be closer to God.

It was the third time Cândida had been given that job, which she had been looking forward to all year, more than Christmas. The sound of the crowd gathered in the square made her tiny body pulse. It was a mixture of fear and euphoria, preceded by an unusual silence, and ending in a powerful wave of applause. Cândida felt like her chest might explode. Last year, my sister had deliberately lingered three seconds longer than necessary holding the crown over the saint so that, after the possibility of disaster, people would clap even harder.

This time my sister would have a new mission. On her wings she would carry the message *Don't go*. Eugênia's salvation would come through an angel.

15

Recife, 1919

Ave Libertas received many requests for help, but none had ever arrived in such an unusual way, on an exquisite lace mantilla veil. Weeks earlier, the paper had received a letter from the same town. In the envelope, there was a vague note, written at the post office counter, which said only: "Please wait for next contact." Attached to the note was a piece of paper where I'd copied down the code created by Eugênia.

The scant details were for safety. If the letter got lost or was intercepted, the content of that note might be traced back to Eugênia Medeiros Galvão. The ladies of Ave Libertas were used to mysterious messages like that and wouldn't find the intentional gaps I'd left strange.

Tremendously active in the fight for human rights in the years leading up to the abolition of slavery, these women had sheltered fugitives in their own homes and dedicated their lives to answering calls for help like this one.

Weeks after the first letter, the ladies received a new letter from the same town, this time inside a larger package, which contained the lace veil. As a precaution, I made a point of posting them a few weeks apart, so they wouldn't travel in the same mailbag. Inside the veil, they found another note, almost as brief as the previous one: "Note the stitches, made especially for you." Again, if intercepted, the veil and the message would not arouse suspicion.

After many years, I found out that the person who opened the package that day was the lady we knew from the photo printed on the page Vitorina had shown us. Maria Amélia de Queirós placed the notes received from the same sender on the table and spread the veil over the wooden tabletop, surrounded by her female comrades.

Understanding immediately what they were looking at, she showed the others the letters she recognized in the stitches, while Bárbara de Mendonça wrote down the sequence in a notebook bound in floral fabric. In under an hour, the ladies were up to speed on Eugênia's story.

I, Eugênia Medeiros Galvão, formerly known as Eugênia Damásio Lima, find myself a prisoner of a nightmare from which I intend to escape. I was forced to marry at age fifteen, to a man I despise and who mistreats me. His name is Colonel Aristeu Medeiros Galvão, a political leader and the most powerful man in the town of Bom Retiro and its surroundings. I have decided to run away, lest I kill him. I have been saving money for some time, earned from the sale of my work as a lacemaker, and with the amount already collected I believe I will be able to reach the city of Recife, where my husband's political influence does not have the same power and where I hope to be able to count on the protection of you ladies, and other groups that value freedom. I don't know a soul in the capital, but, when a copy of Ave Libertas *made its way into my hands here in Pajeú valley, I glimpsed in those printed words a thread of hope. Lace is the only way I have to communicate with anyone, and that is why I am sending you my request through this veil. My intention is to leave Bom Retiro in February and, upon arriving in the capital, seek you out to receive guidance on how to proceed from then on. Any assistance will be welcomed. My despair is such that I do not care about the consequences. Starvation, sleeping out of doors, having to face any other adversity. I cannot continue here. I*

*have faith that I will be able to count on the compassion of you
ladies, who have already done so much for so many wronged
souls. I pray that God will give me health and courage so that
I may soon be free and standing before my benefactresses.*

My sincerest appreciation,
Eugênia
December 10, 1918

When Maria Amélia finished reading the veil aloud, the ladies looked at each other, already knowing what to do.

"We have to send a reply. Who here knows how to make lace?" she asked the others.

Lace, however, was an art dominated by common women, who relied on the trade to survive. Sophisticated urban ladies like them only had to choose which lace would look more elegant alongside the silverware and china at the dinner parties they hosted.

Taking a better look at the stitches on the veil, Bárbara de Mendonça concluded that the stitches could be reproduced with embroidery on a piece of linen.

"I can make a doily with flowers in the center and a message around the hem," she said.

Together, the ladies wrote a reply in which they assured Eugênia that it would be their pleasure to welcome her in Recife. They only asked the girl to proceed with caution, as her prolonged suffering might cloud her clarity of mind and make her believe the dangers were less real. They also assured her they would give her all the help she needed to start a new chapter of life in the capital: legal assistance, if needed, a job, housing. At the end, they saw fit to add a few words of motivation and decided on the phrase *The oppressor may seem strong, but it is not always strength that wins.*

With the text ready, they prepared a template on a sheet of tracing paper, which Bárbara de Mendonça would use as a guide. The message would be embroidered in white, the same color as the fabric, to deceive whoever might handle the piece. Their eyes would naturally be drawn to the bouquet of vibrantly colored flowers covering the entire center.

"That's how magicians do it. They divert attention from what's most important. The message on the edge will barely be visible," Bárbara de Mendonça assured everyone, promising to start work that same night. They could send their reply in one or two days at most, to the sender of the two letters: Inês Flores, the fugitive's trusted friend.

Before reviewing the notes for her lecture on the importance of women in the labor market, Maria Amélia de Queirós decided to hang the lace veil made by Eugênia on the office wall at Ave Libertas, as if it were a flag. The veil from Bom Retiro would remain there, in that prominent location, for many years, even after my friend's death.

16

Nearly a hundred years later, Eugênia's veil, which had spent decades at the Ave Libertas headquarters, was now traveling inside Alice's backpack on the seat of a tour bus. Protected from the heat by the air-conditioning blowing at full blast, Alice watched the sepia-toned landscape past the window gradually turn green as they climbed the mountains of the Borborema Plateau. It was the first time since 1918, when Inês Flores had sent it by post to Ave Libertas, that the veil was returning to the place it was made.

There were almost no tourists on the bus. Most of the passengers were relatives going to visit their families, carrying bags full of gifts and other luxuries that could only be found in the capital. Alice tried to relax on the trip, but she couldn't, bothered by the conversation she heard in the row behind her.

On the previous two stops—and also when she got up to use the bathroom at the back of the bus—she'd seen a serious-looking young woman traveling in row 3, sitting exaggeratedly close to the window, and, beside her, a young man, who'd taken his shoes off and unbuttoned his shirt, his body sprawled in the seat so that he took up almost half the space belonging to the woman.

Before the bus had even left the station, Alice had begun to eavesdrop on the two strangers. The passenger in 3B struck up a conversation about the weather and the journey ahead. "I think it's going to rain." "Still over six hours to go. It's a dirt road, you know?" "Are you hot? I don't think the air's working." Then he moved on to more personal questions: "What are you going to do in Bom Retiro? Do you have family there?" "What's your name again?" "Want some crackers?" "Do you have a boyfriend?"

At first, the female passenger answered his questions politely and went back to her reading. But the guy didn't seem to understand her economy of words as a boundary, and an hour into the trip she stopped responding altogether and sat in cornered silence. At the next stop, Alice watched as the woman from row 3 went to say something to the driver, gesturing and pointing at the man who wouldn't stop bothering her, but the driver just shook his head, as if to say: "The bus is full, there's nothing I can do."

They still had two hours to go before they reached their destination when Alice heard the passenger in 3B say: "I like you. I think we should be together."

Alice leapt up and, turning around, said: "Excuse me?"

The sudden movement woke Tia Helena, who was dozing beside her. The man seemed startled to be approached by a girl like Alice, who, judging by her trendy clothes and her blue hair, must have been from the big city. The woman in 3A also widened her eyes in surprise. She wasn't alone, as she'd imagined.

"You know what?" Alice began, in a sarcastically colloquial tone. "I get sooooo carsick in the aisle seat. Would you mind switching places with me?" She directly asked the girl in 3A, who hesitated for a moment, maybe because she didn't want to put Alice in the same situation she was in. "Please," Alice insisted, almost intimately, looking her square in the eye so she would understand she'd be safe.

Hearing her niece's request, Tia Helena piped up: "If you're feeling sick, Alice, just switch places with me. No need to bother this nice girl. I'll take the aisle seat."

The woman in 3A, fearing she would lose her chance to escape her nuisance neighbor, hurriedly said: "No worries. It's no trouble at all. Of course I'll swap seats with you." As she got up, the girl whispered to Alice, "Thank you."

"Oh, please! You're the one doing me a favor, believe me. I'll be a lot more relaxed now," Alice assured her, stepping to the side so the woman could put her bags in the luggage rack above row 2.

The first thing Alice did when she sat down was plant her elbow on the center armrest, clearly marking her territory. She wouldn't allow intrusions of any kind. She stared at the passenger, who looked away, avoiding her eyes. In a few moments, the man in 3B had put his shoes back on, buttoned up his shirt, and was sitting up straight. Soon after he fell asleep. Or pretended to sleep. It didn't matter, since, in the seat in front of her, the girl was now chatting away with Tia Helena, and the sound of their conversation lulled Alice to sleep until they reached their final destination.

From what Alice had discovered over the previous few days, her ancestors left Bom Retiro shortly after the Feast of Saint Agatha in 1919, and the only one who remained in the house with the blue windows was Firmina Flores. According to Tia Helena—who'd heard the story from her mother, who'd heard it from her grandmother—Firmina refused to leave the ground where her father was buried.

"They left against their will, but then everything worked out," said Tia Helena as they checked in at the bed-and-breakfast in Bom Retiro. "The only thing you can't run away from in this life is death, Alice."

Alice nodded, not quite sure what to think, as she believed there were many things in this world you couldn't run away from.

"I've only been here a few times; can you believe it?" Tia Helena said, already making plans for the next few days. "We can go to Triunfo to see the famous Teatro Guarany, a beautiful building. Then there's the Cangaço Museum. Lampião was born nearby, did you know that?"

They could also visit the Serra do Giz archaeological site, near Afogados da Ingazeira, a forty-minute drive on the PE-320. The very first inhabitants of this land left behind their stories there, recorded in drawings on the sandstone walls.

"But tomorrow is all about the veil. I've already arranged everything with Vitorina."

Tia Helena had been a civil engineer. She was first in her class at the Federal University of Pernambuco, and the only woman in the entire class.

"You have no idea what it was like to pull up to a construction site and have to make yourself heard," she said later on, over a plate of osso buco stew at a local restaurant recommended by the hotel. "When I first started out, I didn't get credit for a lot of projects that came from my drafting table, my male colleagues did. I almost never heard someone say: 'Look at Helena's building.' It was always: 'Look at Geraldo's building, or Silveira's.'"

"Weren't you ever married, Tia?" asked Alice, then thought it best to explain herself. "I'm just asking for the sake of asking. It makes no difference to me. Just curiosity, really."

Alice was afraid her question would sound like a demand, like so many others: "Why didn't you want to have kids?" "Why don't you have a boyfriend?" "Why did you break up?"

Her intention was different.

"You're wondering if someone died because of me, aren't you?" Tia Helena guessed and then started to explain. "Technically, I'm not a direct descendant of Das Dores. My great-grandmother was the younger sister of the so-called cursed bride. Even before the wedding, that part of the family had already left Bom Retiro, so I wouldn't have been under the gypsy's hex. But . . ." She proposed a theory: "Anyone who didn't know that little detail might assume I was too afraid to get married. But it wasn't that. I had a lot of boyfriends, as it happens. I just never found someone to say, 'Till death do us part,' and I'm very happy. I have my apartment, my job, I've traveled all over the world, I have friends who are like family to me, and a bunch of nieces and nephews, including you. I never missed having a long-term partner. Not that I had planned on being single or had anything against marriage, but that's just how things turned out."

Alice felt pleased to be bonding with someone so at peace with her options.

"On the other hand," Tia Helena went on, "Eugênia, the one who suffered the most in this story, was not our blood relative. She was never under the weight of the gypsy's curse, but she met the cruelest fate of all the lacemakers."

Tia Helena sighed, wistfully. "Every life has its share of suffering, and the Floreses, if we think about it, were happy, too. To believe in curses is to believe we have no choice. And we always do."

"Maybe that's why my grandmother chose not to register my mother as a Flores."

"Yes, that's one possibility. My cousin Celina was so upset after her father's suicide, when the Floreses were already living in Recife. But that man was buried in debt, he left a note full of resentment, and, in my opinion, jumping in the Capibaribe is a very personal choice, which has nothing to do with the occult. I think it would be unfair to say your great-grandfather was driven to his death by a curse rather than by failure itself. But you're right," she mused. "Perhaps removing the name from her birth certificate was a way for your grandmother to overcome the pain of losing her father. Celina wouldn't have been the first to try to lessen the effects of that plight. Firmina also tried to protect the family's descendants, with prayer and promises."

They finished their coffee, and Alice signaled to the waiter to bring them the check.

"I think the episode with the gypsy must have really happened," Tia Helena continued. "But if people believed all that, maybe that was a way our ancestors found to be free and go about their business without

149

anyone interfering. Not that they did it on purpose, but, marked by that fate, they could take advantage of people's beliefs. They were independent and could devote themselves fully to the craft of lace. It was providence that everyone believed they shouldn't get involved with them, don't you think?"

"It makes sense."

Walking through the silent cobblestone streets, Alice's thoughts immediately went to Sofia, who, being a woman, was perhaps out of harm's way. To drive the worry from her mind, she shook her head. *Curses don't exist.*

"And the house? It's still there?" Alice asked curiously.

"It's a stationery shop now, but it's still standing. The garden's long gone, but the windows are still blue, as I understand, and they say birds still nest in the ceiling. They never forgot the way. Do you want to go there now?" asked Tia Helena, almost as if she were proposing a prank.

Bom Retiro was fast asleep that time of night, and the full moon lit up the small house, which Alice didn't recognize as the same one in the photos her aunt had shown her. The new owners had built an addition where the garden used to be, and the building now reached the sidewalk. On the front hung a white-painted wooden sign that read, in blue letters, *Papelaria Elegância*. Alice placed her hand solemnly on the wall, a small, improvised ritual to mark her presence in that place to which she was also connected. Beside her, her aunt stood silently, respectful, and they stayed like that for a while, as if paying tribute to their ancestors, before heading back to the inn.

Ironically, after the Floreses left, the town of Bom Retiro became a hub for handcrafted lace.

"When our family left, Vitorina taught the craft to other girls in town and formed a new group of lacemakers. Tomorrow we'll go talk to her. She's going to love meeting a Flores with blue hair," said Tia Helena before they went to bed, not as a criticism but as a compliment.

17

Eugênia received the lace handkerchief with confirmation of her escape plan one morning in January. Odoniel had hand-delivered it to Colonel Aristeu's wife along with three more bolts of fabric she'd ordered. Nobody paid much attention to the handoff or was surprised by Eugênia's presence in the kitchen, 'where she once again insisted on checking the delivery from the store. On the contrary, Dorina was thrilled when she saw the lady of the house enter the room. Secretly, she hoped that one day the two of them would become good friends.

Eugênia waited for the afternoon siesta to read my message. She retired to her bedchamber and, with her handkerchief in her lap, discovered with a mixture of relief and euphoria that a carriage would pick her up at eight o'clock on the night of the festivities, at the second bend in the road after leaving town. Eugênia felt a strong sense of excitement. Everything was going as planned, and she'd never be able to thank me enough for the favor I was doing her.

It would be the first time my friend had left the ranch since her wedding day, and she was determined not to ever return. She would disappear amid the crowds gathered to pay tribute to Saint Agatha and flee until she reached the spot agreed with the driver. The festivities for the feast day of the town's patron saint would be her farewell to Bom Retiro: the last time she would see her parents and friends. She was taking such great care to cover up her real intentions for that day that it was possible Eugênia might not risk giving me a hug, which only she and I would know would be our last.

But the future was bright. When she got to Recife, or if Aristeu's life was cut short, which she very much doubted since, as they say, the devil looks after his own, Eugênia would be able to see us again.

Freedom was close at hand, but until it reached her completely, Eugênia was willing to do her best not to irritate Aristeu. She would show her husband that she'd come to her senses, and he would surely let his guard down. Until the day of her departure, she would be the most obedient wife. In the weeks that followed the delivery, Eugênia tried to act like a gracious and devoted housewife. She checked the table setting each day, and, when she heard the sound of her husband's boots coming down the hallway, she became even more focused on the task. "Don't forget those plates, Dorina. The little ones, please." She also gave directions to the cooks about the day's menu, hoping Dorina would comment on it during the meal: "It was Eugênia who reminded us to make this compote, Colonel."

Finally, to appear even more dutiful, Eugênia talked to the children about religion and moral duties.

"Today I'm going to tell you the story of Saint Agatha, our patron saint," she announced one evening after dinner. "Did you know the saint's first miracle was with a veil?"

The two children pretended not to know and sat at Eugênia's feet, curious to hear more.

"The veil buried with Saint Agatha saved the lives of thousands of people. It was a holy shroud."

The children's eyes widened, aghast at that morbid image of a dead woman wrapped in cloth, perhaps thinking of their own mother, who'd probably also been buried that way.

"Agatha was a rich and noble girl born in a part of Italy called Sicily. From the time she was very little, she used to tell everyone it was her greatest wish to devote her life to God and become a nun. But Agatha didn't know that a very bad and powerful man would cross her path and take away her peace."

Trying to make the story more dramatic and keep the little ones' attention, Eugênia paused and only resumed the story when her stepchildren insisted, hands folded in prayer, anxious to know who that terrible man was.

"A heartless man, children. He wanted to marry Agatha, but he didn't truly love her. He was only interested in her fortune."

Eugênia felt a bolt of electricity run through her body as she dared to speak of an oppressor in front of her own oppressor. But sitting at his desk, Aristeu continued to calmly smoke his pipe and leaf through the ranch's accounting ledger, as if he weren't listening to the conversation.

"When Agatha turned down his marriage proposal, as it was her desire to serve only God, the evil man was furious. He took the girl prisoner and tortured her for days, trying to make her give in to his will."

Eugênia's stepdaughter put her hands to her face, covering her eyes, frightened by the images the word *torture* brought to mind, while her father turned another page in the ledger.

"The more she resisted," Eugênia continued, "the greater the evil that man inflicted, going so far as to rip her breasts off."

Upon hearing the description of such cruel martyrdom, Eugênia's stepchildren let out a wail and started to ask her many questions, perhaps to convince themselves it was just a story, perhaps not as real as their stepmother made it seem. "Ripped off how?" "With a knife?" "Did she cry?" "Did she survive?" "Did no one help the poor thing?"

Eugênia answered each question, but her attention was no longer on the children, but on the sound of Aristeu's fountain pen, which suddenly stopped, hovering over the paper. He'd heard her.

"Was she no longer a woman?" asked her stepdaughter, imagining a woman without breasts.

"Of course she was, my dear," Eugênia assured her, with an air of great wisdom. "Her body was mutilated, but her soul was still intact. Agatha knelt down and prayed with so much faith in her heart that, afraid of God's wrath, her tormentor stopped the abuse and ordered the prisoner to be taken to her room."

Though frightened by the violence of the tale, the children sat spellbound, keen to know how it ended.

"And how was she saved?" asked the stepson.

"She saved herself, didn't she?" The little girl wanted to make sure, fearful.

Eugênia sighed.

"Not in life, my loves. Not in this world. When she returned to the bedroom, nearly losing consciousness from the pain, Agatha had a vision of Saint Peter himself. He heard her prayers and enveloped her with a divine light capable of making all her pain disappear and healing all her wounds. Grateful, Agatha asked Saint Peter to take her to Our Lord, for the world of men did not deserve her."

"So, Agatha died?" asked the stepdaughter, still holding on to a small hope.

"Yes, my dear," said Eugênia, but qualified her answer. "But without suffering and without giving in to her executioner."

At that point, without even turning to look where Aristeu was sitting, Eugênia could feel her husband's eyes on her neck.

"And that very night . . . ," she continued. "Do you know what happened?"

"What?" asked the children more cheerfully, intuiting it would be something less tragic than what they'd heard so far.

"A terrible earthquake ravaged the city."

"Was it the wrath of God?" the little girl asked.

"Exactly. A punishment for those who didn't defend Agatha. At that time, no one suspected she would become a saint, they just thought she was a very devout but ordinary girl. Her power was only revealed later when another tragedy befell the region. This time it was a fire that destroyed houses and crops."

The children didn't immediately understand. "Was that another punishment from God? Wasn't the first one enough?"

"No, my dears. This time it was different," Eugênia explained. "When the fire began to spread, people panicked and ran to Agatha's tomb to ask for protection. The townspeople believed that the deceased girl was close to God and that she could intercede for anyone who prayed to her. When they opened the tomb, they found the girl's corpse exactly as it had been buried. Years after her death, she was still that beautiful young woman, with the same peaceful look on her face."

"Was she wrapped in the miraculous veil?" asked the stepdaughter, remembering the shroud her stepmother had already mentioned. The little girl's hands gripped the hem of her dress, perhaps thinking again of her dead mother. Maybe she was also still beautiful and peaceful in her grave?

"Standing before Agatha's untouched body, the people knew there had been divine intervention, and someone suggested holding up the veil as a shield against the flames. When the fire encountered the sacred cloth, it miraculously stopped in its tracks. All those who took shelter that day under the veil of Saint Agatha, who only became a saint after that event, survived to tell this story."

The children sighed with relief that those lives were saved and that the story told by their stepmother had come to an end.

"And the bad man? What happened to him?"

"He fell off his horse a short time later," said Eugênia, without mentioning the torturer's fate.

In his chair, Aristeu didn't move. Even his expression remained unchanged. Eugênia trusted her husband's own arrogance would prevent him from seeing any resemblance between himself and the Roman prefect Quintianus, who lived in the year 251. In the image he had of himself, Aristeu wouldn't see "a mean man who rips off breasts." He was a husband who respected his wife and gave her all the necessary comforts, in spite of Eugênia's stubborn ingratitude.

"And ever since," Eugênia continued, "people suffering great pain and injustice, as Agatha herself suffered, ask her to cover them with her veil and keep them safe from harm. The first miracle happened on February 5, and that's why, every year, on that same day, we have a beautiful celebration in her honor."

"The procession!" the stepson exclaimed. "We are going, aren't we, Father?"

"A man in my position cannot miss certain engagements," Aristeu replied dryly and decided to send them off to bed.

"I'll go with you, my loves, to give you a kiss good night," said Eugênia as she stood up, but her husband told her otherwise.

"You stay."

"But I thought I'd tell them one more story," she pleaded.

"That one was enough to keep them awake. They don't need another."

Eugênia regretted her detailed descriptions of Agatha's martyrdom and said:

"That wasn't my intention. I thought telling the children about the lives of the saints would teach them good things."

"No son of mine was born to become a bible thumper. Enough."

The children knew that an *enough* from Aristeu was nonnegotiable. They exchanged a knowing look with Eugênia, respectfully accepted their father's blessing, and, without letting their disappointment show, wished them good night and went to their room.

As soon as her stepchildren left, Eugênia cautiously returned to the couple's usual silence. She reached for a lace project she'd been working on and began stitching. They sat in silence for some time until, after finishing his digestif, Aristeu got up and left without saying a word, slightly drunk from the alcohol. Eugênia hoped that tenuous intoxication she identified from the flush on Aristeu's cheeks would keep him out of her bed that night, which is precisely what happened.

In the days that followed, Eugênia devoted herself to preparations for the family's trip to Bom Retiro. She set aside the clothes the children would wear to the festivities and asked Dorina to make a packed lunch, in case they got hungry on the trip. She was acting like the lady of the house for the first time, and this change did not go unnoticed by her husband.

At first Aristeu thought the improvement in his wife's mood was because Eugênia was about to see her mother again. Contrary to his mother-in-law's hopes at the time of their engagement, Aristeu had never invited or allowed Eugênia to invite her parents to visit, much less to spend any time at Caviúna.

Eugênia didn't mind being so far from her family: it would be worse if she had to play her new and unwanted role in front of her parents and be forced to respond to her mother's curiosity and expectations with a smile on her face. The sheriff and his wife were satisfied with their daughter's new circumstances and would not give her the support Eugênia so desperately needed. If she made any complaint about Aristeu, they would take his side. Eugênia had no illusions about that.

Since the beginning of their married life, she had communicated with her mother through letters that never conveyed the truth. Suspecting Aristeu might open them before they were sent, she spoke only of the delights of the ranch and of the children's progress in their studies, and she preferred to ask questions rather than talk about herself.

And so, proudly savoring every word written by their daughter, now the wife of a colonel, the sheriff and his wife became convinced Eugênia had adapted to her new life, despite her initial protests. The decision to marry her off had been the right one.

Although they hadn't gotten as close to the Colonel as they'd wanted, Eugênia's parents remained satisfied with the arrangement and hoped the arrival of a grandson would bring the two families closer together. Whenever her mother asked her about a future heir, Eugênia said only what her mother wanted to hear. She told her she prayed each night to have a baby in her arms. It would be such a joy to the stepchildren to have another sibling. A brother, because her offspring must be male. She intended to name him Aristeu II.

But, contrary to what she said in her letters, every month, without exception, Eugênia secretly chewed on herb-of-grace and added Queen Anne's lace to her husband's coffee, a well-known folk remedy to weaken the male seed.

As a child, Eugênia was lucky to have overheard a variety of whispered conversations from the girls who did chores around her house, giving her the knowledge that would prove so useful to her. One day, one of the cooks was in tears, complaining about not knowing what to do with her life: "What now, my God? I have no means. My father's kicked me out of the house, and this man dared to tell me the child is not his." The older women embraced the tearful young woman, told her how to proceed, and taught her what to do so it wouldn't happen again.

In those late January days, contrary to what Eugênia had hoped, instead of feeling relaxed by his wife's new submissive behavior, Aristeu began to suspect that something was wrong. Her change in behavior had been too sudden. There must be some secret underneath her obedience.

So her husband began to keep a close eye on her. More than once, he caught Eugênia smiling to herself or looking out at the pasture stretching to the horizon. Not knowing what Eugênia was thinking tormented Aristeu, who had become jealous of whatever was going on in his wife's soul, a space all her own, where he could not enter. Though they'd never really taken to one another, ever since he'd met her the Colonel had always found it easy to decipher Eugênia's thoughts.

The girl had hated him from the very first day, when she ran out of her father's sitting room, and he was somehow flattered by this. The anger his wife felt for him filled his entire soul, and Aristeu considered that an achievement. Eugênia was his because she only thought about him. That venomous hatred was heady and pungent, and it exhilarated him more than the placid obedience he first thought he wanted. He craved confrontation because confrontation was the only thing they shared. Bitterness united them.

So, for that reason, on that afternoon when he heard Eugênia humming in the hallway, Aristeu could think of nothing else for the rest of the day. It was not without struggle that the Colonel had turned a blind eye to all Eugênia had put him through those last few months. If it had been anyone else, he would have sent her back after he'd used her. But he'd been generous and patient, and when he finally authorized her to visit her old life—her parents, the city, the lacemakers—she'd defied him like that, humming like a little girl.

At dinner, Aristeu notice an unusual sparkle in Eugênia's eyes, as well as the way she laughed when his eldest son spilled some rice pudding on his shirt. For the first time since she'd set foot on his land, she was content. And it wasn't because of the life he'd given her, the perks of being the mistress of Fazenda Caviúna. Eugênia was happy to be on the eve of returning, even if temporarily, to her life as a single woman.

She was so full of hope—not, as her husband imagined, to be participating in the celebrations, but because the date of her escape was getting nearer—that Eugênia didn't even notice Aristeu's resentful gaze, trying to crush any expression of joy.

That night, her husband came to her. As always, Eugênia lay there motionless, her attention turned to the ceiling, her eyes opaque like those of a taxidermied animal. But this time her husband did not accept her indifference, which surprised her.

The wine Aristeu drank at dinner had loosened his pride, and he didn't mind ordering her around: "Move."

That was new. Aristeu had never humiliated himself to the point of demanding Eugênia's participation in the carnal act. His behavior always made it seem like whether his wife was present or not, he'd have his fill just the same.

When Eugênia remained motionless, he insisted: "Come on, move. I didn't marry a corpse."

Eugênia didn't know what to do. She wanted to tell him the truth, that she'd been dried up inside since the day she'd met him, but she couldn't take that risk, not on the eve of her escape.

Irritated by his wife's inertia, the Colonel attempted to finish, but was unable to. That failure upset him so much that suddenly Eugênia felt her body, naked from the waist down, being picked up, followed by pain from being thrown against the wall.

"You're of no use to me. I rue the day I let myself be convinced by your father. If I could, I'd give you back."

Lying on the ground, a trickle of blood running down her forehead, Eugênia made a grave mistake: "Then give me back! I'm not here by choice."

When he heard this affront, Aristeu walked decisively toward his wife and slapped her so hard she fell silent. Not out of obedience, but disorientation.

"Don't you ever talk back to me again. Your duty is to listen and obey. Your obligation is to serve me."

In that situation, the old Eugênia would have raised her head and confronted him, even if it meant getting a beating. But that night, Eugênia had a plan to regain her freedom scheduled for the next day, a plan she'd been dreaming about for months while she made lace with her head down. Aristeu had to be sure his wife was controlled. So instead of piping up again, she remained silent for a few moments and then looked at him with a sorrowful expression.

"I beg your pardon, my husband," she murmured, and Aristeu seemed disconcerted.

Staring down at the floorboards, Eugênia hoped she might convince him of her fragility. Aristeu grunted, annoyed, still under the influence of alcohol, and, heading for the door, announced:

"You won't be going to the procession tomorrow."

It was as if Eugênia had been dropped into the middle of a storm. Her body shivered, and she felt like she was about to be knocked over. Blood still ran down her forehead, blurring her vision, and she remembered it was past midnight and therefore it was the fifth of February, the feast of Saint Agatha.

Eugênia began to say a prayer in her mind: *Oh, Saint Agatha, you who endured such excruciating pain, give me the courage to stand firm.*

"Aristeu, wait," she called out to her husband, who, without turning around, stopped in his tracks to listen. "I can't miss the procession. I'm . . ." And her entire body contracted in a spasm before she could finish her sentence. "I'm your wife. I have to go. In the name of the Medeiros Galvão family."

Oh, Saint Agatha, you who so bravely withstood great suffering, give me courage to face my own martyrdom.

It was the first time Eugênia had called him by his given name, Aristeu. It was also the first time Eugênia had referred to the family she'd married into, pretending to care about a name she'd spent the past several months disowning. Those words dug into Aristeu's chest, and he immediately felt pulled into the same storm of resentment. The Colonel knew his wife and understood her intentions: she would behave like docile cattle so as not to get fenced in.

"You don't deserve the husband you have, Eugênia. I'll have to appear without my wife in front of the whole town. Yet another humiliation you'll put me through. I curse the day I met you."

Curled up on the floor hugging her knees, Eugênia stared at the scratches in the floorboards that formed random designs, like lace.

Saint Agatha, you who were stronger than your cruel executioners, give me wisdom and faith to keep believing.

If she continued trying to convince Aristeu, he might become even more suspicious, and there would be no turning back. She felt powerless, a spectator to her own life, watching the world crumble before her eyes for the second time, just as she had in the parlor of her father's house when her engagement had been announced. For months she'd clung to the hope of that escape. It was thanks to that plan that she was able to abide her prison and not go mad.

"It's for Saint Agatha, Aristeu," she whispered, still hopeful. Her words came out calmly, the result of her repressed despair, a prisoner's survival instinct.

You, who exposed your flesh to the beatings, come to my aid, oh, merciful . . .

"It would be a chance for me to atone for my sins," she added, making one last attempt.

"Which are many," Aristeu agreed, and Eugênia saw her chance.

"It's for my soul—I'm begging you, my husband. I'll be a better person from now on, I promise!"

Aristeu reflected for a moment, annoyed that she'd called him "my husband" again. But he saw an unusual sincerity on his wife's face. Her pleading eyes, no longer furious, made him uneasy. Perhaps Eugênia truly was sorry. Perhaps they could still come to an understanding. Maybe she *could* be the missing cog in the machine of his life.

But that brief flicker of hope was powerless to reverse the order he'd already given. Aristeu Medeiros Galvão's word stood.

"Then pray at home. It won't make any difference to Saint Agatha." And with that, he left without saying another word.

Eugênia wouldn't see her husband again until the time of her death, which occurred the next day, the feast day of Saint Agatha of Sicily, martyred in the third century by Quintianus. Still too paralyzed by fear to get up, Eugênia shivered on that hot summer night with the cold of the turmoil that made her soul buckle, and went to sleep on the floorboards, chanting a prayer.

Saint Agatha, you who remained confident until the end, even as they knifed your breasts, be my guardian, now and always.

18

The elderly couple well over a hundred years old peered at Alice with curiosity, searching for familiar features. The man couldn't hear very well, but his wife, who was used to it, patiently repeated everything their visitors said. Though she was very talkative, the woman had a constant tremor in her hands, calmed by a firm squeeze of her husband's hand. A give and take.

"Honey, look. These two are related to the Floreses. Tell me this girl doesn't look just like Carmelita? It's like she's right here in front of me. Your family and I were very close; did you know that?"

"I told her everything, Vitorina," Tia Helena explained, then thought it best to add: "Well, almost everything, because only the ones who were there know everything."

Vitorina laughed, flattered, and Alice thought it was a good time to show her the veil.

"Do you remember this, Vitorina?"

Vitorina's keen eyes, now milky white from an unoperated cataract, recognized it immediately. It was the lace veil Eugênia had made, which Vitorina had never held in her hands before and which she only found out about after her friend's death. Vitorina examined the veil without any of the melancholy Alice had expected. Maybe longevity gives the elderly the ability to look at the past as something you had to take a step back from to understand. As the years went by and people felt distant from events, it also gave them the chance—no longer protagonists—to become spectators of their own timeline. Near the end, they might become more confident to look at their experiences without fear, traversing, almost impartially, just out of curiosity, the twists and turns of their successes, mistakes, disappointments, and achievements.

"Well, well, would you look at that," said Vitorina, running her hand over the lace. "This veil is still telling its story all these years later. Isn't it beautiful, old man?"

February fifth was also a memorable date for the couple, the day they shared their first kiss.

"They were stubborn, those Flores women," Vitorina said angrily. "I was, too, it's true. Maybe more than them. If Inês and Eugênia had deigned to tell me what was going on, I could have helped, and everything would have been different. But no. They thought I was irresponsible, impulsive, with a mind of my own, when it was just the opposite. I was always the one with a good head on my shoulders. Isn't that right, old man?"

The schoolmaster nodded in agreement, even though he hadn't made out everything she said, which sounded to him like a song playing in the distance.

"I'm sure you're aware it was me, and no one else, who taught all of them how to make lace? I climbed up that ladder, didn't I, old man? And I got an earful from my cousin, who never forgave me for my snooping. Did you tell her everything, Helena? You did, didn't you?"

"Yes, Vitorina. All the credit goes to you for making Bom Retiro so famous for its lace."

"Even so, your relatives chose to shut me out. It was outrageous."

Vitorina paused for a moment, overcome by a feeling of resentment all those years hadn't been able to shake. She'd tried throughout her life to forget about her sadness over what happened and the longing she felt for her friends, but also tried to bite her tongue so as not to speak ill of those foolish women who'd acted without consulting her. She didn't talk about how hurt she was out of respect for their memory. They were a team of three; they always had been. Why hadn't they come to her at their moment of greatest need?

"The whole town was at the procession for the Feast of Saint Agatha, except for the one person who couldn't miss it: Eugênia," said Vitorina, resuming her story, her voice cracking from time to time. Alice couldn't tell if it was because of her age, or the feelings brought on by reliving those memories. "When Inês saw the Colonel get out of the carriage with just the children and a young woman acting as the children's nanny, she felt her legs give out. Cândida was all prepared to wear the 'Don't go' sign on her angel wings, a ploy Inês had come up with. What nonsense! Even Cândida, who must've only been eight years old at the time, was in on their scheme. They didn't trust me, don't ask me why. I was always the smartest one. What a terrible day that was, my God."

Her breathing suddenly became labored, and her watchful husband clasped her hand in his. The gesture seemed to have a calming effect, and Vitorina soon recovered.

"I had my eye on this handsome gentleman beside me for some time, didn't I, old man?"

Her husband affectionately returned the look his wife had given him.

"My mother was very jealous and didn't want me to date. She didn't want to lose me, you know? I don't blame her. The house would have become a morgue with just my father and brothers, talking about deliveries and merchandise. As far as Mother was concerned, the men of the house were only interested in what was for dinner. They hardly spoke to the poor woman."

Then, she turned to Alice and chided her: "Aren't you going to drink your coffee, girl? It'll get cold."

Alice obeyed, and Vitorina waited for her to empty her cup. Tia Helena and the schoolmaster also downed their coffee, as if Vitorina's order had been addressed to everyone in the room.

"No one could hold me down," she continued. "If you think I'm active now, imagine back then. Not even my parents, God rest their souls. I wouldn't allow them to make decisions for me. So that day, I took advantage of the confusion of the crowd to find a way to approach this handsome gentleman," she revealed naughtily, proud she'd been so bold. "Mother almost died of a broken heart, didn't she, old man?"

This time her husband seemed to have heard what she said, because he smiled at what was surely the sweetest, but also most distressing, memory of his life.

"When this woman wants something, it's best not to get in her way," he said, and Vitorina smiled.

"Isn't that the way it should be? If I don't spin that wheel, who will do it for me? Eugênia was the same: she liked to plot her own destiny. But marrying someone so powerful yanked that right away from her, and that stubborn thing still decided to spin the wheel, no matter the cost. She was confident she could."

"Do you remember what happened after the procession, Vitorina?" asked Alice, careful not to ask her hosts too many questions. She didn't know the appropriate duration for a visit with people of that age, who had long outgrown the category of elderly. "The veil doesn't tell everything. It ends with the plan."

"Right, right. Eugênia had a purpose when she made that veil, to ask some very chic ladies in Recife for help."

The schoolmaster shifted in his seat, and Vitorina stopped to ask if he needed anything.

"Do you want me to open the window? It's too muggy for you today. I told you not to wear that long-sleeved shirt."

Alice offered to open the window. The house was in the upper part of Bom Retiro, and, from where she sat, she could see the red tile roofs of the houses, the church tower, and, in the background, the rock formations so common in the region.

She sat like that for a few moments, trying to feel the call of the valley that her aunt had mentioned a few days earlier in Recife, which she thought she might be able to manifest there, but Vitorina's voice interrupted her.

"What happened next was a series of tragedies. Since Eugênia didn't attend the procession, Inês wasn't able to warn her that the carriage driver would no longer be waiting for her. Inês did everything she could to stop the flow of events. She stayed up all night stitching a message on the wings of her sister's costume, trying to prevent the worst, but Eugênia wasn't there to see it, unfortunately."

Vitorina shook her head, inconsolable.

"You should know, Inês wasn't one of those reckless girls who throw themselves hastily into thoughtless acts. So when I saw my friend distraught like that, I knew it was serious. But I wasn't having the most peaceful day myself."

And, at that moment, she and her husband exchanged a knowing look.

"Inês had decided to ask my brother Odoniel to help her, but her aunt was watching her. Firmina Flores really gave us grief, didn't she, old man?"

"Who's Firmina again?"

"The one who caught us at the store! How could you forget?"

The old man laughed so hard he nearly choked on the cookie he'd been nibbling on their whole visit.

"He's laughing now, but he wasn't smiling then. My mother almost left this mortal coil, and the confusion that ensued kept Inês from her mission to warn Eugênia. My brother wasn't able to help her that day, and, deep down, I think the feelings that were beginning to blossom between them got lost, before they'd cemented. They would have made a beautiful couple. I don't know her side of things. Inês was very discreet and didn't talk to us about matters of the heart. But Odoniel loved her. I witnessed the state he was in when she left. They would've had beautiful children, and today I'd be related to both of you. How interesting."

"At least Odoniel lived well into his eighties. Which wouldn't have happened if he married Inês," said her husband, straying for the first time from his wife's line of thought.

With her trembling hands, Vitorina patted her husband's arm, as if scolding a son who puts his finger in a pie fresh from the oven.

"Oh, don't be silly, old man. That's superstition. A teacher has to set an example, and believe only in what's scientifically proven."

In her mind, Alice replayed the chain of absent men in the Flores family, from the gypsy's wedding visit, until her birth. Just as her aunt said, the names came naturally. Das Dores's husband, who died from a snakebite; Lindalva's husband, who fell from his horse; her great-great-grandfather, who died of malaria; her great-great-uncle, victim of a childhood fever; her great-grandfather, who took his own life in the Capibaribe; her grandfather, whose name she never knew; and, finally, her father, who'd lived in another country since she was eight months old. He was alive, but somehow, he didn't exist.

"The fact is that afternoon marked the end of life as we knew it," said Vitorina. "Even for me, who wasn't involved. A few weeks later, there I was at the altar, getting married to this handsome gentleman beside me. Life is like lace, dear. The facts intertwine and take on their own shape. If those threads had joined together in a different way, the design would have been different. Each story is unique, like the table-cloths and bedspreads we made on those afternoons at your relatives' house. Some more elaborate, the result of planning and dedication. Others are one-of-a-kind, born of distraction or chance. Did you see this doily? It's from that time."

Alice touched the cloth reverently and said: "I'd like to learn some stitches."

"Well, it's been a while since I picked up my lace pillow. My vision's no longer what it was when I was fifteen, when I first spied those stitches from the top of the ladder. But I'll make an exception if it's to teach our art to a Flores. My great-granddaughters can help me."

Pleased, Alice thanked her, and Tia Helena said it was time to get back to the inn. They must have reached the maximum time for visiting people that age.

As Alice carefully refolded the veil to put it in her backpack, Vitorina thought it best to add:

"If it weren't for that veil, Colonel Aristeu's story, that Eugênia fell from her horse and hit her head on a rock, would have become the only truth. That's why your great-grandmother kept it. The veil is proof that things happened as they did. Your great-grandmother was a very special person," the old woman finally said, her eyes now even cloudier, perhaps from her longing for other times.

Her husband was curious: "Who was this girl's great-grandmother? Inês Flores?"

Vitorina was about to answer, but Alice cut her off: "No, my great-grandmother's name was Cândida."

"The blind girl?" he asked, intrigued.

"Yes."

"Your great-grandmother had her own way of understanding things," Vitorina added. "They say that when the Colonel gave the order to kick the Floreses out of town, she was the one who deciphered a doily that came in the mail from Recife. With her nimble little fingers, she told the older ones what was written in the embroidery: an offer of shelter from those chic ladies in the capital. The message was for Eugênia, but there's always room for one more, and the Flores women knew they could count on their assistance and left without looking back in a hired wagon, carrying only one suitcase each. Off they went to the coast, Carmelita and her two daughters, never to return to the Pajeú valley. Close to her chest, the matriarch clutched a photo of her deceased husband and son; Inês carried her lace cushion; and Cândida, a blackbird, which sat perched on her arm without trying to escape."

"Firmina was the only one who stayed, wasn't she?" interrupted Tia Helena respectfully, even though she already knew the answer.

"You think that tough old thing was going to bend to the Colonel? She was very attached to the land. Her blood would boil whenever it came to defending the family name. She always scolded us if we talked about the gypsy's curse and insisted their name was Oliveira, not Flores. You told this girl everything, didn't you, Helena?"

Tia Helena nodded, and Alice noticed the old man looking at her, puzzled.

"I taught your great-grandmother," he said unexpectedly, as his wife had carried the whole conversation.

The old man spoke with a teacher's calm, rationing his words and stretching out each pause.

"I don't know if you know, but even though Cândida had never seen any colors, she invented a method of identifying them by birdsong. It was also a code. If she were here, we'd tell her that her great-granddaughter's hair was the color of a masked gnatcatcher."

The sweetness of the memory made everyone fall silent for a moment.

The old man did the math: "So the girl is Cândida's great-granddaughter, Carmelita's great-great-granddaughter, Lindalva's great-great-great-granddaughter, Das Dores's great-great-great-great-granddaughter—that means you're the seventh generation. Soon you'll be free of the curse."

"Come now, enough of that nonsense, old man!" Vitorina chastised her husband once more, but she couldn't contain herself and praised him proudly. "He was always good with numbers. Was I or was I not right to have had my eye on this handsome gentleman beside me?"

19

Bom Retiro, 1919

The schoolmaster had never wanted any trouble in life. Born in the capital, he lost his parents at a young age and was able to complete his studies thanks to the help of his godfather, who paid for his education at a boarding school, where he lived until he came of age. Because he'd had such a rough start in life, he was determined to ensure his own survival in the world, so much so that he could hardly remember a time when he'd had any interests other than doing his duty: studying hard, then working hard, and so on. He was so careful not to bother anyone or cause any discomfort, so as to never risk his livelihood or the roof over his head.

He tried to make himself as invisible and agreeable as possible. He'd learned this strategy from trying to escape the punishments handed down at boarding school and beatings from the older boys he lived with for so many years—most of them like him, with no home to return to. To stay out of harm's way, he wouldn't stand out. Showing off or reveling in small pleasures might plant a seed of envy in someone's heart, someone who in the future might give in to the temptation to wrong him out of spite.

After his godfather passed away, the schoolmaster, having no one else, threw himself even deeper into his ambition to find security, so he would never go hungry. He convinced himself he didn't need entertainment or pastimes, soft sheets, love, or a full table. He cared only about work and went on about his life in peace.

After he completed his training as a teacher, a colleague mentioned a vacancy at the school in a far-flung town called Bom Retiro, and he immediately took an interest. He'd always thought that life away from the big city would suit him. In the countryside, he could finally experience a tranquility he never knew as a child, sharing the dormitory with dozens of other boys—some of them angry, or noisy, or whiny—whom he battled daily. In Bom Retiro, he could live without fear.

For a while, the schoolmaster rather enjoyed this stability. He would wake up with the sun, make coffee for himself, and eat a piece of corn bread made from toasted cornmeal before walking to school. For him, teaching was not a job, but a vocation. He saw in each student the boy he once was, and it was his wish that all of them, without exception, grow up to become more than they were in the present, and that they would know more as adults than they did as children.

Because he was a good teacher, the most mischievous and distracted ones took a greater share of his attention, since he didn't want any of them to fall behind due to laziness or lack of ambition. His first months in Bom Retiro, the schoolmaster used to go to bed before eight, and he slept so deeply he never remembered his dreams, now veiled and protected by a proper routine and the silence of the valley. He lived in that state of personal satisfaction, exactly as he had planned for himself, until young Vitorina appeared to shake things up.

At first the young man was just alert to the way the grocer's daughter seemed insistent on striking up a friendship he didn't want to have. To avoid her, he reduced his weekly purchases and even avoided passing by the store on his daily commute. But it was difficult to hide in such a small town, even more so from someone as determined as Vitorina. She ambushed him wherever he went. There wasn't a single day when they didn't bump into each other. Over time, terrified by the threat she posed—as such a friendship opened a series of possibilities for unthinkable harm—the schoolmaster gradually started to remember his dreams.

He'd read a scientific study that all human beings have the ability to dream, but they don't always remember them. People who said they didn't dream just didn't register them in their memory. In the schoolmaster's dreams—a territory beyond his control, where the laws of mathematics and physics, time and space, failed to follow established patterns—he would find Vitorina. He'd walk with her beside a creek that didn't exist, and recite poems made up in his mind, free from the shackles of constant vigilance, verses with no rhyme, no meter, no diligence in their choice of imagery, oneiric poems no poet had ever written.

He would awake startled by a feeling of strangeness, longing for the time he couldn't remember any dreams. The impact of that dreamlife with Vitorina only distressed the schoolmaster in those first moments of the morning. It was as if, when he opened his eyes, he remembered he'd carelessly left a pot on the fire the night before and now the whole house was in ashes.

But, as he brewed his coffee, the images from his dreams began to fade and were almost completely erased from his memory by the time he began to write the conjugation of some irregular verb on the blackboard.

But all he had to do was fall asleep again and new dreams would come. They arrived sneakily, but little by little they revealed their mark. The dreams were so constant that the schoolmaster began to think he really did know Vitorina. Not the flesh-and-blood one, that girl who'd spied lace stitches from the top of a ladder and given a trade to so many other women, but the nonexistent Vitorina of his dreams. A placid angel, content to live for eternity in his mind, the opposite of the real Vitorina, who already considered him hers, and there was no way to dissuade her from her goal.

On the day of the procession of Saint Agatha, a sneaky but kind Vitorina, as in his dreams, but also real and therefore determined, kissed him. She was closing the store when she saw the schoolmaster passing on the other side of the street, which he'd crossed to avoid a possible encounter with her. When she saw him, Vitorina waved like someone who had a problem and had just found someone to solve it.

"What luck running into you, schoolmaster. I could really use some help. It's stuck, see," she said, pointing to the door. "I'm not strong enough to pull it closed," Vitorina added charmingly.

My friend knew that feigning weakness made men feel more comfortable in the presence of a woman they found intimidating. Making the schoolmaster not see her as a threat was a predator's trick.

"With great pleasure, Miss Vitorina," he replied, which was both a lie and the truth, since he both wanted and didn't want to be there, so close to her, the real Vitorina, smelling her real perfume, something he'd never experienced in his dreams.

The schoolmaster easily pulled the latch shut, and Vitorina, quick as a heron snatching a fish, stole a kiss. A quick, almost innocent peck.

"Thank you, schoolmaster," she said matter-of-factly, as if she hadn't just kissed him on the lips. "You saved my day."

Then she smiled at him with the same smile as in his dreams, like someone who already knows she's loved.

"Now, come on, we're going to be late for the party," she said, inviting him along, but, as she turned around, Vitorina realized they weren't alone.

20

Bom Retiro, 1919

Tia Firmina knew that love made people lose their minds; she'd seen it happen to a childhood acquaintance who'd thrown herself into the waters of the Rio Pajeú because her feelings were not reciprocated by a neighbor. Docile people turned into ferocious beasts when threatened with being deprived of that intoxicating torpor amorous desire brings. That's why when my aunt noticed my absence during the procession, she decided to go after me, even though she knew it was a grave offense to abandon her role as cantor. She figured she could settle accounts with Saint Agatha later. She'd given her a lifetime of devotion, and that would certainly count in her favor.

One second, she'd seen me beside Cândida, surrounded by other children dressed as angels; the next, I'd disappeared from her sight. Only passion, that selfish and ungrateful counselor, could justify such an impulse, coming from someone with such a peaceful temperament as mine. Despite her warnings and threats, and having canceled the carriage driver, my aunt believed I was still determined to escape with Odoniel.

Moved by a feeling of urgency shooting up her spine, she made her way through the crowd of people that filled the square holding lighted candles and colorful pennants. Hildinha, Vitorina's mother, was a devout woman like my aunt and a fellow member of the lay

Sisterhood of Saint Agatha. She had her hands raised to the sky, with her eyes closed, rolling a rosary between her fingers, when Tia Firmina, whom Hildinha admired as the greatest example of rectitude and common sense, interrupted her prayer, her face flushed.

"Where's your son, Hilda?"

Hildinha hesitated for a moment, perhaps wondering *Which one?* since she had so many, but Firmina had no time for explanations:

"Odoniel and Inês have disappeared," she announced, firmly, with an urgency in her voice. "We have to do something."

Hearing that information, Hildinha dropped the candle she was holding and almost burned the skirt of a lady in front of her, causing a small commotion among the crowd of the faithful.

Not my son, Hildinha probably thought at that moment. Odoniel was the most affectionate of her four sons, the most attentive to her wishes, even more so than Vitorina, who, being the queen of the house, didn't make the same effort as her brother to comfort their mother.

Hildinha could not allow the name of one of her children, especially Odoniel, to be next on the list of Flores casualties. She liked Carmelita and had always had a good relationship with Firmina. Unlike many in town, she allowed her daughter to go to the house with the blue windows and to be friends with Inês. But her generosity toward those cursed women ended the moment they began to pose a danger to one of her own. Odoniel would not die for the Floreses' sins.

The shadow of that risk had already washed over her during Eugênia's wedding party. Hildinha had been tasting a bom-bocado, thinking the filling could have used more coconut, when she realized Odoniel was dancing with Inês Flores in front of the whole town. The sweet pastry turned bitter in her mouth, and she even had difficulty swallowing it.

In the days following the wedding, Vitorina's mother tried not to believe in the possibility. She carefully searched the words spoken by her son at mealtime and the expressions on his face at night when he lay down in his hammock. Hildinha was looking for some change in the boy's behavior, and, finding no signs of falling in love, she tried to put her fear aside. There was nothing to worry about.

Besides, it was unlikely that her son, so cheerful and talkative, would be interested in the eldest Flores, a girl with no particular charms. Inês had an ordinary face, a body with no curves, and a meek personality. Nothing like what she considered to be a girl who stoked passion, like her vibrant Vitorina. The hypothesis was so absurd that, after a while, she scolded herself for having even thought it, and tucked it away in a box deep inside her—at least, that was, until that moment when Firmina Flores came to warn her about their disappearance.

"What are you saying, Firmina?" asked Hildinha, incredulous, though she already knew what was happening.

Her first impression had been right. Some threats seem so dire that we refuse to accept their existence. That's what Hildinha had been doing for years with her daughter: avoiding the thought that one day her youngest would fall in love and leave her. She'd thought so much about Vitorina that she'd sinned by omission with her other children and allowed Odoniel to go unprotected. It was all her fault: she should have heard her maternal instinct crying out at the wedding party. Her fear had made her deaf to it and opened the door to danger.

"There's no time to explain, but they're going to run away together, Hildinha. They may already be far away. Let's go!"

A growing palpitation in her chest made Hildinha think her time had come, but Firmina wouldn't let her faint.

"Save it for later, we have to act before it's too late." And with that, she took Hildinha by the hand, and, together, they headed toward the store. "They're going to take the truck," said Firmina, as they hurried along. "They've had it all planned out for months. They're crazy in love."

"It can't be . . . I would have noticed." Odoniel's mother was still incredulous.

"Mothers see nothing. Just look at Carmelita. She was deceived, too. You always expect the best from your children. God was generous to me, not giving me such a hindrance in my life. I haven't lost my clear head."

Hildinha acted like Firmina wasn't talking about her son and began to pray aloud, asking for divine mercy: "Saint Agatha, you who were exposed to so much torment, deliver me from this grief," she recited. Then she began to improvise: "Ensure we arrive in time to save the fate of these two irresponsible youths. They know not what they do. O Saint Agatha, put sense in my son's head, that he may not be deceived by the promise of the pleasures of the flesh, that he may not pay for the sins that are not his own, which were committed in another time by this girl's ancestors."

Tia Firmina was uneasy with the direction her prayer was taking but allowed her to continue anyway. Saint Agatha might hear that mother's prayer and delay the couple. They took shortcuts, walking quickly with their skirts hiked above their ankles, until they reached the street that led to the back of the store, where the garage was.

Finding no one there, the two ladies turned the corner, and, to their surprise, instead of catching Inês and Odoniel, they saw Vitorina kissing the schoolmaster.

"What's this?!" asked my aunt, perplexed not to find the couple she was expecting, but another.

By that point, however, Tia Firmina was already playing the supporting role in the drama that was unfolding. Beside her, unable to bear what she saw before her, Hildinha fell to her knees on the dry earth, and gave out a heart-wrenching cry.

"Not my daughter!"

Vitorina ran to help her, but her mother was no longer making any sense. If Firmina Flores hadn't witnessed that, Hildinha could have pretended she never saw such a scene. She knew her daughter, smooth talking as she was, would convince her that her tired eyes had somehow deceived her. "Mama, don't be ridiculous! Of course it wasn't a kiss. I was helping the schoolmaster with his tie and I stumbled. If he hadn't held me up, I would have hurt myself badly. We should thank him, actually. I always tell you to take your glasses with you when you go out, but you're so stubborn, you don't listen to me."

Embellished with small details of reality, the lie would give Hildinha room to pretend she believed Vitorina's version, and then nothing about her daily routine would change. She could keep putting off the much-feared separation from her daughter.

But watching Firmina Flores standing there shouting, scolding those two young people for indulging in the middle of the street—"Just look at your mother's condition!"—Hildinha knew there was no going back: they would have to schedule a wedding. She had just lost her pride and joy.

Vitorina hated to see her mother in pain. That hadn't been the plan at all when she called the schoolmaster from across the street. She'd hoped to have a little more time to carefully convince her mother that having a married daughter also had its benefits. But chance had hastened things. But even seeing Hildinha's despair and the pale face of her future fiancé, Vitorina felt pleased with herself: she'd spun the wheel and felt calm with a clear conscience.

She knew her mother and the schoolmaster were suffering for nothing, since the change would only bring joy to both. In a couple of years, Hildinha would have grandchildren to amuse her, Christmas would be livelier, and the schoolmaster would leave behind his lonely life, like a loose thread lying on the ground, with no connection to other threads or other skeins.

Out of respect for their ignorance of the beautiful future that awaited them, Vitorina said nothing. She feigned consternation, but deep down she tried not to smile.

"And Inês? Where is she?" Tia Firmina pressed Vitorina, wanting to know my whereabouts. My friend just shrugged, as she really didn't know where I was.

Kneeling in front of the store, sobbing and moaning, Hildinha was so upset that she'd forgotten she also needed to save her son.

"My girl, my little girl" was all she said, while Vitorina held her up, cradling Hildinha as if she were the mother, and not the other way around.

"I'm here, Mama. I'll never leave you," she promised. Out of the corner of her eye, she watched the schoolmaster, who stood motionless in the same spot on the sidewalk where they'd kissed. Interestingly, he was staring back at her without anger or fear. *Wouldn't you know, the schoolmaster does love me!* Vitorina correctly concluded, with only that look to go on.

When Vitorina's father and siblings arrived at the scene, the schoolmaster remained firm, answering all their questions, assuring them he would fulfill the duties his "inappropriate gesture," as he called it, would entail. At no time did he reveal to his future bride's family that it was not he who'd initiated the kiss. Nor that it was Vitorina who had advanced toward him, nor that he'd even retreated at the moment she approached him, and even kept his lips closed, not because he didn't want to open them, but out of respect for the girl.

Seeing him act so dignified and so faithful to her, Vitorina loved him even more. They would be happy, just as she'd predicted.

21

Tia Firmina was right in thinking that I'd left the procession to look for Odoniel, but she was wrong about why I wanted to find him so urgently. As soon as I spotted him in the middle of the crowd, right after I realized Eugênia hadn't come with her husband, I ran over to him, upset.

"Odoniel! I need your help," I announced, pulling him by the arm.

"Now? But Cândida is about to place the crown on Saint Agatha."

"It's a matter of life and death, believe me," I assured him. Knowing I wasn't one for making rash gestures like that without justifiable reasons, he followed me away from the crowd, where he could get a clearer understanding of the reason for my distress.

"I need you to take me to a point on the road. It's not far from here, but it's urgent."

Odoniel had never seen me in such a state.

"Of course, but what happened?"

I was about to start explaining to him, an abbreviated version so we wouldn't waste any more time, when, at that exact moment, Odoniel noticed his brothers hurrying toward the store. Immediately, his attention was divided between what I was trying to tell him and the sudden activity of his family members, who also seemed to be facing an emergency.

"Something's happened at my house," he murmured, worried, and called out to one of his brothers, who, seeing him, announced:

"It's Mama! Come quick!"

Odoniel turned to me again, now with an indecisive look on his face. I was losing my only chance to save Eugênia.

"Please, Odoniel," I insisted once more, as I'd never insisted with anyone before. "I need you."

In front of me, I watched that young man's face contort with the unresolvable question of whom to help first: his mother or the girl he'd secretly been in love with for months.

"I'll help you, Inês," he said, trying to reconcile the two forces battling it out within him. "We'll go to the store together to see what happened to Mother, and then we'll go. I'd have to stop by the store to get the truck, anyway," he said, holding out his hand.

Together we ran through the streets and soon saw Hildinha, kneeling on the sidewalk, her hair a mess and tears streaming down her face. On one side, Vitorina was consoling her. Up ahead, the men of the family had formed a circle around the schoolmaster.

In a brief moment of clarity, Hildinha looked around and saw Odoniel, hand in hand with me, and she grabbed at him, still on her knees, afraid of losing two children on the same day.

"Son! Thank God you came back."

At first Odoniel didn't understand what was going on, or why his arrival made his mother so emotional, until he heard the words Hildinha addressed to me. "And you!" she said, pointing her finger angrily in my direction, almost forgetting the other drama she was involved in. "Stay away from my son, you shameless hussy!"

"Mother!" Odoniel scolded her, incredulous, figuring it was some mistake on her part.

"Hush, boy," she ordered. "I'm doing this for your own good. One defiled child is enough for today."

Cornered, I looked at Odoniel and Vitorina, both paralyzed, and took a step back, humiliated at being accused of something I hadn't done. Odoniel looked at me apologetically; he wouldn't be taking me anywhere in the family truck.

Across the street, I met Tia Firmina's gaze as she feverishly stared me down, outraged by my behavior and by Hildinha's words. At that moment, however, I had no way to defend myself or explain. Not wanting to waste another second, I turned my back on everyone there and ran toward the road, determined to beat Eugênia to the spot where she was supposed to wait.

As I ran along the hard dirt road in shoes that weren't made for that purpose, my only wish was that a similar string of unforeseen events had also happened to Eugênia, and that my friend had never managed to leave Fazenda Caviúna.

If she was still at home, the matter would take care of itself. As I pressed on, now with bare feet cut by the stones and branches on the road, I tried to convince myself that Eugênia had given up. Knowing my friend, however, I knew she would do anything to stick to the plan. In fact, her absence from the procession might even be a ruse, to get to the appointed place faster.

By that point, back in Bom Retiro, the Feast of Saint Agatha was still going on, but the Colonel, who'd already arrived in town thinking about not participating until the end, was getting ready to leave. Appearing in public without his wife had made him feel a bitterness that was gnawing at him from within. He was agitated and wanted to return to Caviúna as soon as possible to show his wife the harm she'd done him.

He listened in annoyance to the priest speaking to the people, imagining Eugênia, at that exact moment, making her lace in the luxurious sitting room decorated by his mother, with no remorse for having brought him such embarrassment. The role of a wife was to accompany her husband in situations like this, and Eugênia wasn't even able to do the bare minimum.

At the altar in the square in front of the church, the Colonel stood in his distinguished place, but by his side, instead of his wife, was a shabby, poorly dressed nanny, who rested her calloused hand on the shoulders of his two children. He would never forgive Eugênia. Or her parents, who'd tricked him into believing that they had given the girl an adequate education, when, in fact, they'd raised her without giving her the discipline women needed.

Hours earlier, when his mother-in-law approached him to ask about her daughter, saying she missed the girl very much and was worried about her absence—only an illness or serious incident could justify Eugênia not attending the most important event of the year—the Colonel felt uncomfortable and kept on walking so as not to have to hear her voice.

"Colonel? My son-in-law?" She eventually caught up with him. "Where is Eugênia? Did something happen?"

"Yes," the Colonel replied curtly, and his mother-in-law immediately put her hand to her chest, fearing what he might say next.

"God in Heaven! What is it?"

"You didn't raise a strong daughter," he said, and walked away without further ado.

Eugênia's mother tried to keep pace with him, now more alarmed than before about her daughter's well-being. But the Colonel went on his way, ignoring her anguished questions.

In Eugênia's escape plan, being at the open-air Mass and in such a prominent place as the Colonel's wife would be in her favor. Once the priest gave everyone his blessing, when she would be seen alongside her husband, the procession would begin, and, according to tradition, the men would follow the procession on one side and the women on the other. Everyone would be concentrating on their prayers, heads down, hands clutching their rosaries, gazes turned toward the saint on her processional litter. The women around her wouldn't be especially attentive to Eugênia, and there would always be Inês, who, as her accomplice, could cover up any suspicions along the way.

Once her husband realized she was missing at the end of the procession, when men and women normally reconvened, Aristeu would have no chance of covering up what had happened. His wife would be reported missing, and everyone would be witness to her dishonor, which made Eugênia's revenge all the sweeter.

Eugênia had woken up that day determined to improvise as she sometimes did with her lace. Whenever a thread got tangled in the tape or wasn't fixed correctly in the place she'd planned, Eugênia wouldn't throw out her hard work, as the Flores women did. She would use the mistake to create something different: a pulled stitch would become a petal, a murundu, a rosebud. She knew she wouldn't last another day in that prison, and her certainty grew every time she felt the throbbing of the cut on her forehead, caused by Aristeu's aggression the night before.

As soon as her husband left with the children, Eugênia tied a scarf over her hair to hide the wound and went into the sitting room determined to put on a show. When Dorina came in to speak to her, Eugênia looked somewhat mournful and gave a couple of unusual sighs with the aim of grabbing the cook's attention.

"The Colonel said that the lady is sick. Would you like some tea?"

"Thank you, my dear, I'm fine," she said, and, after a considered pause, she added: "But I'm not sure about tomorrow." The maid gave her an apprehensive look and Eugênia continued. "The worst is yet to come, Dorina," Eugênia announced, with a prophetic air, but soon changed her tone, making a gesture with her hand that it was nothing. "Never mind. On second thought, I will have some tea, yes. It might calm my nerves," she said and got up from the table, pretending not to notice Dorina's presence, but knowing she'd already piqued her curiosity.

"What is this worse yet to come that the missus is talking about?" Dorina asked, and Eugênia closed her eyes, pausing for a moment, before confessing.

"Maybe it's silly, Dorina, but I had a dream last night that really left me rattled," she said.

Dorina's eyes widened. Eugênia knew Dorina believed in invisible forces and was in the habit of looking for small signs that foretold of events before they happened. She'd learned of the death of a cousin from a guira cuckoo that had landed on the fence. Around her neck, she wore a piece of garlic tied to a string, which, according to her, protected her from the evil eye.

"Whenever you have a dream like that, it's always good to try to figure out what it's about," Dorina told her mistress. She was worried, but didn't want to frighten her or seem indiscreet. "Tell me about the dream. Do you remember it?"

"I dreamed of Saint Agatha," Eugênia revealed, and Dorina grew even more intrigued.

Dreams about saints were warnings. Her mistress wasn't old enough to understand the importance of that type of message, so Dorina knew it was her responsibility to investigate the matter further.

"Pardon my curiosity, ma'am," Dorina said, in a forced, mundane tone, so as not to alarm Eugênia. "But what was Saint Agatha doing in the dream?"

Eugênia hesitated for a moment, looking doubtful, as if deciding whether she should reveal the details to Dorina.

"It's always good to tell someone. It helps to unburden the heart," Dorina said to encourage Eugênia, who seemed convinced.

"In the dream, Saint Agatha was crying right there at that window," she said, pointing. "Everyone was so sad, and wearing all black, like at a wake."

Eugênia stopped here, looking remorseful.

"Forget it, Dorina. Maybe I'm just feeling guilty for not doing my duty at the procession, because of a silly affliction."

"Yes, of course. That could be it," Dorina said, pretending to agree, though she was still hungry for more details.

She was experienced in these things. When a neighbor dreamed of seven chicks crossing a road, it was she who deciphered that the girl was pregnant and that the baby would be born in seven months. When her father dreamed that his feet were stuck in a small pile of cow dung, she knew he'd soon come into a nice sum of money. It was an ancient wisdom—Dorina didn't even remember whom she learned it from—but it never failed.

"Was everyone in the dream?" she asked probingly.

"I think so," Eugênia replied, unsure. "It was dinnertime. I remember the table was set."

"And how many plates were on the table, ma'am?" Dorina kept digging.

"How many?" Eugênia paused, as if struggling to remember the exact number. "Three, I think . . ."

When Dorina heard that, her face transformed.

"Just three? Are you sure, ma'am?"

"Yes," replied Eugênia, now alarmed, walking over to the table to point out the place settings. "At the head of the table, Aristeu's plate, mine was here, on that side, Lili's." Then Eugênia stopped, despairing: "O Saint Agatha!" she cried out, her eyes widening, searching for Dorina, who had already realized the missing place at the table belonged to the boy.

"Little Durvalzinho," said Dorina, in a pained whisper, not wanting to believe it, but already convinced, from her own experience in matters like that, that the boy was in serious danger.

She had raised those children and seen them through their mother's illness. She'd seen them grieve the death of her former mistress and, later, their joy returning little by little with the arrival of Eugênia. She couldn't allow another tragedy to befall that house.

"No, Dorina," said Eugênia, in a panic, pacing the room. "It was just a dream. Like I said, I was feeling unwell—that's why I didn't go to the procession. Indigestion can cause nightmares."

"It wasn't a nightmare, ma'am," Dorina said. "It was a warning, and it's not wise to risk the boy's life. The procession isn't over yet, and Saint Agatha will forgive you. Go put on your mantilla veil and get ready!"

Eugênia acted unsure and proposed a dozen obstacles to Dorina's orders.

"I don't know if there will be time, Dorina. Besides, I'm not strong enough. Aristeu will be worried when he sees me arriving in town, and he might scold us for me going out feeling so unwell. You know how men are. You know him better than I do."

"I know him so well that I know there's no one the Colonel values more than his son," said Dorina, going to call one of the foremen through the window. "Now, go! I'll deal with him later."

Dorina was the real head of that house, and no one would disavow her. She'd gone to live on the ranch even before Aristeu was born and had helped change his diapers. She'd given her word to the Colonel's deceased mother—a thorn in her side while she was alive, and for that very reason was all the more likely to come back from the world of the dead to collect on that promise—that she'd protect that family. If she didn't watch over that family, who would? Eugênia was kind, a good stepmother, but she was just a girl.

"If you think that's what we should do, then I will. For Durvalzinho's sake," Eugênia finally agreed.

Dorina excused herself, rushed off to speak to one person and another, then put her mistress in a wagon heading into town. She told the foreman to hurry up and then ordered all the kitchen helpers to stop their work to pray for the boy.

Under the steady eye of Dorina, who believed she'd just saved the life of the Medeiros Galvão heir, Eugênia crossed the gate of Fazenda Caviúna, carrying under her skirt a change of clothes and forty thousand réis and, in her heart, hope for a new life that was just beginning.

22

Road to Bom Retiro, 1919

About halfway to town, Eugênia asked the young man driving the wagon to stop for a while, saying she was feeling queasy from all the jostling. She needed to breathe with her feet firmly on the ground and splash some water on her face, even if it was from the nearby creek. The young foreman pulled on the reins to stop the horses and, to give his mistress some privacy, turned to light a cigarette. While he was looking at the horizon, distracted by the plumes of smoke that wafted in the breeze, he didn't notice Eugênia tiptoeing away, silent as a tegu lizard, careful not to step on a dry stick until she finally reached dense woods.

As soon as she was far from the road and protected by the vegetation alongside it, Eugênia lifted her skirt and started to run as fast as she could. Legs and lungs moved by the confidence that I'd suggested she acquire, once, on my collar. "Trust," I'd told her. In a matter of minutes, or even less, the foreman would notice her delay and go looking for her by the creek. Even when he realized what had happened, he wouldn't know exactly which direction to run. If he tried to track her down by footprints or using his woodsman's intuition, it would be almost eight o'clock at night, and by the time he caught up to her, the carriage driver would already have passed the second bend in the road and taken her away forever.

The whole thing wouldn't turn out exactly as Eugênia had planned, but she was adjusting her route according to the circumstances. Sweating, Eugênia arrived at the agreed-upon spot ten minutes before the scheduled time, and her punctuality, amid all the chaos she'd been immersed in since the previous night, filled her with pride and hope. Saint Agatha was by her side, had heard her prayers, and covered her with her veil of protection.

Her confidence that everything would work out never faltered, even when the carriage didn't pass at eight. Nor at five past eight, nor at ten past eight. Eugênia was so confident in my word. I had never failed her. Ever since we were children, there was nothing I guaranteed her was right that wasn't right. Even in our argument about the apple peel ritual for Saint Anthony, Eugênia had always known, though she refuted and mocked me at the time, that I was right.

When we were children, Eugênia used to scold me, arguing that my always being right was incredibly irritating. And when she said that, she elongated the *cre* in *incredibly*, making an already big word sound even bigger, and making me sound more irritating.

"Being with someone who thinks they're always right is so annoying, Inês. You make everyone else look dumb. So we're at a disadvantage," she'd say, and I'd shrug.

"What do you want me to do? Keep my mouth shut and not say what I'm thinking?"

"You might try to think like me for a change."

I wanted to think like her, but I couldn't.

Although Eugênia and I were often at odds as children, when we grew up, I stopped trying to impose my opinion on her, the way I did when I was little. Over time, especially after Cândida's accident, I developed a conciliatory nature, not out of submission, but out of the desire to please everyone around me, just as I'd done with my father—an unattainable goal, I would later realize.

I never suspected that my unconditional concession to the wishes of others would ever have harmful consequences. It was only much later, living in Recife, that I had the courage to ask myself the following questions, though I knew I would never have the answers: "What if I hadn't supported Eugênia that day? Would she still be alive?"

Once, when we weren't even eleven years old, we were walking home after school when we passed a house with a mango tree heavy with fruit. Eugênia spotted the tree from afar and called our attention to it: "Look at those mangoes! I'd give anything for one right now."

Vitorina's mouth was watering, too, and she suggested we jump over the wall and steal some.

"Let's go, before someone walks by. It'll be easier from the side," she suggested, but Eugênia vehemently disagreed—after all, she was wearing a new dress and didn't want to ruin it climbing trees like a tomboy. Besides, maybe Vitorina had forgotten, but she was the sheriff's daughter, and she couldn't be caught stealing, even if it was mangoes. Vitorina made a face but accepted Eugênia's arguments and began to think of alternatives.

Being defied but still getting what she wanted was like a challenge for Vitorina. Ever since she was little, our friend never got upset with anyone who told her no, because she didn't believe in no. For Vitorina, the word *no* was a tease, an "I dare you," a jest that would be revealed later. *How could anyone say no to me?* she used to think. That's how it was with the schoolmaster, and time proved her right.

"What if we poked the fruit with a branch? We wouldn't be stealing or trespassing. The mangoes would fall on the ground, outside the fence. They'd be ours by right," she declared, sounding like a judge.

Eugênia weighed the idea, tending to agree with her, but on one condition:

"All right, but you're the one who's going to pick up the fruit. I'm not going to humiliate myself or be an accomplice to brazen acts."

The condition imposed by Eugênia irritated Vitorina, who argued that she didn't do her bidding and Eugênia was not her mother to be giving orders like that.

In the middle of their heated debate, which I'd only been following in silence, a practical question kept repeating in my mind. It was so obvious I decided to just blurt it out:

"Why don't we ask the lady of the house for the mangoes?"

Vitorina and Eugênia immediately stopped talking and looked at me as if I were a child asking misguided but adorable questions.

"Are you crazy, Inês?" Eugênia said, scolding me. "Veridiana doesn't get along with my mother. She'll just say no, out of spite."

"Okay, okay," I agreed, trying to come up with a new plan, one in which the existing animosity between those two women would be easily circumvented. "If Veridiana's problem is with your mother, all you have to do is hide, Eugênia. Vitorina and I will go and ask. She has no quarrel with our mothers, as far as I know."

Eugênia snorted when she heard my idea. She didn't want to be left out.

"Veridiana will think you're a couple of beggars, that's for sure. And I'll be seen as the friend of a couple of beggars."

"I don't look like a beggar," said Vitorina, defending herself.

We were still wearing our school uniforms: neat button-down shirts, pleated skirts, and polished buckle shoes.

"And my hairband is still new!" she added, stiffly.

"Veridiana won't think we're beggars, Eugênia," I replied calmly, knowing she was just coming up with excuses to cancel the whole escapade. "Vitorina's father owns the grocery. There's no lack of food on your table. Stop being stubborn and go hide. Do you want the mangoes or not?"

Eugênia looked at me sour faced—she didn't even want the darned mangoes anymore. When she'd pointed out the fruit, just minutes before, she was expressing a diffuse desire, a desire that didn't necessarily need to be filled. And now, thanks to her two friends, Little Miss

Practical and Little Miss Eager, she found herself in an awkward situation, about to be humiliated by Veridiana.

That's how our little trio worked: Eugênia was the dreamer, Vitorina acted, and I looked for solutions, which were neither as romantic as Eugênia's aspirations nor as courageous as Vitorina's actions. For that reason, years later, even though my lace, mathematically symmetrical, always got the highest praise, it never seemed to kindle the same emotions as the pieces made by the other two.

"To err is human. When we make a mistake, the piece becomes something unique," Vitorina had said, when a flower she'd been working on came out crooked, and she didn't have the patience to redo it.

"I don't want any mangoes anymore," Eugênia muttered. "I didn't mean it."

"Perfect. Then I'll eat yours," Vitorina teased, already making her way toward the gate.

"You'll do nothing of the sort," I said, holding Vitorina by the arm to keep her there until the three of us had settled everything. "We'll ask for two. One for each of us, since Eugênia claims she lost her appetite. Isn't that right, Eugênia? Are you sure you really don't want any?"

"Well, hurry up, then. I don't want anyone to see me acting suspiciously." And she shooed us away, annoyed. Soon Vitorina was clapping in front of Veridiana's gate, shouting, "Anybody home?"

"Let me do the talking," she told me, because she knew she was better at the art of convincing others.

When the lady of the house appeared at the gate, we put on our best good-girl smiles.

"Good day, Veridiana. I'm Vitorina, Hildinha's daughter. And this is Inês Flores."

Veridiana looked at me suspiciously, as I expected. Even when I was a young girl, my reputation as being cursed made many townspeople look at me that way.

"What do you want?"

"We came to pay you a compliment," Vitorina began kindly. "Your backyard is so beautiful. You can see the well-pruned trees all the way from the other end of the street. The jackfruit tree, the lemon trees. I think my father would be interested in selling your fruit for you. And the mangoes, as well. They would be a real hit at the store."

The old woman let her guard down a little when she heard Vitorina's charming words.

"Goodness, I'm so sick of that smell, and they make such a mess when they fall. I'll give you a bag full. Come on, girls."

"Are you sure, Veridiana?" asked Vitorina, just for fun. "There's no need."

"Of course, girl. What did I just say? I want to get rid of the ripe ones, they attract a whole swarm of flies. Here. And take one to your father. Who knows, maybe we'll do some business."

Vitorina accepted and glanced at me with a victorious smile, which I returned in kind. I was also proud of myself for having given the idea that led us to that moment.

While we selected our fruit—"Take them all, I really don't need them"—Eugênia waited for us at the corner, hiding so no one would think she was a beggar. Or the friend of a beggar.

When she saw us leaving through the gate, carrying a basket with more than ten mangoes, she came out of hiding, still angry for having been left out of the plot.

"Look, Eugênia," said Vitorina, taunting her. "Five for me, five for Inês. Too bad you didn't want to go with us."

"Stop it, Vitorina," I scolded her. "We have plenty, and we're going to share."

"I'm not going to share mine," said Vitorina, annoyed, with an air of injustice. "Eugênia didn't do anything, so she doesn't deserve our kindness."

"Here, Eugênia." I offered her two mangoes, thinking that would put an end to it. "Now nobody gets left out."

But Eugênia really had lost interest.

"I don't want it, I told you," she said, pushing my hands away. "If they were on the ground, they must be rotten. You'll both have a stomachache tonight. You'll be writhing around all night with cramps, I bet."

Vitorina laughed with mango stuck in her teeth, her mouth smeared with orange juice running down the sides of her chin.

Eugênia made a disgusted face. "You really are a slob. I can't even look at you, Vitorina." And with an exaggerated look of revulsion, she began to walk faster to keep ahead of us.

Anyone watching us from afar wouldn't be able to say for sure that the sheriff's daughter was even with us. A few steps ahead, Eugênia plodded firmly down the street in her waxed buckle shoes.

She was the one who'd spotted the mangoes. And she was the one who'd put that desire in us, and now she was forced to witness our joy, unable to surrender or enjoy the fruit.

The sweet smell of the mangoes rose in her nostrils, increasing her suffering, but Eugênia would never backpedal, or try to find a resolution. So, years later, as I rushed to try to help her, I was certain she would have found a way to be at the appointed place and time for her escape.

Even in that great distress and with my emotions racing, the practical solution I'd found to save Eugênia, the friend who'd always wanted more than me—if she had somehow made it to the second bend in the road—was to find her before her husband did. All I had to do was tell her to turn around. "Let's leave it for another day. There won't be any carriage today." Eugênia would complain, maybe walk a few steps ahead of me, upset that things hadn't gone as she wished, just like that day with the mangoes, but at least she would be safe.

23

Second Bend in the Road, 1919

The Colonel found the wagon from the ranch parked on the side of the road with no one around. He slammed on the brakes, hurriedly got out of the car, and walked around until he found the foreman. With an anxious look in his eyes as he imagined the terrible consequences he would suffer for having turned his back for a few moments to light his cigarette, the foreman gulped before telling his boss in a trembling voice that the mistress had disappeared. Contrary to what the young man imagined, the Colonel did not attack or reprimand him. He just ordered him to take the children home in the wagon and not to say anything when he got to Caviúna.

"What happened, Daddy? Where's Eugênia?" the children asked, and the Colonel, slapping the horse's rear, shouted: "Go on! Take them away!"

As soon as he was out of the children's sight, Aristeu took his pistol from its holster and ran into the woods after his fleeing wife. At that moment, somewhere in the valley, I was also running, thinking that knowing Eugênia's exact location would give me some advantage. I was counting on the Colonel still being in Bom Retiro, attending prayers. When I approached the second bend in the road, however, holding on to one final hope, I saw Eugênia struggling to free herself from her husband, who was pulling her by the hair.

"Goddamned whore! Where is he? Where's your lover, you wretch?" shouted Aristeu, pointing the revolver randomly at the woods. "Speak, you good-for-nothing swine!"

"There is no lover. I was on my way to the procession, I stepped away from the road a bit when we stopped, and I got lost," she lied, trying to save herself.

Her husband snapped back, furious: "Do I look like a cuckold to you? Today's the day I end you, you ingrate!" He slapped her so hard he knocked her over again.

Having fallen to the ground, Eugênia could no longer contain herself.

"Then go ahead and kill me! Kill me once and for all and put an end to my torment."

She looked him right in the eye, head held high, abandoning the shrinking posture she'd adopted since spotting him minutes before.

Aristeu pointed the gun at Eugênia's head, determined to pull the trigger.

"Shoot me!" she screamed at him, fearless, her bloodshot eyes filled with a hatred more powerful than her instinct for survival.

"Don't defy me, woman. You won't have time to ask forgiveness for your sins. You're a disgrace."

It was at that moment that I approached, running ahead and shouting: "Colonel! Please!"

He turned the gun away from Eugênia and pointed it at me. Eugênia looked at me, surprised but also relieved by my presence, since I always brought her solutions.

"What's this other whore doing here? Are the Floreses in on this?" he asked, recognizing me, veins popping out of his neck.

The Colonel wasn't known for having a violent temper. Reserved and soft spoken, he was a man who ordered others to kill for him. Until that February afternoon, his wealth had given him the privilege of not having to get blood on his hands very often.

"Have mercy, Colonel," I begged him, trying to reason with him. "You know how Eugênia is. She has these whims, but it always passes."

In my desperation, I sputtered out any excuse that came to mind, relying on my hunch that some men see women as nothing more than girls to be disciplined, who start to behave right after a little punishment, no longer hopeless cases.

If I could make the Colonel believe Eugênia's escape attempt was just another stubborn act, and that with age and a little discipline she could change, maybe he would spare her.

"I gave everything to her," he said to me, in an unexpectedly confessional tone that threw me off. "Everything. But nothing is ever enough for this ungrateful wretch."

At that moment, I realized Aristeu had strong feelings for Eugênia, and I believed he loved her. I grabbed on to that unexpected discovery to try to save my friend.

"You're right, Colonel. Eugênia has always been spoiled. Blame it on the way she was raised. Her parents raised her like a princess and made her believe she was the boss in the house. Can you believe such foolishness?"

Eugênia understood what I was doing and remained silent in anticipation. She couldn't endorse what I was saying, but she didn't have the courage to contradict it, either.

"I'm in charge of my house," we heard the Colonel say. "I'm the one who gives people orders."

"Of course, of course. She understands that now. Don't you, Eugênia?"

I knelt beside my friend, whose eyes were glazed over with terror, blood streaming down the side of her face. The slap he gave her minutes ago had reopened the wound from the night before.

As I felt her body trembling in my arms, I realized she really didn't know what decision to make; her options had run out. My instinct was to pull her up by the hand to make her choice easier.

The Colonel was calmer now and didn't react to my gesture. He didn't want to kill her, and there was his dilemma. His desire was to tame Eugênia but to also be loved by her. If his wife died, he'd never get what he wanted so badly. If he squeezed the trigger, that angry ocelot would die without being bent to his will.

"It's getting late, and the children must be worried," I started again, calmly, making Eugênia take a step toward the road. "At the ranch, everything will be settled. The car is right there. Come on, Eugênia, let's go."

Aristeu's silence seemed to signify agreement with my suggestion. He really was considering giving his wife another chance. "This will be your last chance, you hear?"

But, after taking the first step, Eugênia stopped and gave me a look I'll never forget. She knew, after everything that happened that day, that once she got into her husband's car to return to Fazenda Caviúna, there would be no escape.

"Go on, woman," Aristeu barked without even looking at us, and, at that moment, Eugênia made her choice.

"No."

"Eugênia, please . . . ," I begged her softly, and she smiled at me, saying goodbye.

The look on her face expressed all the gratitude she felt for everything we'd experienced together until that moment. Childhood games, afternoons making lace, help in times of need.

"I can't," she mumbled, and only I heard her. "But thank you for trying."

Then she straightened up, haughtily, like the Eugênia I knew well, who never backed down from a decision, and announced: "I'd rather die than live by your side, Aristeu. You disgust me."

When the Colonel heard those words, his face twisted into a scowl. I held Eugênia's hand as hard as I could, but, possessed, that man came toward us, yanking his wife away and throwing her to the ground.

"Then go to hell, you demon!"

And he shot her in the chest. And again. And again.

Against such brutality, I looked to my friend's face, to at least be with her in her final hour, but the Colonel's boots were in the way. Standing there, he stared down at his wife's lifeless body and, in a reflex, perhaps remembering my existence, turned to me. He pointed the gun at me and ordered me to get out of there if I didn't want to suffer the same fate as that harlot who betrayed his trust.

I ran for my life, until, already at a safe distance, I ventured to look back. I saw the Colonel cradling Eugênia's body, like a baby. In his lovesickness, Aristeu regretted having lost the piece he once thought would make his life whole again.

24

"Dead."

"She's dead," I told them, panting, desperate, out of breath, feeling like the ground had just dropped out from under me. "Eugênia is dead," I repeated, and my mother and Tia Firmina, eyes bulging, asked me empty questions that wouldn't change what happened; they wanted to know how, where, why, but I couldn't answer any of these questions, since the implacable truth that had been thrust upon us, like a rock falling from an embankment, was that Eugênia was dead. So much life, so many dreams, so much anger, so much hope, so much stubbornness. All dead.

While my mother was checking that I was still in one piece, something I'd never be again to the end of my days, a man knocked on our door at the behest of the Colonel. The message he gave the lady of the house in a low voice was to inform her that we had until the following day to leave town. When she heard that, my mother burst into tears.

"We're not going anywhere. This land is ours, too," Tia Firmina told the man, who was still standing in the doorway.

His job was to give the message and make sure it was understood. He had just returned from the sheriff's house with the same task. On her knees, the wife screamed, "My daughter, what did that man do to my daughter?!" But her tears didn't prevent her husband from understanding what had to be done.

"Horse accident, ma'am. The animal got spooked, and the mistress fell," he told Eugênia's parents.

Holding up his wife, who murmured, inconsolable, "Eugênia, my love, how could I have allowed this?" the sheriff nodded to the man, to show that he had understood and that soon his wife would understand the situation, too. Due to his position, the sheriff was familiar with the unspoken rules of the Sertão, and, as soon as he shut the door, he ordered his wife to start packing. It was urgent they leave Bom Retiro that same night. "But who will watch over and bury the body of my pride and joy? I have a right to see my girl one last time." To which her husband said: "We lost that right when Eugênia married the Colonel. Now pull yourself together and go pack."

"The Colonel only warns you once," the man repeated at the house with the blue windows, perhaps because he considered us women with no men to protect us or make us understand the gravity of things. On my mother's face I saw a bit of the innocence of her elderly mother who'd stayed in the backcountry and whom she hadn't seen for years. "Don't be long," he thought fit to say and, tipping his hat, bid us farewell before getting back on his horse.

We knew our time in Bom Retiro was over. In that land, when the powerful ordered exile, there was no bargaining. Whole families would leave overnight, and the other townspeople would simply stop talking about them, deleting them from their shared memory, as if they'd never existed.

If, from time to time, out of honor, courage, or stubbornness, anyone dared to confront a ruling handed down by the powers that be, it would be met with death, ambushes, and burned-down houses. The exception was when the other family involved also owned land and held power. Then it was different: violence multiplied, and, in most cases, a war began that could go on for years.

But for us, lacemakers with little income, with no father, husband, brothers, or sons—just a widow, a devout spinster, and two single girls—the path was to disappear without a trace. We would simply be erased, forgotten like unused objects, whose history dust and time tried to cover up. It was the law of the land.

My mother's face remained static, in anguish, her eyes bleary as she silently wept, imagining what would become of us. She wept for me and for Cândida. We would have no future. The lives of her daughters had been stopped in their tracks.

"It's my fault," I said finally, breaking the silence. "I tried to help Eugênia escape," I confessed.

My mother gave me a look I'd only seen her give once, when my father confessed his mistake when putting the eye drops in their youngest's eyes.

"Eugênia wasn't my concern, I know," I said, trying to explain myself, even though I knew it was impossible to justify the unjustifiable, but Tia Firmina interrupted me.

"She really wasn't. You've just destroyed your mother's and sister's lives by meddling in other people's business."

Aware of my mistake, I threw myself on the couch, destroyed, but my aunt continued.

"Do you realize where your recklessness and stubbornness have led us?"

"Enough, Firmina," my mother said, her voiced raised, and stared at her sister, then took my trembling hands in hers.

"You did the right thing, my dear. The Colonel is wrong, the world is wrong the way it is. Eugênia was your concern. She was all our concern. Her murderer is who's wrong."

Then, Cândida, who'd been silent and was still wearing her angel costume, handed me an embroidered cloth: "Inês, read this. It was at our door when we returned from the procession."

Cândida was holding a doily that didn't belong to us. Made of unbleached linen by what were certainly amateur hands, with triple skein threads in bold colors. In the center, a bouquet of flowers in chain, daisy, and rococo stitches and French knots.

"Where did that come from, girl?" asked Tia Firmina, but Cândida spoke only to me.

"Read it to them, Inês."

Tia Firmina was getting annoyed.

"And since when can people read cloth, Cândida? Have you lost your mind like your sister? This is a very serious situation we're in here," Tia Firmina said gruffly, but my mother stepped forward and stroked Cândida's hair, the warmth of her affection unwavering.

"It's embroidery, my love. It's not for reading."

Cândida's fingers moved along the edges of the piece, stitched in fine white thread, with stitches so small that they were almost imperceptible, even if you looked at them very carefully.

"Feel it, Inês. We have somewhere to go," my sister told me hopefully. "Let's go to Recife. They're calling us."

Furious that Cândida insisted on talking nonsense at such a critical moment, when everything was slipping away, Tia Firmina approached her younger niece and snatched the cloth from her hands. It was no time for games, a young woman was dead, the ground beneath the house with the blue windows had just cracked under their feet. "This girl is making up stories. It can only be a punishment," she decided, disillusioned. "Because Inês and Eugênia invented this sinful plot on the day we were supposed to pay homage to Saint Agatha."

"Saint Agatha has no reason to punish any of us, Firmina," my mother told her sister, again in our defense. "She suffered a similar fate. Her heart would take pity on Eugênia, and us, too."

Tia Firmina fell silent for a moment, because she knew her sister was right, and I took the opportunity to take the embroidery from her lap. A package had been delivered to our door by a postal worker in the morning. But there had been such turmoil that day that the package was only discovered that evening, lying outside the house, when Cândida tripped over it on her way back from the festivities.

As I glanced at the understated hem of the work, I quickly deciphered the message that had come from the capital and understood what my sister meant.

"It's true, Cândida. We do have somewhere to go."

"Didn't I tell you?"

"It says here it's from Ave Libertas, which means 'Hail freedom' in Latin," I announced as I read the stitched signature on the doily's border.

"What are you talking about?" my mother asked, coming closer to examine the embroidery.

"It's a code, Mama." I pointed to show her better. "Eugênia came up with a way for us to communicate through lace without the Colonel noticing. See, each stitch is a letter. A few months ago, we sent a request for help to a group of very distinguished ladies in Recife, in the hope they would welcome Eugênia. And here is their answer. They embroidered a message with the same code Eugênia created."

My mother studied the discreet line of unusual stitches.

"They're the same as the ones on Eugênia's collar," she said, recognizing it right away. "And the wedding veil, too."

Tia Firmina refused to look at the piece we were talking about. She turned toward the outside. Her gaze fell on the distant Baixa Verde Mountains, in the background of the Pajeú valley, framed by the already-peeling blue paint on our windows.

"The help these ladies were going to give to Eugênia might be of use to us," Cândida said. "Help is for those who are in need, isn't it, Mother? 'Do unto others as you would have them do unto you.' Isn't that what you always say?"

My mother smiled in agreement as I continued to decipher the message.

"They're saying they can give us the support we need. To just go and see them at the address we already know."

As I glimpsed the possibility of a way out, I felt the air reentering my lungs. But the euphoria I began to feel was not shared by my relatives. Sitting in the armchair, now with the embroidery in her hands, my mother plunged into catatonia.

"I can't leave this house."

"I know it's painful, Mama," I said, trying to comfort her. "But it's necessary," I insisted.

Cândida joined us, taking my mother's hand to give her strength. "We'll be fine, Mama. Everything will work itself out. Like always."

Then my mother broke down in excruciating sobs, hugging her two daughters. Little by little, her breathing calmed, and the idea of moving to Recife became more bearable. We just had to wait.

Cândida was used to listening carefully to the breathing around her, which became agitated and then calmed down again, in a continuous cycle that only ended with death.

Distressed by the silent tears uniting us at that moment, Tia Firmina shut the window and began to tidy up the room, fluffing pillows, straightening a vase, lighting the lamp.

"Do what you want, but I won't budge from here. Especially not to pay for the acts of two numbskulls. Eugênia didn't learn to bear the burden of her marriage, and I'm not about to lose my father's house because of that girl's lack of dignity."

"Tia! Have some compassion," I said, scolding her for speaking so unmercifully of Eugênia. "Eugênia is dead. Dead!"

"Well, she wouldn't be if she weren't so willful," she snapped, looking back at me with rage. "If she'd accepted her fate, she would still be alive. And another thing, Inês: if you hadn't tried to help her, the outcome would also have been different for your friend."

Her accusation caused my breath to hitch once more. I had to sit down for a moment from the weight of my guilt crushing my bones. The image of my mother looking ten years older than she had minutes before was mixed with the last look Eugênia had given me. "Thank you for trying," she'd said, but deep down I knew I wasn't worthy of her gratitude.

If I hadn't dyed that damned dress yellow, confirming my commitment to help her, if I hadn't taken her the money, if I hadn't arranged transport for her, Eugênia would still be alive. Not even the best-laid plans are guaranteed to turn out the way we want. We are all always surrounded by chaos, and there is no way to predict how events will chain together.

"As is my duty as a practicing Catholic," Tia Firmina resumed, with a stern expression, "I will pray for Eugênia's soul. But that's about as much as I can do for that fool. And I will pray for you too, Inês, that God will forgive you for being so careless. For not having weighed the damage this tale could bring forth. Carmelita, the decision is yours. You never really listened to me, you raised these girls as you wanted, and this is the result. But there's no colonel alive on this earth who will take me from the land where I was born."

"We need to go, Firmina," my mother finally said. "There's no other way."

Since childhood, those two had never been apart, and perhaps that was why, at that moment, they both had the confused look of someone unsure how to react when a part of themselves gets ripped away so violently. Like in an accident, they felt the pain of their own flesh being ripped apart, bones turning to dust, all while their survival instinct impelled them to seek some makeshift solution to keep going, even if torn to pieces: "What now, without her? Who am I without her? Is there a crutch so I can walk without my leg? Without my familiar and beloved leg? Only my leg bears the marks of my stumbles, only my leg keeps me upright and balanced." Firmina and Carmelita Flores knew they would be forever incomplete without each other.

"Colonel Aristeu won't forgive Inês, Firmina," my mother continued, trying to stay focused on what needed to be done. "He might forgive me, you, and even Cândida. But never Inês."

By helping Eugênia, I had vainly sealed the fate of the people I loved most, and my friend was still dead. My only comfort at that moment was feeling Cândida's small hand snuggling into mine, like a baby rufous-bellied thrush in its nest.

"Forgive me," I stammered, even though I considered myself unworthy of absolution. I knew I would never experience a worse moment in my life. Not even at the time of my death or the death of my mother would I tear myself up so much inside.

"What were you and Eugênia thinking?" Tia Firmina came toward me once more, indignant. "That you could stand up to a man like the Colonel? You can't! And you never will. It's been that way since before you were born, girl. Before me or your mother. You young people are fools. You don't listen to those who've lived longer and have suffered more."

As I listened to Tia Firmina's accusations, a flicker of hope flashed across my mind, like a poorly sketched pattern for a piece of lace.

"Unless . . . ," I said in an almost cheerful tone, as if changing the subject, which made my mother look up. "I go to Recife alone. If I'm far from Bom Retiro, the Colonel will ease off and allow you to stay."

It seemed like a magically simple solution, and a wave of excitement, born of that slight nod to a way out, coursed through my whole body. If I sacrificed myself by leaving Bom Retiro, my family would be spared. What could two ladies and a blind girl have done that was so bad? They were obviously oblivious to Eugênia's plans. The choice to help my friend had been mine, not theirs. I would be the outcast. It was fair.

I got up with new momentum. We had some money in the bank, from selling our lace, and there was also the offer of accommodation from the ladies at Ave Libertas. The life Eugênia had dreamed of for herself would now be mine. Like those relay races on field day, where you pass a baton so your teammate can finish the race in your place. I could almost see Eugênia's baton reaching out to me.

I would live by the sea. I, who'd never left that land of dry earth, cracked and rutted with lines like lace. I, who didn't have as many desires as Eugênia and only yearned for the peace and quiet of my needle going up and down on hot afternoons in the valley. I, Inês Flores, would leave and become somebody else. I would honor Eugênia's memory by living for her.

"No daughter of mine is going anywhere without me," my mother announced suddenly, putting an end to my reverie as Tia Firmina looked on, surprised. "Cândida and I will go with her."

"Are you crazy, Carmelita?" Tia Firmina scolded her sister.

"You belong in this house, Firmina," replied my mother, affectionately. "But I belong with my daughters. All I ask is that when we are in the capital, you send us the money through the bank for our lace."

When she heard this request, Tia Firmina's face twitched. There was no more money. She'd spent it all to pay off the driver. For a few moments, my aunt weighed whether she should be honest about her mistake and reveal to her sister that her new life would be even harder than she imagined, but she decided not to confess, so their farewells might be free of resentment.

Keeping secrets from Carmelita wasn't something new for Tia Firmina. She'd kept quiet about the gypsy's curse for so many years to spare her sister that, now, she had no difficulty in staying silent again. She wanted to postpone the disappointment and anguish of a future life without means.

"I will do just that," Tia Firmina agreed, lying, and my mother, with her characteristic calm, wiped her tears and began to collect the few objects she intended to take.

She started by taking the picture of my dad with my baby brother off the wall. Tia Firmina was still staring at the rectangular mark the frame had left when she felt Cândida's hand brush against her arm.

"Are you sure you won't be sad, Tia?" my sister asked, wanting to confirm.

"Now, girl, stop being silly. Go help your mother," she replied, not shedding a single tear.

"Remember, my little birds will stay here, and you won't be alone," Cândida said, trying to comfort her. "You can keep putting out the scarlet eggplant and the birdseed. Once a day is enough. Their singing will keep you company. Would you do that for them? Would you do that for me?"

Tia Firmina remained silent, and Cândida took her silence as a yes. Reassured by the arrangement, she went to the bedroom to pack her bag.

It was getting late, but we were too exhausted to light the oil lamp. Lit by the moonlight that came in through the blue windows, it was just me and Tia Firmina in the sitting room, standing in silence for I don't know how long.

The anger had disappeared from her face. She knew that outcome was also a consequence of her own actions.

"Inês?"

"Yes, Tia."

"That carriage driver," she began hesitantly, as it wasn't like her to ask questions, but to tell the truth. "It was for Eugênia, wasn't it?"

I nodded, and Tia Firmina sighed.

"There's something I have to tell you about the money, but you have to wait until you're all safe to tell Carmelita. I don't want to alarm her any more."

I pretended to understand and listened calmly to the story she proceeded to tell me, not accusing her of taking money that didn't belong to her, as her suffering was also great. In an attempt to cheat fate, Tia Firmina had made her own mistakes. That was the only time I ever saw her cry, and it was also the last time I saw her alive.

Epilogue

Because her eyesight was no longer as sharp as it was in the days when she climbed ladders to eavesdrop, Vitorina enlisted the help of two great-granddaughters to teach Alice Flores the basic stitches for making lace, now known as Bom Retiro lace and even exported abroad.

Cândida's great-granddaughter's goal was to be able to stitch, onto Eugênia's original lace veil, the piece of the story that hadn't been told yet.

"I can't believe you ruined that veil, Alice," said Vera when she saw her daughter adding colorful synthetic ribbons to that hundred-year-old relic, back in Rio.

"I'm not ruining it, Mom, I'm continuing it," replied Alice, minus her usual defensive tone.

Vera, somewhat remorseful for the unnecessary criticism, made out of habit, said: "Well, if it looks bad, you can just undo it."

The two of them were more patient with each other, perhaps because of the discoveries Alice had made about their family history, which Vera's mother had never told her.

Instead of white cloth tape, Alice plaited a golden cord and threaded beads Sofia had bought days earlier at the Saara street market. After a few weeks of work, the piece still had its classic, decorous essence, but it now displayed a burst of sparkle and vibrant, neon colors.

The veil had become an art installation that bridged two eras.

In the center of the piece was a square measuring one meter by one meter, stitched by Eugênia, née Damásio Lima, in 1918, asking for help with an escape she would not be able to make. The same veil that hung in the offices of Ave Libertas for decades, until Maria Amélia de Queirós gave it to Inês when the office changed its address.

Along the sides of the veil, now multicolored and less elaborately stitched, the code summarized what happened in later years. This time, it was signed by the representative of the seventh generation of the family since Das Dores Oliveira's wedding: Alice.

Guests gathered at the Bom Retiro Cultural Center for the opening of the exhibition titled "Lace Code: Breaking Female Silence Today and at the Turn of the Twentieth Century." Alice's objective in bringing together all that material was to allow the story of the lacemakers of Bom Retiro to be shared not only with their descendants, as their ancestors had done, but with as many people as possible, both men and women.

Alice still didn't feel the call of the valley, as Tia Helena had once suggested, but maybe she just didn't know how to identify it. After all, from the moment she received the veil as a gift, that morning when she woke up dizzy with a hangover, Alice hadn't stopped making her way toward that place, perhaps already obeying the call.

Still very much a beginner at her ancestors' techniques, it took Alice months to stitch the events that occurred after Eugênia's escape attempt: the arrival of her great-grandmother Cândida in Recife, accompanied by her mother and her sister, Inês; the financial hardships of their early days in the big city, having lost their savings; and then getting back on track with hard work and a good clientele.

On the veil, Alice also related the courageousness of Firmina Flores, who, days after her relatives departed, personally went to Fazenda Caviúna to call on the widower Colonel Aristeu, to whom she claimed to be an old, God-fearing woman who greatly disapproved of her niece's behavior and, therefore, would live out her days in the house where she was born. If the Colonel decided to commit one more injustice, he would have to answer to Our Lord Jesus Christ when his time came. "Fare thee well, and I'll be on my way."

The Colonel seemed to accept the ultimatum, since he never sent another messenger to the house with the blue windows. The widower also never remarried, although several families were interested in presenting their daughters to him. He died young, at forty-five, of a twisted gut.

Talking to the residents of Bom Retiro, Alice discovered that, in the years that followed the incident, Firmina Flores never stopped putting out birdseed and scarlet eggplant for the birds in the house, exactly as Cândida had asked her. That's why the animals still live there to this day, bothering the new owners and soiling the newly arrived notebooks at Papelaria Elegância.

Firmina Flores also played a leading role in an episode involving Virgulino Ferreira, a cangaceiro born in the region who formed his own band of outlaws the same year Eugênia died. On his way to Bahia—where he would later become known as Lampião, the most wanted outlaw in Brazil until his death two decades later—Virgulino, along with his men, had planned an attack on Bom Retiro. Instead of armed officers and residents, however, the band of cangaceiros were met with a veil stretching over twenty meters wide in the square, acting as a shield.

Behind the veil was the statue of a saint with honey-colored hair. Not a single living soul was around. People said that when Ferreira came across that scene—as disturbing as it was mysterious—he decided not to challenge that warrior saint, who, even inanimate, threatened him with forces unfamiliar to him. Out of respect for the patron saint of Bom Retiro, the gang continued their path of violence in other places, and the town was left in peace.

The ruse was thanks to the cleverness of Firmina Flores, who had the idea to set up the physical but also mystical barrier, loaning the shroud she'd devoted herself to since her youth, to be used to defend her land. Until her death, activities at the church kept Firmina Flores busy. Even though she missed living with her family, she was convinced it was safer for her nieces to be raised far from the Pajeú valley. Maybe the gypsy's curse wouldn't reach them near the sea.

When news of her death reached Recife, Inês read the letter to Carmelita and Cândida, who listened, hand in hand, to the detailed description of the wake written in the meticulous handwriting of Hildinha, who'd been by her side until the end. "Firmina was smiling, wrapped in the most beautiful shroud you've ever seen, and which had even defended us from the terrible Lampião." Alice had retrieved the letter from a box of keepsakes belonging to a cousin on Tia Helena's side.

After that first trip to Pernambuco, Alice returned a few times to both Recife and Bom Retiro to try to locate those first pieces to contain the code: the dress collar, the sachets, the table runner, and the napkins. Firmina Flores had donated almost everything to the church.

Rummaging through the drawers in the sacristy, Alice even found, folded in tissue paper, the dainty nightgown that was part of the cherub costume—so small, almost like for a doll—that had belonged to her great-grandmother Cândida. She wanted to take it home but didn't. What she inherited was something else: the belief that no destiny is lost before the fact.

In her curse, the gypsy never said that only the women of the family would suffer, but that's the way the curse was understood, because, in the end, it's typical to assume it's women who should pay for everything. It's been that way ever since a certain someone ate an apple she wasn't supposed to. Alice was convinced the story of the curse was meant to show how we must always be careful with our words. A son of a bitch is just an asshole. There was no point in offending the guy's mother.

At the entrance to the exhibition, hanging against a bloodred wall, was the veil that Eugênia had worn at her wedding and that had been returned to her family after her death. When the Colonel arrived back at Caviúna, holding his wife's body in his arms, he ordered everything belonging to Eugênia burned. But Dorina, knowing the Colonel's story about an accident wasn't true—and feeling a twinge of guilt for encouraging the girl's misbehavior, believing, until the end of her life, that it was out of love for Durvalzinho—took one more risk.

She defied her boss's orders and had a trunk with Eugênia's belongings delivered to the sheriff's house before he and his wife left town. Dorina believed the memories of their deceased daughter might serve as some consolation for those two unfortunate souls, alone in their old age. Instead of turning to ashes, those clothes, combs, and handkerchiefs would turn into comfort.

Inside that same trunk, tucked inside a book, was also a bloody lace rag. One of the exhibition plaques, fixed to the wall just below the rag, read: "In this piece, the words *fear* and *hatred* in code."

Interviewing the daughter of a cousin of Tia Helena, Alice discovered that Inês Flores had never married. This cousin, now deceased, had become very close to Inês in the 1940s and 1950s, and her daughter remembered the Flores women well. According to her, Inês always talked about a boy from her hometown, who once even went to visit her in Recife, when she was already in middle age.

"It was a funny name with an *O*, but I don't quite remember. Otônio, Otilio."

"Odoniel," said Alice. Ironically, *O* is an initial that would have easily been formed from an apple peel, if Inês had ventured to join in on Eugênia's ritual.

"That's right," Alice's interviewee confirmed and then told her what happened: "Apparently they just didn't hit it off. I remember Inês that day, after the meeting, saying too much time had passed."

The name Inês Flores also appeared in some copies of *Ave Libertas*, where she wrote articles on fairer wages for women who earned less than their male counterparts doing the same job. Despite never having invented or named a lace stitch of her own, something she'd once planned to baptize "creek," "dew," or "dawn," it was Inês Flores, her great-great-aunt, who was the great narrator of this story of Eugênia and the Flores women.

In a vital records office in the capital, Alice found the marriage certificate of her great-grandmother, Cândida, married at the age of eighteen to a merchant who would later commit suicide in the Rio Capibaribe after watching his small business go bankrupt, causing his daughter Celina to permanently break ties with the family and move to Rio. Celina had blamed the family curse for her father's death and for that reason didn't register her daughter, Vera, as a Flores, unaware the cursed bride was an Oliveira—a detail that time, silence, and the choices made by those who came before her had covered up.

The death certificates of the three women, who, being from Bom Retiro, were recorded in the same registry book, were also retrieved. Carmelita: 63, of cardiac arrest; Inês, 82, a stroke, which Alice found out happened while she was sleeping peacefully; Cândida, 90, of multiple organ failure. Reading those ages, Alice couldn't help but feel sad. Her great-grandmother had lived so long, the two might have known each other had it not been for her grandmother's determination to forget her roots.

In the last few months, Alice insisted Vera try to remember any stories she'd heard as a child, but her mother said Celina never spoke about the past.

"Whenever we asked about our origins, my mother always grumbled and changed the subject. She even tried to hide her Pernambuco accent."

There was one detail Alice remembered well: when people asked her grandmother where she was from, Celina was always proud to say, even if it wasn't true: "Rio de Janeiro, born and raised. Just like my daughter and granddaughter here." It was as if the mere intonation of her voice could awaken her ghosts.

"I couldn't find anything in the old folders," Vera told her daughter, sincerely sorry. "Only passports with lots of travel stamps. We never had anything old in our house. Your grandmother considered anything over ten years old to be junk, and she was always throwing things away, buying new things, redecorating rooms. My mother had no attachment to physical objects. 'You have to keep moving forward, I'm not a crab' was what she used to say."

Vera laughed, thinking about that memory, and Alice was grateful for her mother's effort and intentions. They were forging a new way of coexisting, which just might work.

The story still had a lot of gaps, and Alice knew it would always be that way. The identity of her maternal grandfather, for example, was still hazy. Her grandmother had never revealed that information to her mother, who suspected he was a married man or someone with whom Celina had had a brief affair or a single encounter that resulted in pregnancy. Was he still alive? Had he been the victim of a premature death, too, like the other men who got involved with the Floreses?

Even without all the answers, Alice felt close enough to that family tree she'd never even heard of until just a few months ago. So much so that she'd started signing her name "Alice Ribeiro Flores." She wasn't a piece of fruit that had sprouted straight from the ground.

Even the descendants of Aristeu Medeiros Galvão attended the event. Nearly a hundred years later, it was public knowledge that the Colonel was responsible for the death of his runaway wife. The story told by her husband back then was that Eugênia had died after a fall from a horse. The priest was called to give last rites that same night, and Eugênia was buried the following morning in a sealed coffin, right at Caviúna, without a wake and without the presence of her parents, who'd left the city "out of grief," the Colonel had said. At the time, everyone pretended to believe that story, though they all knew things had not happened that way.

"It was femicide, but back then they didn't call it that," Alice told one of the Colonel's descendants, who was listening to her with interest. "My family was also banished from the town at the time, and, quite frankly, a fall from a horse doesn't create so many enemies."

Fazenda Caviúna was now an experiential resort, managed by the great-grandson of the little boy, Durvalzinho.

"I'm sorry for what happened in the past between our families," said Aristeu's descendant, slightly embarrassed by his ancestor's crimes. "Whatever I can do to help clarify anything about the case, do let me know. You're welcome to be our guest at the hotel. We've kept everything pretty much as it was back then. Guests like it that way. It's like taking a trip back in time. They call it immersive tourism."

Alice smiled in appreciation, and the young man added: "My great-grandfather spoke very fondly of his stepmother Eugênia. He considered her a mother. They lived together for a short time, but they were very close, and she was very affectionate with her stepchildren. Once, when he was very old, he even told me that he never forgave his father for what he did to her."

Spending some time at Caviúna wouldn't be a bad idea: it might help with the research Alice was now thinking of turning into her final thesis. Staying in the main house at the ranch, now it would be her boots causing the creaks in the wooden floor, the noise Eugênia feared so much, a sign her husband was approaching. She could also visit the place where Eugênia had been buried and where, in a way, she was still imprisoned. Alice figured she could pay tribute to her. Eating a juicy mango and then digging a hole in the ground next to her tombstone, then letting a mango tree sprout there, just for Eugênia.

Among the crowd of guests, Alice saw Vitorina in a wheelchair, admiring the main work of the exhibition, the original Mass veil, now on display with Alice's bold interventions, something only possible because of the stitches that old lady had spied so long ago and then taught to so many people. The schoolmaster hadn't left the house in years.

"So, Vitorina? Do I pass? Am I a lacemaker?"

"Oh, it turned out beautiful!" She smiled at Alice. "You managed to insert some joy in that veil, which until today had only made people cry."

And, pulling Alice closer to her, so she could hear her better, Vitorina whispered:

"Wherever Eugênia is, that hothead must be laughing."

"Why?" Alice was curious.

"Eugênia was always against making white lace. And she was right, you know? We could have used any color, but it wasn't considered proper at the time. But who's to say what's right or wrong, anyway? Lace can be yellow like canaries, as your great-grandmother Cândida would say. Red like the plume of a red-cowled cardinal, blue like . . ." The old woman was going to say, "like your hair," but when she looked more closely at Alice, she was surprised again. "Hey, is it pink now?" asked Vitorina, amused. "You Flores girls. Always trendsetters. Don't ever lose that!"

Alice smiled in appreciation of the compliment. She was getting used to them.

Discoveries, Feelings, and Motivations

I wanted to set the fictional story of the lacemakers in a period when the debate around women's issues and their achievements was just beginning. At the turn of the twentieth century, several women's rights groups emerged in major cities across Brazil, including Recife, and this movement intensified into the 1920s. In 1916, a bill was passed that allowed legal and physical separation in certain situations; divorce, however, would only become legal in Brazil in 1977.

Meanwhile, in the rural interior of the state of Pernambuco, more specifically in the Pajeú River valley—a region marked by feuding families and the oligarch-based *Coronelismo*—an era of great violence was also beginning, with the rise of the *Cangaço*, when nomadic bandits roamed the hinterlands seeking money, food, and revenge. At the same time, however, there was a desire for progressive, forward-thinking ideals among the local middle class. These aspirations are symbolized by the construction of the elegant Cine Teatro Guarany in Triunfo, which opened in 1922. The fictionalized town of Bom Retiro symbolizes precisely this dichotomy: backwardness and culture, brutality and courtesy, male and female, dust and lace.

Almost a hundred years later, in 2010, our modern character, Alice, practices another type of activism, more focused on social and behavioral change than on legislative achievements. Other figures included in the book, such as Maria Amélia de Queirós and the Ave Libertas association (formed in 1884), are also real, even if they are used in a completely fictitious way in the novel. In both cases, there are also some slight mismatches in timeline (for example, there is no confirmation that the group was still operational in 1918, and the date of Maria Amélia's death is also unknown). Even so, I kept these elements because I believed they would enrich the story and because they were within the range of the time period I wanted to re-create.

—Angélica Lopes

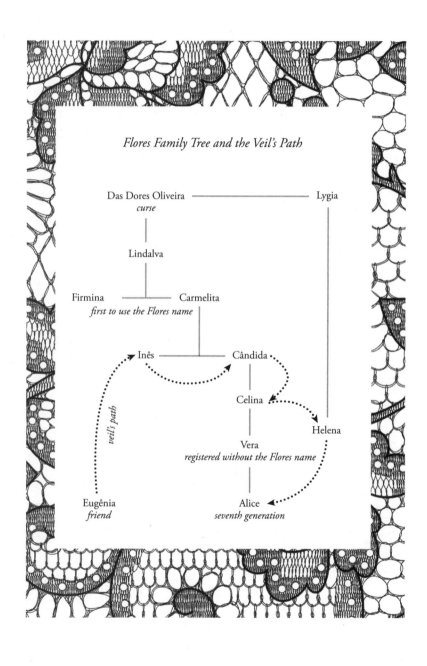

Flores Family Tree and the Veil's Path

Das Dores Oliveira — Lygia
curse

Lindalva

Firmina — Carmelita
first to use the Flores name

Inês — Cândida

Celina

Helena

Vera
registered without the Flores name

veil's path

Eugênia
friend

Alice
seventh generation

About the Author

Angélica Lopes is a novelist, screenwriter, and journalist from Rio de Janeiro with over twenty years of experience in writing fiction. Her dramatic vein came from writing Brazilian soap operas, known worldwide for attracting millions of viewers daily. She is also an award-winning author of YA novels and has written scripts for films, TV series, and comedy shows. *The Curse of the Flores Women* is her first adult novel and was sold for translation in France and Italy even before being published in her native Brazil.

About the Translator

Photo © Bruno Ribeiro

Zoë Perry has translated the work of several contemporary Brazilian authors, including Emilio Fraia, Ana Paula Maia, Juliana Leite, Clara Drummond, Veronica Stigger, and Carol Bensimon. Her translations have appeared in the *Paris Review*, the *New Yorker*, *Granta*, *Astra*, *n+1*, and the *New York Times*. Perry's translation of Ana Paula Maia's *Of Cattle and Men* was awarded an English PEN grant, and she received a PEN/Heim grant for her translation of Veronica Stigger's *Opisanie świata*. She is currently based in Miami.